"Men like you really can't care."

His brows shot up in surprise. What the hell? Men like him? What was with this woman? Did she have any idea what she was doing to him? How she was making him care? About her, about what she thought of him? Caring for a woman once had cost him everything. He refused to take that risk again.

"You know jack about me, Sarah. Now get into that river. Get yourself cleaned up, and then take off your shirt."

Dear Reader,

The leaves aren't the only things changing colors this October. Starting this month, you'll notice Silhouette Intimate Moments is evolving into its vibrant new look, and that's just the start of some exciting changes we're undergoing. As of February 2007, we will have a new name, Silhouette Romantic Suspense. Not to worry, these are still the breathtaking romances—don't forget the suspense!—that you've come to know and love in Intimate Moments. Keep your eyes open for our new look over the next few months as we transition fully to our new appearance. As always, we deliver on our promise of romance, danger and excitement.

Speaking of romance, danger and excitement, award-winning author Ruth Wind brings us *Juliet's Law* (#1435), the debut of her miniseries SISTERS OF THE MOUNTAIN. An attorney must depend on a handsome tribal officer to prove her sister's innocence on murder charges. Wendy Rosnau continues her arresting SPY GAMES series with *Undercover Nightingale* (#1436) in which an explosives expert falls for an undercover agent and learns just how deceiving looks can be.

You'll nearly swoon as a Navajo investigator protects a traumatized photojournalist in *The Last Warrior* (#1437) by Kylie Brant. Don't miss Loreth Anne White's new miniseries, SHADOW SOLDIERS, and its first story, *The Heart of a Mercenary* (#1438), a gripping tale with a to-die-for alpha hero!

This month, and every month, let our stories sweep you into an exciting world of passion and suspense. Happy reading!

Sincerely,

Patience Smith
Associate Senior Editor

Please address questions and book requests to:
Silhouette Reader Service
U.S.: 3010 Walden Ave., P.O. Box 1325, Buffalo, NY 14269
Canadian: P.O. Box 609, Fort Erie, Ont. L2A 5X3

Loreth Anne White

THE HEART OF A MERCENARY

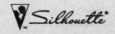

INTIMATE MOMENTS™

Published by Silhouette Books

America's Publisher of Contemporary Romance

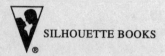

SILHOUETTE BOOKS

ISBN-13: 978-0-373-27508-3
ISBN-10:   0-373-27508-0

THE HEART OF A MERCENARY

Visit Silhouette Books at www.eHarlequin.com

Printed in U.S.A.

Books by Loreth Anne White

Silhouette Intimate Moments

Melting the Ice #1254
Safe Passage #1326
The Sheik Who Loved Me #1368
*The Heart of a Mercenary #1438

*Shadow Soldiers

LORETH ANNE WHITE

Loreth Anne White was born and raised in southern Africa, but now lives in Whistler, a ski resort in the moody British Columbia Coast Mountain range. It's a place of vast, wild and often dangerous mountains, larger-than-life characters, epic adventure and romance—the perfect place to escape reality. It's no wonder it was here she was inspired to abandon a sixteen-year career as a journalist, features writer and editor to escape into the world of romance fiction.

When she's not writing, you will find her long-distance running or skiing on the trails, and generally trying to avoid the bears. She calls this work, because it's when some of the best ideas come. Loreth loves to her from readers. Visit her Web site at lorethannewhite.com.

As always, to Susan Litman.
Without her I wouldn't be here.

To Marlin, who keeps me focused
on the importance of story in our world.

To the rest of my family for
too many reasons to mention.

And to Meretta and Toni, for just being there.

Prologue

The doctor's head sagged sideways. His eyes glazed into a fixed stare behind his protective goggles, and blood dribbled slowly down from the corner of his mouth, soaking into the white surgical mask bunched beneath his chin.

Sarah Burdett wriggled out of the coffin-size hole in the floor and scrambled frantically over the packed red dirt to where the doctor lay slumped against the leg of his autopsy bench.

She grabbed his shoulders. "Dr. Regnaud!" she whispered, her breath hot and damp under her own mask, sweat trickling down between her breasts. She tried to move him, to get a sense of his injuries, but as she did, his body flopped back onto the dirt and she caught sight of the dark crimson stain blossoming out over the fabric of his lab coat. Her breath caught sharply in her throat.

With shaking fingers she ripped off the clumsy plastic bags that covered the surgical gloves on her hands. There were no neoprene or rubber gloves in the makeshift clinic, no proper bio-safety gear. They'd had to make do with what they had. "Doctor…" She felt his wrist through her latex gloves. Nothing.

She yanked at his mask, searching for the carotid arteries at his neck, praying to find the faint beat of a pulse under her gloved fingertips. There was none.

Her heart plummeted. Dr. Guy Regnaud, a brilliant, kind, generous, warm-hearted man…was dead.

She was alone.

The soldiers had killed everyone. They'd stormed the compound, slain the nurses, the two nuns, the priest, even the patients. And they'd taken the seven autopsied bodies before dousing the palm-thatched roofs in petroleum and torching the mission compound.

Sarah lifted the doctor's goggles up onto his head with trem-bling hands, and looked into the fixed stare of his blue eyes. Even in death they seemed to drill into hers, driving home the urgency of the mission he'd handed her just seconds before the men had stormed the medical hut and shot him dead.

"Whatever happens, Sarah, get these samples to the CDC," Dr. Regnaud had whispered as he'd shoved her and a sealed bio-hazard container into a hole in the floor of the baked-mud hut. *"And trust no one. This is the Congo. Everyone has a price."* He'd concealed her tomb with a plank and a reed mat, while outside, gunfire peppered the compound and gut-wrenching screams sliced the air. Then the soldiers had burst in….

Tears welled in her eyes. Dr. Regnaud had saved her life, and it had cost him his own. The trembling in her hands intensified, shuddering uncontrollably through her entire body. Her protective goggles misted with tears and body heat. She fisted her hands against the fear. If she lost control now, she'd be as good as dead.

As she tried to focus, she slowly became aware of thick smoke billowing from the thatched roofs of the adjoining buildings. The air was growing black and bitter as the choking haze filled the clearing and hung low in the thick equatorial heat. Flames crackled louder, closer, brighter, engulfing the compound. The sound was so close.... With a dull jolt of panic she realized the roof of the hut she was in was also on fire. But she couldn't move. She felt dazed. Time stretched, slowed, warped. She couldn't begin to comprehend what was happening. Why had soldiers with assault rifles stormed out of the jungle in hazmat suits? Why had they taken the autopsied bodies?

"This is big, Sarah. Nothing science has seen before..." She latched on to Dr. Regnaud's words. For some reason, she alone had been spared death. She had to hold on to that. She had a duty now. She had to somehow get those biological samples to the Centers for Disease Control in Atlanta. She would not—*could not*—let the doctor down.

She made a quick sign of the cross over Dr. Regnaud's body, gently closed his eyes and then scrambled on her hands and knees toward the radio on the desk near the door.

She had no idea how to use it. How could she have been so stupid, so naive not to learn how to do this simple thing? She tried to tell herself she would've learned in a few more days. But the villagers had begun to arrive with symptoms of the horrific disease, and chaos had erupted. She hadn't had the luxury of time to even begin to understand this bizarre jungle environment, let alone figure out how to use the darn radio.

She fiddled with the dials and buttons, trying to recall what she'd seen Dr. Regnaud doing. Static crackled. Her pulse leaped. Her heart hammered.

"Mayday! Mayday!" Sarah yelled into the transceiver. Did people even say that anymore? Was it only for ships at sea? Or planes? Or old movies? *"Mayday! Help! Help!* 9-1-1—" Oh God, she was panicking again. This was Africa. They didn't know about 9-1-1 here. She cleared her throat, wiped the sweat from her forehead with the back of her sleeve, tried to get hold of herself. The smoke was scorching her nasal passages even through her mask. "This…this is Sarah Burdett. Emergency. Can anybody hear me? I'm a nurse from Ishonga clinic…northeast of Ouesso near the Oyambo River. Unidentified deadly virus…we've been attacked. Soldiers—"

A chunk of burning thatch crashed through the roof and exploded onto the floor in a shower of orange sparks. Acrid smoke instantly engulfed the room. Panic gripped her. *"Help me! Please, oh God, someone help me!"* The fire leaped to a stack of papers and crackled through a wicker basket. She dropped the handset, leaving it dangling by a wire from the desk. She had to get out or she'd be as dead as the rest of them.

Trying to stay beneath the pall of suffocating smoke, Sarah groped her way to an overturned metal cabinet. She'd seen a flashlight in there. She wildly fingered the dirt floor, searching the scattered contents of the drawers. She found the flashlight, stuffed it deep into a pocket under her plastic apron. She found another drawer, groped around inside, felt the doctor's handgun, jammed it into her other pocket. The soldiers had ransacked the room, but hadn't taken a thing, not even the gun. Whatever they'd been looking for, they hadn't found.

They had to be searching for the tissue samples in the bio-hazard container.

She crawled across the dirt floor, reached into the hole,

grasped the handle of the aluminum canister and yanked it free. Clutching her deadly package, Sarah stumbled blindly through the hut, out the door.

She froze in her tracks.

Blackened skeletons of charred wood and the shocking smell of burning human flesh seared into her brain. The wooden roof of the tiny clinic church burned fiercely, shooting a shower of orange stars into the night sky. She swayed on her feet as her vision blurred.

Move, Sarah. Do this for them. You owe them this much.

Gripping the container, she forced one foot in front of the other, woodenly making her way toward the periphery of the clearing, toward the living, breathing, inhospitable jungle. Her sneakers were still encased in plastic bags tied at her ankles, her hair still tucked into a cotton head covering, her protective apron still smeared with the doctor's blood.

She was only vaguely aware that her path was lit by burning huts, that night had fallen, fast and complete, around six o'clock, as it did every day so near the equator.

Twelve hours of blackness loomed ahead of her. And with it came sheer, sickening terror.

She was truly alone.

Chapter 1

Hunter McBride floated silently through the thick air, the nylon chute above him a dark blot against the star-spattered heavens.

As he descended, the sounds of the rain forest swelled to a soft chorus below him. He could hear the shrill chirp of crickets, the hollow drumming of chimps hitting buttress roots of trees as they hunted in the predawn. Moist heat and the rich scent of fecund growth wafted up on soft currents of air as the jungle itself seemed to exhale, alive and hungry and waiting below.

His nostrils flared sharply at the familiar scent of primordial life. Somewhere down there was the American nurse, Sarah Burdett.

And a deadly pathogen.

His job was clear. Find the nurse, dead or alive. Locate the pathogen and get it back to the Force du Sable base on São Diogo Island off the coast of Angola, where a level 4 biosafety lab was being set up to identify it. And he had to do it quickly, because the clock was ticking down on a global threat of almost incomprehensible proportions. Failure at any stage of this mission would trigger a series of events that could topple the U.S. government, bring death to millions and end democracy as the world knew it.

The Force du Sable—a highly secretive and deadly efficient private military company that Hunter had helped found—was all that stood between the status quo and a grave new world order. And they had until midnight on October 13—just twenty-one days from now—to complete what, until they'd intercepted the nurse's distress call, had appeared to be a mission impossible.

He double-checked his GPS coordinates and guided his chute toward the Ishonga clinic clearing, skimming over spiked raffia palms and towering Bombax giants that punched up through the forest canopy. The FDS knew the pathogen was being tested somewhere in central Africa, but they hadn't been able to pinpoint where. The nurse's Mayday had changed that. Now they had a location, and possibly even a witness—*if* the nurse was still alive.

Hunter landed with a soft thud on the packed dirt along the outskirts of the compound. He adjusted his night vision gear and quickly gathered his chute. He removed his combat pack, extracted a respirator, positioned it carefully over his nose and mouth and checked the hose connections. From the intel they'd received, the pathogen was not likely airborne, but they weren't sure. They knew only that it was one hundred percent fatal.

He checked his watch and pulled neoprene gloves over his hands. Almost immediately the extra gear peaked his core temperature, and perspiration dampened his torso. The humidity in this region didn't allow a body to cool itself. But Hunter knew how to handle the heat. Guerrilla warfare in tropical climates was his area of expertise.

He made his way toward the charred, skeletal ruins of the clinic buildings, where wisps of smoke still trailed up from hot spots. Burned corpses were scattered across the hardened earth between gutted buildings, the bodies twisted into shapes made all the more grotesque by the eerie gray-green monotones of his night scopes.

Hunter hunkered down next to one corpse, then another. He noted with detached interest that the bodies were untouched by machetes. These people had been shot and then burned—*not* the usual practice of local rebels. The victims had been massacred by someone else, for some reason other than civil war or tribal conflict.

He worked his way methodically through the compound, looking for signs of life, for clues, for the nurse. He found the burned-out radio in what appeared to be an operating room, and stilled. This must have been where she'd sent out her Mayday call. The FDS had traced her immediately to the Aid Africa organization, which had provided her electronic file instantly. Sarah Burdett, 28, divorced, a pediatric nurse from Seattle, had been the lone American stationed at Aid Africa's Ishonga clinic. She'd signed on with the nongovernmental organization only three months ago and had arrived in the Congo exactly two weeks ago. She was a complete neophyte in some of the most hostile terrain known to man.

The digitized image of Sarah Burdett suddenly sifted into Hunter's brain, and for a second all he could see were her soft brown eyes gazing down from the LCD screen in the situation room. Warm eyes. Innocent eyes. His jaw tightened.

That woman was *not* equipped to deal with whatever had happened here.

He quickly scanned the rest of the room. Broken vials and medical equipment were scattered everywhere. A metal cabinet had been toppled and the door of a generator-operated fridge hung on its hinges. Hunter noticed a hole had been dug in the dirt floor, a plank and a bunched-up rug pushed to the side. Had she hidden in there while her colleagues were massacred within earshot? Where was she now?

Hunter found more bodies in what must have been a hospital ward, judging by the wire beds and smoldering mattresses. The bastards had even killed the patients.

He crouched down and studied the victims. They were not likely to be harboring the disease. If the pathogen had indeed found its way into the general population and to this clinic, the soldiers would have gone to great lengths to remove the infected bodies. They'd have wanted to leave no trace of the pathogen's existence. He suspected that was the reason behind this attack.

He needed to find the nurse. She alone held answers that could help save the U.S. president and his nation.

Hunter picked his way to the outer buildings of the compound. In all, the fire had been swift and superficial, fueled by an accelerant, probably petroleum. Parts of one building on the east end had barely even burned. It looked like a storage shed.

He made his way over to the structure, pushed aside a fallen rafter, and poked at the blackened edges of a packing crate with the barrel of his AK-47. The charred container fell open in a cloud of soot that cleared to reveal tins of baby formula.

Hunter stared at the cans. The cherubic face of an infant on the labels smiled happily back at him in ghostly green night-vision hues. His throat tightened. He shut his eyes, and for a brief instant lost the rhythm of breathing through his respirator. It shocked him instantly. His eyes flashed open and he abruptly turned his back on the tins, on the smiling babies.

Keep your cool, buddy. Stay focused. Locate the critical personality. Extract the package. He'd done it a hundred times. It should be no different now.

So why had soft brown eyes and an infant's face suddenly rattled him? He drew a breath in slowly, willing his body to calm. He didn't want to think about why. He didn't want to recall the unborn child in his dark past. He didn't want to think about what the woman he'd once loved with all his heart had done. He had no intention of going anywhere near those ancient memories. They belonged to another man, the man he used to be. He checked his watch again. He needed to keep moving. The sun would rise in less than three hours.

He quickly broadened his search to the perimeter of the compound, and almost immediately spotted something small and white lying on the ground along the edge of the thick jungle fringe. He crouched down, lifted it with the muzzle of his gun. It was a surgical mask. A pair of protective goggles and bloody latex gloves lay next to it.

He studied the ground carefully. He could make out faint scuff marks in the packed earth, small footprints strangely blurred along the edges, as if the shoes were covered with something. His eyes followed the odd trail. They led to a break in the vegetation up ahead, a path.

Hunter skirted along the forest fringe, following the tracks to the path entrance. He dropped to his haunches. Someone else had been here. Several sets of heavy military boot prints virtually obliterated the smaller sets of fuzzy ones. He studied the new tracks, the crushed vegetation, and he saw something else in the dirt. He lifted it carefully with his fingers, sniffed. A hand-rolled cigarette.

He looked up.

If these smaller prints belonged to Sarah Burdett, she was being followed by at least three men. And they weren't far behind her.

04:58 Alpha. Congo.
Monday, September 22

She was drenched in perspiration. Her heart hammered so hard she could barely breathe. She couldn't go on. She had to rest, hide somewhere.

Sarah groped blindly at the dank soil as she crawled through the foliage, and felt something hard and smooth under her fingers. Roots. Using them to feel her way toward the base of a monstrous Bombax tree, she maneuvered herself into a sitting position and pressed her back deep into a crevice formed by the giant buttress roots. She dragged the biohazard container close to her feet and tried to remain still, but she was still shaking uncontrollably.

She'd been moving as fast as she possibly could for what seemed like hours, stumbling wildly down a crude forest path, guided only by the tiny halo of her flashlight. She'd heard men coming after her, yelling. And then she'd tripped and fallen onto damp ground and lost the flashlight. She'd crawled off the path, into heavy primary jungle where there seemed to be less undergrowth to hamper her movements. She'd kept going, blindly fumbling through the darkness, dragging the heavy container behind her, stopping only to listen for the soldiers. They must have heard her distress call and come back for her. She had no doubt they would kill her if they found her.

All around her she could hear sounds of terrifying, unidentified things, but the shouts of the soldiers seemed to have faded. She must have lost them by leaving the main path.

Her breathing began to slow a little, but with the momentary respite came a sinking sense of utter despair.

How in heavens was she even supposed to get out of this jungle, let alone get this container all the way to Atlanta?

Perhaps she could get it to a U.S. embassy. But the American embassy in Brazzaville was closed because of violence in the capital, the staff operating out of the embassy in Kinshasa for safety reasons. Even if she managed to get as far south as Brazzaville, she'd still have to take a ferry over the Congo River to Kinshasa in the neighboring Democratic Republic of the Congo. And even if the unreliable ferry service was running, she still didn't have the Brazzaville exit permits she'd need to get out of the country, *or* a visa for entry into Congo-Kinshasa…or the money she'd need for bribes to get the necessary travel papers.

She didn't even have a passport now.

The U.S. State Department warnings began to play through her head. *Travel to these regions is not recommended…. Night travel outside of towns and cities should be avoided….* She looked up into the impenetrable night that surrounded her. Who was she kidding? She couldn't even begin to think of getting through this *jungle*. She didn't know a damn thing about surviving in it. She had no compass. No map. *Nothing*. She'd been flown into this darkest heart of Africa by chopper and dumped into a patch of dense equatorial jungle barely known to Western man. It was an area still steeped in Marxist dogma, tribal sorcery and civil violence.

What *had* she been thinking even coming here? She didn't know anything about Africa, or aid work. She was a pediatric nurse who lived in civilized Seattle, a misty and *cool* city with paved streets, electricity and water you didn't have to boil before drinking. A city where leaves were turning gold and days were getting short and crisp. She should be there now. She should be shopping in a mall, wearing lipstick and a coat, buying something nice for dinner…and eating chocolate. Tears welled in her eyes.

Don't delude yourself, Sarah. You know exactly why you came here.

She'd come to escape that old life. She was trying to piece herself together after a bitter and humiliating public divorce. She was trying to hide from the echoes of an emotional nightmare she'd embarrassingly endured for years at the hands of her ex, trying to come to terms with the reality that she'd never have what she'd always wanted—children of her own, a loving husband, a big family, a white picket fence…the whole shebang. Her dreams had been shattered and she'd gotten lost somewhere back in that old world. So she'd run away, to Africa, to find some *real* purpose in her life, to validate herself as a worthwhile human being. To do some good for people who actually needed her…

Sarah blinked back hot tears. Now she was more alone, more blind, more lost than ever—not just emotionally, but physically. Coming to the Congo had been the boldest move she'd ever made, and it had turned out to be a terrible mistake. She'd never find her way back now, not unless God dropped some angel from the sky….

A soft sound jerked her back to her senses.

Sarah held her breath.

Then she heard it again, a quiet crack of twigs, barely distinguishable from the other noises. Her heart leaped straight back up into her throat and hammered hard. She peered into the solid blackness, trying to identify the source, but she couldn't see a thing. And she couldn't run.

She was trapped.

She pressed her back deeper into the roots of the Bombax

and slid her hand into her pocket. Quietly, carefully, she drew out the gun. She grasped the handle with both hands, found the trigger, curled her finger around it and aimed blindly into the darkness with shaking hands, praying she wouldn't have to use it. She'd never fired a gun before.

She stayed like that for what seemed like forever. Sweat trickled over her body as she listened for the noise. She'd never been more petrified in her life. The perspiration that soaked her skin began to cool, and she started to shiver violently. Something crawled slowly up her neck—some kind of caterpillar. She could feel hundreds of little hairy legs. She gritted her teeth, tried desperately to hold still as the worm inched up toward her hairline. But suddenly it stung like all hell. Sarah stifled a scream and flicked it off with her hand.

The movement cost her. Something rustled sharply in the leaves to her right. She swung the gun toward the source of the sound.

Then she heard it again.

She scrunched her eyes tight and squeezed the trigger. Sound cracked her eardrums and shrieks ripped through the jungle canopy as monkeys high in the trees scattered. Sarah screamed in reflex.

A huge hand grabbed her wrists, so tightly that she dropped the gun. She opened her mouth to scream again, but another hand clamped down hard over her jaw. She choked in fright. She felt her eyes bulge in terror, but she was blind in the blackness. All she could do was feel him. And her attacker was definitely male. He was down on the ground beside her, leaning his body into hers, his weight forcing her painfully against the roots. She could taste the saltiness of his palm pressed against her lips, feel the power and strength in his limbs. He was huge, solid like iron. And she was one dead woman. She was certain of it.

"You could kill someone with that gun," he whispered, his voice low and warm in her ear.

Her heart kicked into her throat. He wasn't one of the soldiers. They'd been yelling in French and Lingala. This man spoke to her in English.

She felt his hot breath against her ear again. "Shh, it's okay, I'm not going to hurt you."

She whimpered slightly.

He waited, his hand still pressed firmly over her mouth. "You gonna be quiet?" he murmured, his lips so close to her ear she could feel them brush against her lobe.

She nodded.

He slowly removed his hand from her mouth, grasped her chin between powerful fingers and turned her face toward his. But she could see nothing. She could only sense the size of him, feel his breath on her lips.

"Sarah Burdett?"

He knew her name! She choked back a hysterical sob. A maelstrom of emotions swamped her exhausted brain. Somehow, in this alien place, it mattered incredibly that someone knew her name.

"My name is Hunter McBride," he said softly. "I'm here to take you home, Sarah." He grasped her hands in his and coaxed her gently to her feet. She wobbled as she tried to stand.

"Can you move? Are you hurt?"

She didn't know. She'd been running on autopilot. She hadn't even begun to think about the pain in her body. Her neck was burning like fire. Her face was cut. Her back, near her left shoulder blade, ached deeply. Her knees and shins stung. Every nerve ending in her body was raw.

"Sarah, can you hear me? Are you hurt anywhere?"

She could detect a soft Irish brogue in his hushed words. *Irish.* Like her grandmother. And thinking of her gran made her think of home, of Seattle, of cool mist and rain, of comfort and the ocean and music....

Her knees sagged under her.

05:07 Alpha. Venturion Tower, Manhattan.
Monday, September 22

He checked his watch. Just after eleven on Sunday night. The sun would be rising in the Congo in precisely one hour. He pushed his chair away from his desk and stalked over to windows that yawned up from the polished mahogany floor. Hands behind his back, he stared out over the glittering skyline of his city, its lights like diamonds scattered over velvet. He liked to think of it as his. He'd been born here in New York City, grown up here. He'd conceived and constructed his global empire from here. It was from here that he and his fraternity had helped shape senators, congressmen, presidents and kings...and topple them.

He smiled ruefully. Usually the view contented him. But he was edgy tonight, unusually so. What they were putting into action now went way beyond the realm of the usual. It was bold. Unprecedented. And it had been decades in the making.

Only President John Elliot stood in their way now. The man's resilience had surprised them all and had necessitated a dramatic change in plans.

And there was another glitch. A small one, true, but he didn't tolerate glitches, no matter the size. Somehow the pathogen had infected villagers near Ouesso. Villagers who were *not* part of the trials, who were not supposed to be part of the warning sent to President Elliot. Villagers who'd ended up dying at the Ishonga clinic—a clinic that just *happened* to house Guy Regnaud, one of the world's most renowned epidemiologists.

Of all the damn luck.

He shoved his hands deep into the pockets of his crisply tailored pants. He'd ordered the local militia on his payroll to immediately eliminate every damn living thing at that clinic and to remove all evidence of the infected corpses and the disease. But he'd just gotten word that a nurse had managed to get out a distress call before escaping. Now she was missing. So were the samples that Dr. Regnaud had taken from the autopsied patients.

He told himself it was nothing. If the militia didn't kill her, the jungle would. And even if by some bizarre twist of fate she got out of that godforsaken place, it would take days, weeks, months even, before anyone in the U.S. even began to realize the implications of what she'd seen, or what was in that bio-hazard container, if at all. And by then it would be too late.

She was harmless, he told himself. Nothing would stop them now.

Nothing could.

Chapter 2

Hunter grasped Sarah's shoulders and steadied her on her feet, surprised at how slight—how right—she felt in his hands. He looked into her face. She was clearly terrified, her eyes huge and vulnerable. His chest tightened. She looked even younger than she had in the digital photo he'd seen. "Sarah, how badly are you hurt? Can you move?"

Her eyes flickered as she searched the dark for his face. "I…I think so."

He began a quick assessment of her condition. Her face was cut and bleeding just below her left cheekbone. A torn piece of fabric covered part of her hair; the rest escaped in a wild tangle of curls. She wore a ripped plastic apron over a long-sleeved blouse and a skirt. The apron was smeared with blood. She had thin cotton pants under her skirt. They were shredded, bloodied and muddy at her knees and shins. Ripped plastic bags covered her runners. It looked as if she'd been wearing at least two bags over each shoe. That explained the odd footprints he'd found.

Hunter recalled the surgical mask, goggles and gloves he'd seen lying at the edge of the clearing. Sarah Burdett had been wearing makeshift biohazard clothing. She'd obviously adapted whatever had been available at the compound. She must have been working with the infected patients before the attack.

An odd spasm shuddered down his spine. This young nurse and her colleagues had been working to save lives when those lives had been brutally taken. She was a healer. And he knew too well how the sight of pointless death cut to the quick of a soul born to heal.

Hunter steeled his jaw. Sarah Burdett had been through hell and back tonight, and by some absurd twist of fate she'd survived. But she was far from out of the woods, and his job was not to coddle her. Now that he'd found her alive, his job was to extricate her, and more importantly, extricate the pathogen he suspected was in the biohazard container at her feet.

"Sarah," he whispered against her ear, the contact sending a frisson over his skin, "can you tell me what's in the container?"

Her eyes flicked wildly around as if looking for escape.

His heart kicked against his ribs. "Tell me *exactly* what's in there."

"T-tissue, fluid, brain samples…from…" Her voice wavered and she began to tremble again.

He steadied her shoulders firmly. "Focus, Sarah. *Who* are the tissue samples from?"

"From seven villagers near Ouesso. They…they presented at the clinic with symptoms we didn't recognize. It…it, oh, God…"

She took a deep breath. "They all died. It was horrible, so violent. They began to attack themselves, us, anything that moved."

Hunter's pulse kicked up another notch. "Where are the bodies now?"

"They took them. Just the autopsied ones." A dry sob racked her petite frame. "They killed, burned everyone else—the patients, nurses, priest, even…Doc…Dr. Regnaud. He…he saved my life."

Hunter's grip tightened on her shoulders. "*Who* took the bodies?"

"Soldiers. They had automatic rifles…and were wearing hazmat suits."

Hunter clenched his jaw. This was exactly what they'd been looking for! This woman had just shaved days off their mission. He had to get her and the samples to a clearing where he could get decent satellite reception and where they could bring in a helicopter. He could patch up her injuries while they waited for evacuation. She could get a thorough exam at the FDS clinic on São Diogo.

"Sarah, we need to move—"

She jerked away from him suddenly. "Who *are* you?"

"Later. Right now we move, fast."

She backed away, shaking her head, clutching the canister tightly against her body.

Frustration nipped at him. "Sarah, there were at least three men tracking you before you left the path. I've taken care of them, but their bodies will be found by daybreak, and that's in exactly one hour. There'll—"

Her eyes went wide. "You *killed* them?"

Frustration snapped harder at Hunter. He did not have time for this. "I did what was necessary to keep you alive, Sarah. And there'll be more coming after them. Now if you want to live, you'd better move. Come—" He reached for the handle of the biohazard container.

"*No!*" she shrieked, yanking it away from him. "That's mine! I've got to get it to the CDC!"

Monkeys screeched and scattered high in the canopy above them. A dead giveaway.

"Damn it, Sarah!" Hunter hissed, seizing her upper arm. He dug his fingers hard into her flesh, jerked her body up against his and leaned close to her frightened face. He dropped his tone to a low growl. "Keep your voice down unless you want to die. Got it?"

She went dead still in his arms.

Guilt stabbed his chest. He softened his tone slightly. "I know you've been through hell, and I know you're not thinking straight, but you've *got* to trust me. Your life depends on it. Am I getting through to you?"

She clenched her jaw, said nothing.

Exasperation peaked in him. "Look, we have to get that container to a level 4 lab and get the contents identified ASAP. *That* is why I'm here and that is why you're going to do *exactly* what I say."

He moved his mouth so close to her ear he could feel the soft fuzz of her lobe against his bottom lip, and again a tinge of awareness caught him by surprise. "And that means no questions, no second-guessing, or you'll get us *both* killed. Do you understand me?"

She choked as if she was going to throw up. Hunter's heart twisted sharply in his chest. But he swallowed the discomfort. This was the only way to get through to her, to get her out alive. "Tell me you understand me, Sarah. I want to hear you say it."

Her eyes pooled with moisture but her jaw remained tight. "Yes," she said softly through clenched teeth. "Yes, I understand."

"Good." He prised the container from her fingers as he spoke. "Now here's the deal. I have night vision gear, you don't. I can see, you can't. I need you to hook your hand into my belt webbing here...." He grabbed her hand, guided it to his back, tucked her fingers into his belt. "I'll lead. I'll be your eyes. You just hang on and try to keep up. We move till daybreak, then we take cover and wait for the helevac."

He began to edge forward, but she resisted immediately. "Where are we going?"

He drew a breath in slowly, straining for patience. "The Shilongwe River, where we can get the chopper in."

"I...I was going to the Oyambo River," she protested. "I was going to—to the village there, to get help."

"So was your tail," he snapped. "You ready now?"

She made a faint little sound he took as an affirmative. "Stay directly behind me. Don't want to connect you with a backswing if I need to use the machete to clear a path, understand?"

He took her silence as acquiescence, and he started to move. She stumbled instantly, dragging down hard on his belt, but righted herself just as quickly. Hunter moved slowly at first, picking the easiest route across small gullies, around ferns and raised roots on the forest floor. Sarah managed to find an awkward if staggering gait behind him, and he took it as a sign to increase the pace. They moved like that for the better part of half an hour before the earth turned boggy and began to suck and drag at their feet.

He felt Sarah begin to falter again, and then she stumbled, her hand slipping free of his belt. Hunter reached behind him, snatched her wrist and caught her. He tucked her hand back into his belt—and this time registered how slender and soft her fingers were, how fine-boned her wrist. It felt...*like Kathleen's hand.*

The thought exploded like shrapnel through Hunter, so sharp he stumbled.

He stopped, caught his breath, and killed the memory instantly. But the fact it had even entered his head rocked him to the core.

He blew out a long, slow breath as he tried to focus. He thought he'd totally terminated the memories. The past. The blackness. Himself. But now...now the murdered memories were sifting up like haunting mists from a decaying swamp, the dread rising inside him, making him feel things again. What in hell was wrong with him?

Hunter gritted his teeth. There was no freaking way he was going to start seeing ghosts in this forest. Not after so many years. Not after coming this far. This hadn't happened to him on any other mission. So why this one?

Deliver the package and move on. Another job. Another day.

He picked up the pace, knowing he was going too fast for her, yet unable to slow himself down.

Sarah could barely keep her balance as her rescuer suddenly upped the pace, and she was so out of breath she could hardly speak, let alone find some kind of logical order to the fragmented images and questions slamming through her brain. But she had to ask. "Why...are they after my container?"

"Later. Save your breath." His words were clipped.

"Who...will send a helicopter?"

"Friends. Keep moving."

His dismissive tone frustrated her. And she couldn't keep up at this pace. But she was terrified of protesting, of letting go, of irritating him to a point that he'd take her container and just leave her in the jungle to die. She had no idea who he was or who he worked for, and she didn't trust him any more than those murderous soldiers back at the compound. But right now he was her only salvation, her lifeline through the dark. She *had* to hang on.

The forest undergrowth grew thicker. Sarah could literally sense the tangle of vegetation knitting itself around her, creeping ominously closer. She stumbled again and again. Thorns and twigs and leaves tore at her clothes, scraped her skin. Tears of sheer exhaustion began to stream down her face. "Could…could you slow…down a little? I—"

"Keep moving!"

Her toe hooked under a knot of vines, and this time she wasn't able to brace herself. Her hand wrenched free from his belt and she went down hard and fast. Her chest slammed into the ground and air crunched from her lungs in a violent whoosh. Sparks of pain radiated through her torso, and for a terrifying instant, she couldn't breathe, or even move.

She felt him drop instantly to her side, felt his hands on her, easing her up into a sitting position. She gasped wildly for breath, but her lungs wouldn't open up.

"Easy, easy, Sarah. You're winded. Don't panic, just relax." His voice was calm, strong, quiet. He gathered her to his chest and gently rubbed her back as she struggled to breathe, until her lungs could take in air again, until the acute panic began to ebb and she realized she was going to be okay.

She expected him to release her then, but he didn't. He fell silent and continued to hold her against his body, a brooding, encompassing presence in the dark. She could feel the rough hair on his forearms and the hair at the base of his neck where his shirt was open. She could smell his masculine scent amid the rich layers of jungle smells. And she could sense him studying her. It made her feel naked, yet in a strange way, she felt a sense of refuge in his arms, a basic human comfort.

He placed a callused palm against her cheek, a confident, tangible strength transferring through his touch, as if the man was magically infusing her with the calm to do what she needed to do. "Are you okay?"

There was something about his voice, something in his touch

that made her want to believe she was. "Yes," she whispered. "Yes, I—I think I'm okay."

But the tears trailing furiously down her face must have betrayed her. He brushed them away with his thumb. The gesture made her heart twist and her tears flowed all the harder. Absurdly, she just wanted to stay in his arms. She wanted to bury her face against his chest, drink in his masculine scent, fold herself into his embrace.

"You've made it farther than most people could, Sarah," he whispered against her cheek. "You're strong, and you're going to be just fine as long as you hang in here with me for another twenty minutes or so. It'll be light by then. We should be in the clearing, alongside the Shilongwe. And once we're there, we can get you cleaned and patched up. Here…"

She felt something being pushed up against her lips—the mouth of a canteen. He cupped his hand around the back of her head and tilted the canteen toward her. Water trickled over her lips and down her chin and neck. Sarah gulped at it, but he pulled it away before she'd had enough. She groped in the dark for more.

"Not so fast," he said softly. "Need to save some for later. Ready now?"

She wiped her wrist over her mouth and nodded, feeling strangely refueled by his touch, by the fact that he actually seemed to care. As much as he terrified her, Sarah needed this man on a very basic human level.

He helped her to her feet. "The going will get a bit rougher from here, but not for long. Stay right behind me, clear of the machete." He took her hand and once again guided it around his back, hooked it carefully into his belt.

She heard the sickening sound of a blade being unsheathed, then the first two rapacious strokes as metal met vegetation. He began to move forward again, pulling her along, more slowly now. She edged after him, feet tentatively testing ground before transferring weight.

Gradually, gray shapes and shadows began to emerge from the cloak of pure blackness as dawn broke somewhere beyond the forest canopy. Fresh energy surged through Sarah. She'd made it through the night! She was going to live to see another day.

But almost instantly her flare of excitement was quashed as the indistinct shadows morphed into monstrous, prehistoric-looking trunks, knotted vines curling up them, nests of vegetation growing in the forks of their branches. Tangled lianas looped down from the canopy, some of them thick as her wrist, some with inch-long thorns. Stems and leaves and vines all mixed so chaotically in the eerie dawn light that she couldn't tell where one plant ended and another began, what was growing up or what was growing down. There was absolutely no sense of order. And all around her, heat and sound began to swell. Birds, monkeys, other unidentifiable creatures, all rising to a riotous, raucous cacophony that tore at her ragged nerves. Sarah's heart began to pound even harder.

Being blind to what was around her had been better than actually seeing it all. Seeing made her predicament too stark, too real. This wasn't some horrendous dream from which she could waken. She was stepping out of the blackness into a living nightmare.

And as more light began to filter down through the canopy, the man in front of her took an even more formidable form than she'd imagined in the dark. He was well over six feet tall, with an unruly mess of pitch-black hair. He was wearing a combat vest, camouflage gear and black army boots. He had a military pack on his back and an assault rifle slung across his shoulders. It was the same kind of gun she'd seen both soldiers and rebels carrying since she'd arrived in the Congo. Yet despite his military gear, she could see no official markings on his clothing. Whoever he was, she'd bet her life he did not belong to any conventional army. And judging by the hypnotic swipe of his machete, the way he never lost the rhythm or power of his stroke, she'd also bet that he'd done this kind of thing many, many times before.

It made her hunger for a look at the face that went with the body, with the voice, with the powerful tenderness in his touch—the contradiction that was this man.

Then, so suddenly it shocked her, they broke out of the forest into a clearing. Sarah jerked to a stop, instantly blinded by light. She scrunched her eyes tight against the white pain, feeling as disoriented as a mole that had just been spat out of moist, black ground.

"Your eyes got accustomed to the dark," he said. "Give them time to adjust."

She stilled.

This time there was no harsh whisper or growl from his lips. The man had the languid and mellifluous bass tones of a late-night Irish DJ. Sarah became even more desperate to see him. She lifted both hands to shield her brow and angled her head, squinted one eye open. Then the other.

Her heart stumbled. She blinked once, twice.

And could only stare.

Chapter 3

Black camouflage paint covered his face, making the whites of his eyes leap out in contrast. He was studying her with those eyes in a relaxed, almost lazy fashion. His mouth, sensually sculpted, was absolutely devoid of expression as he appraised her.

A predator, that's what he was, acutely aware of everything going on around him. She didn't doubt for an instant that he could strike to kill in the blink of an eye.

Sarah swallowed the odd mix of awe, fear and admiration rising in her throat. She felt suddenly more powerless in front of this elemental male than she had in the deep jungle night.

He raised his machete and sheathed it slowly behind his

back, his eyes never breaking contact with hers. She had a sense she was being weighed, judged.

He reached for the canteen hanging at his hip, twisted off the cap, held the water bottle out to her, and smiled. The sudden whiteness of his teeth against the camouflage paint was predacious.

Sarah cringed instinctively toward the protection of the jungle foliage. A flock of birds scattered from the reeds along the river and fluttered squawking into the sky, exposing the red underside of their fanned tails. The surreal flurry of color in her peripheral vision, the sudden brightness of daylight after twelve hours of blackness, was overwhelming her senses. She stared at the water bottle in his huge, tanned hand, aware of her thirst, yet unable to move.

"You okay?"

Her eyes lifted slowly, met his. *"Who are you?"*

He smiled again, more gently this time, and the sunlight caught his eyes. A distant part of her brain noted the color of them, an unusual blue, so dark it was almost indigo.

"Here…" He pushed the canteen toward her. "Have some water. You look like you need it."

She moved to take the canteen from his hands, but as she did, she caught sight of the huge hunting knife tucked into a leather casing strapped around his massive thigh. There was dried blood on the hilt, and on his pants. Lots. She froze, thinking of the three men who'd been following her…. Her eyes shot back up to his.

"They would have killed you, Sarah," he said softly. "If I hadn't taken their lives, they would have taken yours."

She shook her head, not wanting to think about what this man had done with that knife. For her. She didn't want to be responsible for death…for anyone's death. She believed in life, in protecting it at all cost. That's what had driven her to be a nurse, a caregiver. Hugging herself, she backed toward the wall of vegetation they'd just come through, as if it might offer refuge from stark reality. But Sarah knew it held only darkness and danger. There was no going back. She had no choice. She had to go forward. *With him.*

He took a step toward her, placed his hand against her neck. Sarah caught her breath. She could feel a latent power almost vibrating through him.

He curled his fingers around the back of her neck, placed his thumb under her jawbone, and tilted her face, forcing her to look back up into his eyes. She had no doubt he could snap her neck in an instant, yet his touch had a solid warmth that seemed to flow right into her, that somehow went beyond protective into the realm of darkly seductive. A shiver rippled through her body at the conflicting sensations generated by the contact.

"Sarah," he murmured. "I'm on your side. I'm going to get you home."

Home?

A hiccup jerked painfully in her chest as she tried to choke down a sob. Wasn't that why she'd come running to Africa? Because her idea of home had been utterly demolished by Josh, the cold, powerful man she'd once thought she'd loved with all her heart? Her ex-husband had crushed her world. He'd taken everything from her.

She had no home.

"Trust me, Sarah." Hunter gazed into her eyes. "If anyone can get you out of here, I will. I promise you that."

She wanted to tell him it was not possible. No one could get her home. Not in a way that mattered.

He pushed the canteen into her hands. "Now here, drink."

le wrapped her fingers around the bottle. "You need to stay ydrated. Take what you need—we'll be out of here soon. In he meantime, I'm going to head out into that clearing over here—" he pointed to a patch of grass that grew luminescent reen and tall in the sunlight "—where I can get a decent satellite signal. I'm going to call for our helevac and then we can et you cleaned up while we wait for the chopper, okay?"

She nodded numbly.

He turned and made his way into the clearing—with her biohazard container. The long grass parted around his sleek, powerful form, his hair glinting blue-black in the sun.

"Trust me, Sarah."

Could she? She sank onto the trunk of a massive fallen tree and drank deeply from the water bottle as she studied him in he distance. He crouched down among the tall grass and took what looked like a stubby phone out of his combat vest, pulling a thick antenna out the top.

"Trust no one. This is the Congo. Everyone has a price." What was this man's price? What on earth had she gotten mixed up in? Her brain didn't want to think. Couldn't. She was too tired to even formulate the questions.

She set the canteen down on the log beside her and clasped her hand tightly around the small gold crucifix that nestled at he hollow of her throat, seeking comfort in the familiar shape. Her grandmother had given her the small cross for her fourteenth birthday, her first birthday after her mother died, and Sarah had worn it ever since. It grounded her, reminded her of he good things she'd had in life. Sarah clutched the keepsake, closed her eyes and lifted her face to the sun.

Then she heard Hunter's voice in the clearing. He was speaking in fluent French. Her eyes flared open. The soldiers who had attacked the compound had been yelling in French.

She listened more closely. The inflection and resonant intonation of his words were no different from the haunting sound of the locals. Her chest tightened. Was he allied to the soldiers who'd attacked the compound? She hadn't been able to see anything of them other than their black hazmat suits. Had he come after her because he'd known she had the pathogen? Was this all just a ploy to get her container? But then why hadn't he killed her back in jungle?

"Trust no one."

He signed off, pocketed his phone, looked sharply up in her direction. Something had changed in him. She could see it in his posture. Her mouth went dry.

He stood in a fluid movement, a gleaming panther rising out of the grass. And in that same liquid motion, he adjusted the sling of his assault rifle, swinging the weapon from his back to hang ready at his side. He picked up her biohazard container and stalked through the long grass toward her, until the shadow of his huge frame blotted out the sun that had warmed her face.

"Chopper will be here within the hour." His voice was gruff and there was a new razor-sharp glare in his eyes. He seemed somehow less human, and the change frightened her.

She shrank back. "Will you *please* tell me who you are, who you were talking to out there?"

He didn't answer. He grasped her arm, lifted her brusquely to her feet and moved her closer to the jungle fringe, his eyes scanning the far edges of the clearing as he moved.

"What is it?" she asked nervously.

"Stay close to the forest cover. We need to move down to those flat rocks at the river's edge, under that tree. We can clean and patch you up there while we wait for the helo."

Hunter escorted Sarah down to the water, every sense alert.

He scanned the far bank of the wide, sluggish river for the slightest signs of movement as they went. Jacques Sauvage at the FDS base had just informed him there'd been a coup in Brazzaville early this morning. Insurgents had stormed the president's residence before dawn. President Samwetwe was now missing, and all borders were shutting down. Sporadic fighting had already spread as far north as the Shilongwe. That meant rebels could be anywhere at this very minute. And it meant that he and Sarah were suddenly fair game from all sides of this war. They were running from not only the militia who had razed the Ishonga compound, but also from unidentified rebel cadres as well. They had to get out of the Congo, fast. The whole place was set to blow.

He sat Sarah down on a slab of rock near the brown waters of the Shilongwe and squinted toward the sky. The chopper would come in from the north, from Cameroon. There was a wide sandbank about twenty yards into the shallows. It would land there. If his guys made it into Congo airspace undetected, they should be here in about forty-five minutes.

That was already cutting it too close.

He turned his attention back to Sarah. She was watching him intently. Tears, dirt and blood streaked her cheeks, and her eyes were huge with fear. *Of him.* She didn't trust him. Who in hell could blame her? What horror had those big brown eyes seen?

Hunter felt an odd little spasm in his chest. He recognized it for what it was: anger. Protective anger. Anger at the people who'd done this to her. Because this woman was *not* equipped to handle the situation. She did not deserve this. How she'd managed to get this far was beyond him.

Then he saw what she was nervously fingering at the hollow of her throat—a small crucifix on a delicate gold chain. His jaw tightened and he stared at her fingers. In this merciless jungle, where you had to take life in order to live, where dark spirits and primal forces ruled, she was seeking the comfort and protection of her civilized God.

The sight forced him right up against the acid memories of his past. And for a fleeting moment his mind was touched by a sense of déjà vu, the distant sensation of icy mist trailing over his face on the night he'd fled Belfast—the night the police had come to arrest him for allegedly killing his fiancée. He shook off the poisonous memory. Why was he even thinking about this garbage? It was ancient history.

But he couldn't tear his eyes away from her hand...from her. She looked so out of place against the backdrop of tangled primordial forest. She didn't belong in this dog-eat-dog world. Her God wasn't going to protect her from this jungle. What on earth made Hunter think *he* could? Something swelled so sharply in his heart it hurt.

He clenched his teeth. He didn't want to feel these things, these protective urges. Not again. Not now. Not ever. That was not who Hunter McBride was anymore. That man had been dead and buried for fifteen long and bitter years.

"Are you going to tell me who you are now?"

For a nanosecond he wasn't sure who the hell he *was* anymore. He mentally shook himself and crouched down in front of her. "My name is Hunter McBride. I—"

"Are you one of them?"

"Them?"

"The militia. The soldiers who attacked the clinic were carrying the same weapon as you, were speaking the same language."

"Sarah, there's a reason everyone out here carries an AK. You can jam it with mud, water, whatever, and it'll still shoot straight without blowing up in your face. And the French…" He shifted slightly on his haunches, the sun hot on his back. "It's one of the country's official languages. My colleagues and I speak it, along with just about everyone else in this region."

"But you're not with the French—or Belgian—armed forces." It was an accusation, not a question. "Who *are* you with?"

Hunter's lips twitched. He hadn't expected the Spanish Inquisition. In spite of what she'd just been through, this woman still had spunk. "You're right, I'm not with the Belgian or French military, but I *am* French—"

"You sound Irish." She made it seem as though she almost wished he *were* Irish. And absurdly, it made a part of him want to say that he was. It made a part of him want to explain. He bit back the urge.

"I'm a citizen of France," he said bluntly. And then he cursed himself for saying it at all. It was none of her damn business where he came from, what passport he carried and why. And it wasn't his job to tell her. His job was to get her—and the pathogen—out. That was all.

"Look, I'm just going to give it to you straight. That canister contains a bioweapon that will be released over the three biggest cities in the United States in exactly twenty-one days. That's New York, Chicago and Los Angeles."

He could tell from the skeptical look in her eyes that she didn't believe him.

"We've been looking for that pathogen, Sarah. We knew it was being tested somewhere in central Africa, that unethical clinical trials were being conducted on innocent villagers, probably under the guise of a vaccine program. But we didn't know exactly where until we intercepted your call. It seems that those clinical trials went sideways and villagers outside the control groups were infected. They found their way to your clinic and died there. The soldiers were sent to cover it up."

She shook her head. "This can't be true. I…I don't believe you. I *can't*."

He shrugged. It wasn't his job to make her believe. He just had to make her cooperate.

Despair clouded her gaze. "Who…who would *do* such a thing?"

"We don't know. Yet. But our intelligence tells us there *is* an antidote. Once we identify this disease, we can begin to think about locating that antidote. That in turn could lead us to whoever is behind this, but we don't have much time."

She shook her head again, her eyes looking strangely distant. "Our patients died within days. Within twenty-four hours they all showed signs of advanced dementia. Then they lost coordination, reason, and became psychotic." She paused, her features growing tight. "They lashed out at anyone who tried to help them, scratching, biting like wild animals. Even at themselves, tearing their own flesh. It…was terrifying. We had to restrain them or I'm sure they would have killed us." Her eyes flashed up to his, desperation in them.

"What happened then, Sarah?" he asked, a little more gently.

"A painful and messy death. Lots of hemorrhaging. It was something Dr. Regnaud had never seen or heard of before in his life. And he is…was…a world-renowned epidemiological specialist, you know."

Hunter nodded. "I know. And this *is* the disease we've been looking for, Sarah." The FDS had seen film footage of the effects, footage sent to President Buchanan as a warning. He jerked his chin toward the canister. "That's a cryogenic container. How long have we got?"

"Dr. Regnaud preserved the samples with enough liquid

nitrogen to last maybe two weeks. He'd planned to fly the canister out on the next chopper." She looked at the biohazard container, then at him. "Hunter, if this gets released in the U.S.—"

"We can't let that happen, Sarah. We must do everything in our power to stop this, and you can help us."

A frown furrowed her dirt-smudged brow. "Us?"

"My team, the Force du Sable. We're a private military company based on the island of São Diogo off the northwest coast of Angola. We contract out to various countries and organizations. This time it's the president of the United States."

"You're *mercenaries?*"

"Right."

"I see." Her jaw tightened ever so slightly and a hint of disapproval shifted into her eyes. For some reason the change in her expression really bothered him. He opened his mouth to speak, to defend himself, his profession. Then he shut it abruptly. He didn't have to justify himself to this woman. To anyone. He didn't even know why the hell he even felt compelled to do so.

"I promised to get the container to the CDC in Atlanta." A note of defiance now laced her voice. "I *have* to get it to Atlanta."

"Can't use the CDC. Can't use anyone or any organization within the United States—they've all been compromised. It could trigger the biological attack. We have to use an outside source. There's a level 4 lab being set up at the FDS base on São Diogo. We're taking it there."

"I don't understand. Why would going to the CDC trigger the attack?"

Hunter pushed out a soft breath of frustration. In spite of the need for secrecy, he had to tell her what he could. She'd be more likely to cooperate if she understood the scope of this thing.

"The threat comes from a group *within* the U.S. An inordinately powerful cabal we believe is comprised mostly of Americans, some with very significant connections to the country's power structure. Until we know who they really are, we can't be sure who is connected to whom or what. If they are tipped off, if they get even a hint of the fact we now have their pathogen and are attempting to identify it, they will launch the attack immediately, and *that* is why we can't risk using the CDC."

Her eyes flickered. "I…I just can't imagine why Americans would kill their own people. What do they want?"

"We don't know," he lied.

"What about the soldiers who attacked the compound? How do they fit in?"

"Hired by the Cabal."

She narrowed her eyes. "You're a mercenary. I know men like you, Hunter. You work for whoever has the cash. How do I know you aren't working for this group, just like those soldiers back at the compound? Why should I trust *you?*"

"Because you don't have a choice, do you?" He leaned forward. "And there's one thing you'd better believe. If I *did* work for the Cabal, you'd have been dead hours ago."

Alarm flared in her eyes.

Guilt spiked in Hunter. The woman was in shock. She was doing her best to think straight, to protect herself, and here he was, taking offense. What in hell was wrong with him? It wasn't her fault mercs had a bad rep. And she was right—she had zero reason to trust him. But he didn't need her trust, just her cooperation. Yet an absurd part of him *wanted* her trust, wanted her approval.

He hadn't felt that in a long, long time. And it made him angry. With himself, and indirectly, inexplicably, with her.

He gritted his teeth, focused on reining in his emotion. He needed to keep his mind clear if he wanted to get her out of the

Congo alive. And that meant he had to get her wounds cleaned and patched up as soon as possible, because infection in this climate was a very real—and very deadly—risk.

He cleared his throat. "Come on. You need to rinse that dirt off in the river so I can get a good look at your cuts and sterilize them." He touched his fingers to the gash on her cheek. "And this here needs a butterfly suture or two."

She sat rock-still as he touched her face, her eyes wary, and in them he could read the beginnings of distaste, for *him,* for what he was.

And suddenly it cut him. It rankled beyond all reason. He'd just saved her life. She had no right to judge him like this. She didn't know a damn thing about him.

Hunter got to his feet. "Look, Sarah," he said coolly. "I don't need your trust. I don't need you to like me. All *you* need to know is that because of what I am, I have the goods to get you and that container out of this jungle. And yes, I'm getting paid to do it. I intend to get the job done."

"I'm…just a job," she said quietly.

"You got that right." And that's exactly how he was going to think of her from now on. No more dead memories. No more sappy feelings. He was going to get her into that chopper, deliver her safely to São Diogo. Mission over.

The others could take it from there.

She looked down at her hands in her lap and began to fiddle with her fingers. "Men like you really *can't* care, can you? It's always about the bottom line."

His brows shot up. What the hell? Men like *him?* What was with this woman? Did she have any idea what she was doing to him? How she was making him care? About her, about what she thought of him? Jesus, she was even making him think about Kathleen.

Caring for a woman once had cost him everything just short of his life. He refused to take that risk again.

"You know jack about me, Sarah." He grabbed her arm, pulled her to her feet. He ignored the righteous flash of indignation in her eyes as he marshaled her down to the water's edge.

"Now get into that river. Get yourself cleaned up and then take your shirt off."

Chapter 4

Sarah spun round as he released her arm. "What did you say?"

"I said take your shirt off." He turned his back and made his way over to the rock. Slipping off his pack, he crouched down and set his rifle at his side. He extracted a first aid pouch from his pack, rolled it open and began laying out equipment on the flat, iron-red stone. The sun glinted off his glossy blue-black hair.

"My…shirt?" she asked, suddenly deeply uneasy.

"The wound on your back is bleeding." He didn't look at her as he spoke.

Sarah lifted her hand over her shoulder and fingered the spot where her back throbbed. With surprise she felt tacky wetness, torn fabric…and a deep gash. When her hand came away, there was fresh blood on her fingers. She'd thought what she was feeling was deep muscular pain. She hadn't realized she'd been wounded.

"And your knees. Need to see those, too. Roll up your pants, rinse the muck off, then get back over here." He still wouldn't look at her as he spoke. He'd written her off in some fundamental way.

Sarah turned from him and stared at the ominous, swirling currents of the Shilongwe. She couldn't see below the surface. She couldn't even begin to imagine what parasites, protists or primitive bacteria lurked beneath the milky, rust-colored waters. The Congo was full of unidentified microscopic killers. And macroscopic ones. She shuddered, turned back to look at Hunter McBride—a killer of another kind.

"The water…it's brown. It's—"

"As hygienic as you're gonna get." He tore open a sealed packet of suture strips, attention focused on his task. "The color's mostly from minerals in the soil."

But when she didn't respond, didn't move, he glanced up. Sarah swallowed. His eyes had gone cold and his blackened features were hard, almost brutal. The change was unsettling. It was as if the man inside was suddenly gone.

Had *she* done that to him? Had she actually managed to offend this powerful mercenary and somehow shut him down? For an instant, Sarah wondered what really made him tick. But just as quickly she pushed her curiosity aside. Why should she care about Hunter McBride? Sure, he'd saved her life, but this was his job. She meant nothing more to him than that. He'd said so himself. Besides, she abhorred what he did for a living. It went against every fiber of her being.

His hard eyes held hers and a muscle pulsed softly under the black paint at the base of his jaw. The sun beat down on her head and she felt her face begin to flush under his scrutiny, but she wasn't able to look away, break the intensity of his stare.

He shrugged suddenly. "Hey, stay dirty if you want." He turned his attention back to his task. "Get infected, maybe die. Or clean up and live. You're a nurse, Burdett, you know the odds out here. Your choice."

The use of her last name, the sudden bluntness of his words, winded her. There was absolutely no hint of feeling in his deep, gravelly voice, no nuance of the compassion she'd detected earlier. His sudden offhandedness hurt, much more than it should. Sarah hadn't realized just how much she'd needed a sense of connection to another human being in this foreign, hostile and very frightening environment.

She clutched her arms tightly over her stomach and a cold loneliness began to leach through her chest. It was a feeling she knew too well; the same dead sensation had filled her when she'd seen the tabloid photos of Josh and his heavily pregnant mistress under the big black headline that blared Twins. It was the same hollow ache that had swamped her when she'd learned she would never be able to bear children. It was the same sick feeling that had gripped her when Josh had told her she was a fool for not realizing their marriage had been over for years.

Sarah hugged herself tighter. Josh had been right on that count. She *was* a fool for not having recognized the coldhearted psychopath lurking behind her husband's charming smile. She was a fool for allowing him to abuse her emotionally for so long, for allowing him to make her feel like a barren failure of a woman.

Men like Josh didn't know how to care.

Tears pricked her eyes at the sudden unbidden and overwhelming memories. Sarah turned to face the river. She hated herself for what she'd allowed Josh to do to her. She hated *him*. And she detested his Machiavellian drive. He was a mercenary. Like Hunter. Sure, Josh didn't look like Tarzan here, and he didn't carry guns and knives. He wasn't paid to kill—not in a physical way. But he destroyed lives nevertheless. And like Hunter, he did it for cash. Josh was a mergers and acquisitions giant. His jungle was concrete and his weapons were stocks, bonds, coercion, fast cars and pretty women. And one of those pretty women was now carrying his babies—a famous model-of-the-moment who was attracting tabloid attention and dragging Sarah's pain into the public eye.

Sarah furiously blinked back her emotions. She was *not* going to let Josh haunt her so many miles away. She would never allow a man to make her feel like that again. She steeled her jaw, ripped off her bloodied apron, bent down and yanked her torn cotton pants up over her shins. She scooped up the reddish-brown water and splashed it over her legs, wincing as she tried to wipe away the memories along with the dirt.

She didn't know why she'd let Hunter's bluntness get to her. Maybe it was the incredible tenderness she'd glimpsed briefly in his eyes, felt in his touch…and the way she'd reacted to it. Another wave of emotion threatened. She cupped the warm river water in her hands and splashed it angrily over her face, gasping from the pain that radiated from her cheek. Whatever she'd glimpsed in Hunter, it was gone now. And she wasn't going to let it affect her. She'd come to Africa to kill that emotionally abused and needy part of herself. She'd come here to grow strong, to play a vital role as a human being, a woman.

She froze as the reality of her situation slammed home. She glanced at the bloody apron bunched up at her side. Lord, she was damn lucky even to be alive, to have been given a second chance. Her stomach churned as images of the carnage at the clinic hit her again. She stared numbly at the mesmerizing, slowly swirling water, but couldn't make the pictures in her mind go away. They churned in her head like the curling current of the river, making her dizzy, sick.

What was taking her so damn long? Hunter glanced up from his first aid kit and stilled. She'd stopped undressing. She was just standing there like a zombie, brown water lapping at her shoes, her pants rolled up under her skirt, her arms clutched tight to her waist. Then he realized she was trembling like a bloody leaf.

He reached for his rifle, slung it over his shoulder and pushed himself to his feet. He took a step forward, then held back. No. He'd shut down, shut her out, and he was going to make damn sure he kept it that way.

Deal with it, Burdett.

But she didn't deal with it. Instead, she turned slowly to face him. Hesitatingly, lifting her eyes to meet his. She looked absolutely haunted, lost. Crushed. Even the bright, feverish fear that had lit her eyes was gone. She'd been completely, emotionally demolished in the space of a few minutes. The muscles in his neck bunched tight.

Guilt and compassion tangled in his brain, making his mind thick. Hunter shook off the sensation. He was determined to feel zip. She was a package. He'd get her delivered. That was it.

She took a step toward him. "Hunter…"

He held his ground, said nothing.

"Hunter, I—I'm sorry, I… My buttons…" She held her hands out apologetically. "I can't seem to make my fingers work. I…I can't stop the shaking. Could you please help me with my blouse?"

He blinked sharply. She wanted *him* to undress her? His mouth went bone-dry.

"Could you help me?"

"Ah…sure." They were just buttons, right? How many times

in his life had he undone a woman's blouse? Too many to count. So why in hell was he actually *afraid* to touch her again? This was beyond ridiculous.

She stepped closer and his heart began to thud. He adjusted the sling of his rifle, swallowed hard and lifted his hand, moving it up to the valley between her breasts. He gripped one teeny, round button with his fingers before he realized he'd need his other hand, too. He swore softly to himself—you'd think he'd be able to undo the buttons of a blouse without thinking this hard. He slipped the pearly button out of the fabric, moved his hands down to the next one, purposefully avoiding her eyes, trying to keep a laser focus on this simple task.

Then the back of his hand brushed against the soft, warm swell of her breast, and his control was shot. Heat speared his belly and began to stab with each beat of his heart. Hunter moistened his lips, forced himself to concentrate. He moved his hands to the next button, barely able to breathe. "There." He blew out the breath he'd been holding, and looked into her eyes.

Was he imagining what he saw there? A flare of need? A yearning? A connection that went beyond the physical…words that needed to be spoken, but couldn't be? His heart beat even faster. But she averted her eyes and turned away abruptly.

He used the momentary privacy to swipe the back of his hand hard across his mouth. Sweet heavens this woman had a crazy effect on him, not just mentally, but physically. He hadn't seen *that* one coming.

With her back to him, Sarah hesitated, then slowly slipped her long-sleeved blouse off her shoulders, exposing a thin white cotton camisole with a hint of lace around the edges. Hunter was transfixed. He couldn't have looked away if he'd tried.

He noted the ragged slash in the fabric, the fresh blood. A vengeful fire began to smolder deep within him. The wound wasn't that bad, but it looked rudely invasive against the virginal white of her cotton top. He fingered the hard lines of his weapon, seeking mental clarity in the familiar shape. *Cool. Stay cool.*

She lifted the camisole up over her head, the movement lengthening the long muscles that cradled her spine. She wasn't wearing a bra. He swore softly to himself as perspiration pricked under the paint on his face and dampened his back. It was getting damn hot out here. Watching Sarah undress wasn't making things any cooler. But he'd be damned if he could look away. He swiped his wrist over his forehead and moistened his lips, forcing himself to concentrate clinically on the gash across her left shoulder blade.

It wasn't deep, but needed to be cleaned and sterilized. And it required several surgical strips to pull the edges together. He tried to clear his throat. "Here, sit on this rock so I can work on you from behind."

She acquiesced in silence. Hunter crouched down behind her, shifted his gun to his side and took a tube of disinfectant gel from his kit. He rubbed it over his hands before moistening a gauze pad with a ten percent solution of Povidone iodine. He touched the disinfectant-soaked pad to her skin.

Her body jerked in reflex.

He hesitated. He knew it stung like all hell. He wanted to tell her to take it easy, to relax. He wanted to talk her through it. But he couldn't. He needed to think of her as a job. Anything else was dangerous. Besides, she was a nurse; she knew what was coming. He touched the pad to her skin again and wiped the wound clean. He could see no debris in it, but to be safe, he irrigated the cut thoroughly with a strong stream of the same antiseptic solution from a syringe. Sarah gasped, but still he said nothing. In silence he applied antibiotic ointment, then forced the edges of the now-clean gash together, holding them down tightly with three suture strips. He made sure her skin was dry and then covered the whole thing with a transparent, waterproof bandage, sealing the wound completely. This was necessary in wilderness environments, especially tropical ones. In places like this, even a small nick could end up killing a person.

"Done," he said.

She reached for her torn camisole, and as she stretched out her arm, Hunter caught sight of the smooth, full roundness of her breast, the profile of a dusky pink nipple. An involuntary spasm rippled through him.

He looked sharply away. But it was too late. Desire was already swelling and surging inside him. He bit it back, clenched his jaw. He checked his watch, the riverbank, the dense wall of foliage, the sky…*anything* not to look at that sweet ridge of spine down the center of her back as she slipped the camisole over her head. He had to keep his cool. He still had to clean the cut on her cheek. He had to touch her again.

She turned to face him. Hunter avoided her eyes, motioned for her to sit back down on the rock. He knelt in front of her, poured antiseptic solution onto a dressing and began to wipe the dirt from the cut on her cheekbone. She shivered and closed her eyes as the burn of the solution met her skin. His body responded instantly to her movement. Again, he fought off the unwelcome sexual longing.

He carefully picked a few embedded bits of dirt out of the cut with forceps, conscious of her breath on the back of his hand as he worked. Then he used the syringe to flush the cut. She winced, but still he said nothing. He applied the antibiotic and then sealed the edges with two suture strips.

"There you go. Wasn't as bad as it looked."

Her eyes fluttered open and Hunter's heart tripped. Up this close he could see tiny flecks of gold in the chocolate-brown, and he could see that her lashes were honey-brown on the tips. She truly was beautiful, in a very natural and pure way. A golden angel.

Jesus, he was losing it.

He ran his wrist over his forehead again, then silently cursed. The movement had transferred greasepaint onto his hands. He'd have to disinfect them again because he still had to tend to her knees and her arms.

He clubbed his errant thoughts aside, rubbed more sterilizing solution over his hands and began to work on cleaning and disinfecting the smaller scrapes and cuts on her knees and arms. She sat motionless, watching his every move.

He finally rocked back on his heels and looked up into her face. "There, that'll keep you going for a while."

She gave him a brave smile. "Thank you, Hunter."

He couldn't help but smile back. Without thinking, he reached up with both hands and removed the ripped blue-and-white cotton cloth from her hair. Tangled mahogany curls tumbled down around her face and fell to her shoulders, the sunlight bringing out burnished auburn highlights. For an instant, he could do nothing but stare. Sarah Burdett might look as soft and gentle as a broken angel, but inside this woman was a surprising core of iron-willed strength. He'd seen it.

She'd lived through a brutal massacre, escaped her attackers. She'd taken hold of that biohazard container and fled into the dark jungle with every intention of somehow getting her lethal cargo all the way to Atlanta. It was an impossible task. How in hell had she planned on doing that?

And to top it all, in spite of her fatigue, after all she'd been through, after *he* had saved her life, she still had the moral fortitude to question his profession and subtly show her disapproval. It made Hunter want to know more about what drove this woman, what really fired her from the inside, what had *really* brought her to Africa.

But he wasn't about to ask.

The less he knew about Sarah Burdett, the better. Because in a couple of hours they'd be on São Diogo Island and she'd be out of his hands. He turned abruptly away from her and began to pack up his first aid kit.

"You'd make a good doctor, you know?"

He didn't look up.

"You have a healing touch. I've worked with enough medical professionals to know."

He clenched his jaw, flipped the kit closed and reached for his gun. He shoved himself to his feet and stared up into the haze of viscous heat that hung over the river. The chopper would be here any second, and not a moment too soon.

Sarah frowned. Something was eating this man big time, something that had wired him with low flash points. She studied his rough profile as he scanned the sky, and a small ping of regret bounced through her heart at the thought that she'd never find out what it was. It was in her nature to want to help, to make people feel better…. But as fleetingly as it had come, the notion was gone. What she really wanted more than anything was to get out of this place and to get Dr. Regnaud's container to safety. It was the one thing that had kept her going through the night. And it was holding her together now. Barely.

She watched Hunter scanning the sky, then the wide ribbon of brown water, then the grassy clearing behind them, his eyes moving gradually toward the thick wall of vegetation at the far end. He tensed. Sarah's heart skipped a beat. She peered into the haze above the trees, trying to see what had alerted him, but couldn't make out a thing. Nerves skittered through her stomach. She stood, came to his side. "What is it?" she whispered.

He lifted the muzzle of his gun, pointed to a spot just above the canopy. "Smoke. Over there."

Sarah shielded her brow and squinted into the distance. "Where?"

Then all of a sudden she could see it. A faint wisp of white separated from the haze and curled up out of the trees. It grew dark and acrid as she watched. Then it began to billow and boil into the sky, black and furious—just like the smoke at the clinic compound had.

"Oh my God," she whispered.

"It's a village along the Oyambo." Hunter studied the smoke with narrowed eyes, not a hint of emotion on his face. "They're looking for you."

Her heart dropped like a cold stone. "But…but why are they burning the village? If they didn't find me, why would they *do* such a thing?"

He said nothing.

She clenched her fists in frustration and glared at Hunter. *"Why?"* she demanded. She needed an answer, needed to understand.

His features remained implacable. "They'll backtrack now. They'll pick up our trail before long."

Horror swamped her. This could *not* be happening. She couldn't take any more. No more. Not another second in this awful place.

Hunter turned his back on the smoke and scanned the trees along the opposite bank of the Shilongwe. "Sarah?"

She couldn't answer, couldn't talk. Couldn't think. All she could do was stare at the billowing black smoke and think about what had happened at Ishonga.

"Sarah—" he grabbed her arm "—listen to me! *Focus*. The helo will come from there, see? From the north. Look."

She moved her head woodenly. He was pointing his gun upriver.

"When it does, we have to move fast. And I mean *fast*. Do *everything* I say. No questions. Got it?"

She stared at his blackened face. It was totally expressionless, showing no glimpse of compassion for what was happening in that village along the Oyambo. The man was inhuman.

Resentment pooled in her stomach. She wanted to get away from him, from this place. Far away.

"Do you understand me, Sarah?"

She forced herself to nod numbly.

"Good. Now see that sandbank, just beyond the shallows?" He pointed into the river. "That's where our guys will land. As soon as the chopper approaches, we wade out there. You hang on to me. Got it?"

Before she could answer, Sarah heard the distinct and distant chop of helicopter blades, the sound expanding and contracting through levels of humidity along the river. Her heart began to jackhammer. The machine materialized, silver in the shimmering, white-hot sky. It banked and flew in low along the course of the brown river. The sound grew louder. Deafening. Water rippled and flattened out in concentric circles as it closed in. Trees bowed. Leaves flew and birds scattered.

She felt Hunter's hand grip hers. Her heart tripped in a panicky lurch of fear and relief. In a couple of hours she'd be out of this hellish place, away from this man and everything he represented.

The helicopter hovered over the sandbank, and she could see the pilot inside giving a thumbs-up. Hunter yanked her forward. "Head down," he yelled over the roar of the lethal rotor blades as he pulled her into the river.

Warm water filled her shoes instantly and thick silt sucked

at her feet. He drew her in deeper. Faster. The brown water was now above her waist. It was deeper than she'd thought. She could feel the current dragging at her clothes. The downdraft from the chopper plastered her hair onto her head and whipped the ends sharply against her cheeks. Tears streamed from her eyes as she squinted into the force of the wind. Hunter dragged her in even deeper. She hung to him for dear life. They were almost there. Then she heard a crack.

Hunter froze. So did she.

Then another sharp crack split the air.

Gunshots.

Terror sliced through her heart. "Someone's shooting at us!" she screamed, the vortex of wind and sound sucking up her words and flinging them out over the water.

A bullet pinged against the chopper, then another. Everything blurred into slow motion. Sarah registered the pilot making signals to Hunter. He gestured back. The chopper lifted, veered sharply up to the left and climbed high over the treetops.

Sarah stared in dismay as the metal beast, her only hope of rescue, her lifeline, disappeared, becoming a silver speck in the shimmering heat of the Congo sky.

A bullet slammed into the river right next to her, shooting a jet of water into her face. She opened her mouth to scream, but before any sound came out, Hunter's hand hit her hard on the back of her head, knocking her facedown into river. She spluttered, choking in a mouthful of water that tasted like sand. She tried to wriggle free, to gasp for air, but Hunter yanked her under. She held her breath. She couldn't see. He drew her down deeper, and suddenly she could no longer touch the bottom. Water swirled around her, tangling her skirt up around her hips, her hair over her face. She was running out of breath. She tried desperately to fight Hunter's death grip, to reach the surface.

But she couldn't. He held on, keeping her under. Her lungs were going to burst. *He was drowning her! She was going to drown!* She felt herself being pulled sideways as the current merged with another and doubled in strength. Then it tripled, sucking her into a cold deep channel, dragging her to the bottom.

And everything went black.

Chapter 5

"We lost McBride's signal there, 'bout thirty klicks south of the Cameroon border." December Ngomo pointed at one of the LCD screens mounted along the wall, his heavily-accented voice reverberating through the FDS situation room.

Jacques Sauvage moved closer to the screen. He narrowed his eyes, studied the terrain in silence, his concentration pulling at the scar that sliced down the left side of his face. "That where the pilot saw them go under?"

"Yebo," Ngomo said in his native Zulu.

Rafiq Zayed looked up from the report in his hands. "Any chance he lost coverage when he went back into dense bush?"

"Negative," said Ngomo. "The signal was lost right there, in the Shilongwe River."

Sauvage cursed under his breath. The satellite phone that emitted McBride's GPS signal may have been damaged.

Or worse.

They all knew Hunter had a backup radio, but breaking radio silence now would be suicide. It would broadcast their location to anyone who had the equipment to tune in. They had no way of knowing now whether their man had taken a bullet and gone down.

Sauvage turned to Zayed. "You have the chopper on standby in Cameroon?"

Zayed nodded, his liquid eyes intense under hooked brows. "But sending it in now would be a death mission. Airspace has completely shut down in the north. Whole place is set to blow, and anyone with half a brain is getting the hell out."

Sauvage checked his watch. "Then we wait." Time was not a luxury they could afford, but they had little alternative now. "If McBride is okay, he'll head north, to the border." He turned his back on the screen and engaged the eyes of first Zayed, and then Ngomo. The corner of his mouth curled slowly into his characteristically crooked smile. "It was looking too smooth, *non?* Trust Irish to take the tough way out." Sauvage used their affectionate tag for McBride. But apart from his Irish accent, the men knew nothing about Hunter's past. McBride, Sauvage, Zayed and Ngomo *never* talked about the past. Not in a way that mattered. It was an unspoken pact among these men. It went to the heart of the bond between them.

All they knew was that Hunter had arrived at the gates of the Légion Étrangère—the French Foreign Legion—fifteen years ago with a thick Irish brogue and a look of murder in his strangely colored eyes. That look had eventually left him.

Mostly. But the brogue had stayed, only softening, becoming veiled after years of his speaking only French.

These disparate men had understood each other back then, as they did now. For hidden reasons of their own, each had been driven to the gates of Fort de Nogent in Paris, desperate to seek asylum with the notorious "Legion of the Damned," where a man could bury his past in order to fight for France. If he survived his contract, he could come out with a new identity and a French passport. A shot at a new life.

They'd all earned their second chance by coming close to death in the name of a country that was not their own, fighting with a crack army of foreigners, the biggest and most legitimate mercenary force in the world. They'd served in places like Bosnia, Rwanda, Zaire, Chad, central Africa, Lebanon, Somalia, the Gulf. They'd developed the Legion mind-set, where soldiers of many nations and many pasts had to set aside differences and stand by each other and die for a foreign nation. The resulting bond that had formed between the men was formidable, sealed with discipline, trust, solidarity and respect for tradition.

It was this mind-set, this philosophy, that McBride, Sauvage, Zayed and Ngomo took with them when they left the Legion to form the Force du Sable, an efficient, lean, private military company that over the last ten years had developed a reputation for having trained some of the most skilled and dangerous soldiers on earth—fearless warrior monks who now served as a model for future rapid-action units in a modern world of limited-intensity conflict and terrorism.

Zayed's eyes flashed back to the LCD screen and he gave a soft snort. "Tough way out? That terrain between the Shilongwe and the Cameroonian border is some of the most hostile known to man. Plus he's got the nurse with him."

"McBride's come out of worse," Ngomo said simply, and turned back to his computer, his massive hands dwarfing the keyboard.

08:03 Alpha. Shilongwe River.
Monday, September 22

As the river widened and the current slowed, the drop in velocity and Sarah's limp weight began to drag Hunter down. Wet clothing didn't help. At least the sealed biohazard container was buoyant, as was his waterproof pack. With the container in one hand and his other arm hooked across Sarah's chest, he gave slow, powerful scissor kicks, swimming diagonally across the current, using it instead of fighting it.

As he moved downriver, he scanned the wall of tangled vegetation that crowded the banks for any signs of movement, but saw none. The forest was dense along this stretch. There was likely no one about for miles.

Hunter soon found what he was looking for—a break in the vegetation. He aimed for a gentle slope of white beach about a hundred yards downstream. At least they were moving in the direction of the Cameroonian border.

He neared the bank, sought footing in the silt, dragged Sarah up out of the water and laid her down on the sand. He immediately checked the seal on the biohazard canister. To his relief, it was secure. His rifle and machete were also still strapped across his back. He shrugged off his pack, glanced around. The place was deserted. They'd be safe for a while.

He turned his attention to Sarah, and his heart stalled. There was froth around her mouth and nose, and her skin was going blue. He dropped to his knees, felt for a pulse.

There was none.

Guilt rammed into his heart. He hadn't realized she was this far gone. He'd been too worried about being shot at, too worried about losing the pathogen. He quickly opened her mouth, clearing away foam, checking for any foreign material. He placed one hand on her forehead, tilted her chin back with the other, opening her airway. He pinched her nostrils shut, sucked in a deep breath of air and put his mouth over hers.

He blew a slow and steady stream of breath into her, his eyes fixed on her chest, watching for a sign that air was getting into her lungs.

He waited two seconds, saw her chest rise and sink as the air expelled from her lungs. He sucked in another deep breath and once again positioned his lips over hers, keeping his eyes trained on her chest as he blew. He saw it rise again. He quickly located her breastbone and began chest compressions, alternating compressions with breaths, again and again.

Hunter's whole body ached. He was wet with river water and sweat, being steamed alive under the equatorial sun. His vision began to swim, and the guilt in his heart was nearly overwhelming. He'd thought of the biohazard container first. He'd thought of the mission, of the millions of people who would die if he didn't get the pathogen out of the jungle. But perhaps, just maybe, if he'd tended to Sarah a second earlier... Hot anger swirled through the cold guilt in his chest. He'd be damned if he was going to let her die!

He gritted his teeth. He'd gotten her this far. Now he was going to take her *and* the pathogen all the way.

He sucked in another deep breath of air and forced it steadily it into her lungs, mechanically pumping her heart.

And then suddenly, he felt the small flutter of a pulse. Hunter's heart stumbled, kicked hard against his ribs. Her limbs spasmed and her stomach began to heave. He quickly flipped

Sarah onto her side and she retched violently, expelling river water and lumps of foam.

Relief, thick and sweet, surged through his veins. He held her as she heaved. Color was returning to her skin, oxygen getting into her blood.

Hunter's eyes burned hot with gratitude. His jaw went tight with the sense of triumph over death, and he lifted his face to the sky. And for an instant he almost found himself yelling thanks to a God he no longer believed in.

When he looked at her face again, she was watching him, her eyes dark hollows in a pale void. He wiped her mouth with the edge of his wet shirt and tried to smile. "You made it."

She said nothing, just stared at him.

He sniffed back the strange cocktail of emotions burning in him, and lifted a wet ribbon of hair from her brow. "I'm going to move you up the beach to some shade, okay?"

She closed her eyes, nodded.

She felt like a wet rag doll in his arms as he carried her up the small strip of sand. He laid her down in the shade of a palm, but as he tried to step away, she grabbed at the fabric of his shirt, balling it in white-knuckled fists, her eyes wide like an animal snared in headlights. She was terrified he was going to abandon her. She saw him as her lifeline.

If only she knew.

"Hey, it's okay, I'm not going to leave you," he said, lowering himself onto the sand beside her, knowing that if it really came down to it, he couldn't keep his word. He lifted her head, rested it on his lap, tried to stroke some of the sand from her damp hair, and while he did, racked his brain for some comforting reassurances he could whisper to her.

But nothing came to him. He felt totally useless. He could satisfy a woman physically, knew what places to touch, how to drive her to such dizzying sensual delirium that she would scream out for release. But emotionally? This was uncharted territory for Hunter McBride. He had no idea how to simply make a woman feel safe. Christ, he'd barely managed to keep her alive.

The tang of remorse stung his tongue. He told himself he'd done the right thing, he'd kept his priorities straight. And if it truly came down to the wire, if he was literally forced to choose between Sarah Burdett or the pathogen, he'd *have* to go with the latter. There was no option. That was his job. Black-and-white. Pure and simple. Because if they didn't get this lethal bug into a lab and find an antidote, millions would die three weeks from now—people just as innocent and unprepared as Sarah Burdett.

One life to save millions. Law enforcement agencies the world over dealt with equations like that on a daily basis and made the same decisions.

So why did he feel like crap?

Sarah stirred on his lap, moaned softly, the soft weight of her breast rubbing against the inside of his forearm. Heat speared through his belly.

Hunter angrily swallowed the sensation. Jesus, this was not the time. He looked away from the transparent fabric of her camisole, away from the dark outline of her nipple under the wet cloth, and forced himself to breathe. To plan. To think clear, hard, cold logistics.

He wasn't going to be able to move Sarah for a while. She was going to need rest. And then she'd need food, water. They'd be safe here for a few hours, but they would have to get going by nightfall at least. He needed to contact the FDS base.

Hunter reached for the front-left compartment of his flak jacket. His fingers met fabric, and his heart skipped a beat.

The flap had come undone.

He thrust his hand into the pocket. Empty. He cursed under his breath. His satellite phone, their one and only secure link to the outside world, was gone. He must have lost it in the Shilongwe. How could the flap have come loose? Had he even secured it? He cursed aloud in French. If he'd been totally focused on the job this would never have happened.

Now he was stuck with Sarah in the middle of bloody nowhere, with no contact with the outside world, just the two of them in a war-torn country set to blow. And over their heads hung the threat of a biological attack, and responsibility for the lives of millions of Americans who would die if he failed to make it out alive, and soon. It didn't get much better than this.

He swore again. Wasn't much he could do about it now apart from waiting until she was up to moving again. They were going to have to make it out on foot. No question about that. He and Sarah were going to have to physically hack their way to the Cameroonian border, and because of her, the going would be slow. Real slow. Time he didn't have. Time the president of the United States and his people didn't have.

Hunter squinted into the sky, checked the angle of the sun. He figured they couldn't be more than thirty miles from Cameroon, if they went along the river. But that wasn't an option. The route they'd have to take would work out a lot longer than thirty miles, and a lot tougher than following the course of the river.

He looked down at Sarah. She was asleep now, breathing easily. He'd need to get her out of those cotton pants so they could dry. Things had a nasty way of rotting against your body out here. But there was no freaking way he was going to try undressing her again. She could do that herself when he woke her up again in a few minutes. In the meantime, he had his own gear to dry out.

He rolled out from under her, stood up, then hesitated. Her wet sneakers *would* have to come off now. Drying her shoes and socks out before nightfall was a priority. Fungus, bacteria and rotting skin were some of the biggest hazards in the jungle, and she was going to need her feet if she wanted to live. He figured he could handle her shoes without coming undone.

He crouched down, untied her wet laces and removed her sodden sneakers, along with the wet tennis socks she was wearing. He paused, looking at her feet. They were narrow, with beautiful arches. Her skin was pale, and her toenails were painted the white-pink of spring blossoms. Nail polish in the jungle? A smile sneaked across Hunter's lips and tenderness blossomed softly through his chest.

He wrung the water from her socks and spread them out on a rock in the sun to dry. He stared down at them and shook his head. They had a pale yellow trim and little yellow pompoms on the back. Pompoms in the jungle? Maybe they'd come in handy as fish lure when they got hungry.

He shrugged out of his combat vest and shirt and draped them over the rock next to her socks. Then he squatted on the hot sand and began to toss stuff out of his pack, checking to see if anything was wet. He kept his rifle at his side and a constant eye on the river and jungle border.

Sarah squinted into the harsh daylight, the movement pulling at the bandage on her cheek. She touched it, confused. Where was she? Images sifted into her mind—the helicopter, her lifeline disappearing into the shimmering sky…the shooting. Water. *The container!* She jerked upright. Where was Hunter?

He was a few yards from her, sitting on a rock by the water, cleaning his gun. He was naked from the waist up, a darkly tanned and potent figure against the white glare of the sand. Sun glinted on his black hair, and his body gleamed with perspiration and humidity.

He stilled, looked up suddenly and smiled. "Hello."

Sarah's jaw dropped. The black face paint was gone, and what was left was magnificent. Not beautiful. Magnificent in a gut-slamming, powerful male kind of way. How he was looking at her, how the light caught his eyes, clean took her breath away.

She closed her eyes. Maybe when she opened them again, life would seem more real. But he was still there when she flicked them open. She was still on the banks of some brown river in the heart of the Congo, with one of the most dangerous-looking males she'd ever seen in her life. Panic licked through her. She struggled to get up, but the world spun and she sank back.

"Hey, take it easy," he said, pushing himself to his feet in a fluid movement. Holding the barrel of his rifle in one hand, he stalked over the shimmering-hot sand. The dark hair that covered his pecs glistened with moisture and gathered into a sexy whorl that trailed down the center of his rock-hard belly and disappeared into the belt of his camouflage pants. Sarah just stared. Her brain wasn't working right. Everything looked surreal.

He crouched beside her, rummaged in his pack and handed her a foil pack of army-style rations and a canteen of water. She noted with relief that the biohazard canister sat alongside the pack, right next to her in the shade.

"Get some fuel into your system," he said. "And then we can get you out of those pants."

"I beg your pardon?"

A twinkle of amusement flickered through his eyes. "We need to make sure your clothes are dry, Sarah. We move at nightfall. As soon as the sun sets, we're off."

"What?" Alarm flared in her. "At night? Why? Where are we going?" She sat up stiffly. "Where *are* we, Hunter?"

"Still on the Shilongwe. We washed a couple of miles north. We need to try and make it to the Cameroonian border now."

"Cameroon! How?"

"We walk."

"You have *got* to be kidding!" But even as she spoke, she could see by the look in his eyes that he was dead serious. Tongues of panic licked through her. She could *not* go through another night in the jungle. "Why…why can't you just call your people and get them to fly another helicopter in like you did before?" She looked around frantically. "It could land here…couldn't it?"

Hunter cocked a brow. "My people? The ones who get *paid* to do this sort of thing?"

"Yes, them." Being rescued seemed a pretty good option right now, by mercenaries or not. But judging by the expression on his face, that was not going to happen anytime soon. A cold dread seeped into her chest. "You…you're not going to call them, are you?"

"No."

"Why not?"

"Lost the phone in the river."

"Oh my God. So we're…"

"Yes, Sarah. We're on our own."

She looked up at the sky. It would be dark in a few hours; the sudden cloak of pure blackness dropped at precisely 6:07 local time. Panic edged into her throat. She couldn't do this again. It had taken everything just to survive the night before.

He was watching her intently, appraising her on some fundamental level, deciding if she had the mettle to make it to Cameroon. The fact sobered her. It reminded her of why they were here, of what was in the biohazard container, of Dr. Regnaud. She swallowed, tried to find her voice. "How…how long will it take?"

"Maybe three days, if we're lucky."

Three days! And this morning she'd believed she'd be out of the Congo within the hour.

"It would be quicker if we went down the Shilongwe, but we can't risk that. There are settlements, people along the riverbanks. We can't chance being seen. We can't trust anyone right now, Sarah."

"Why not?" She wasn't sure she even wanted to know the answer.

"There was a coup in Brazzaville this morning. The entire country is in a state of civil war and we're foreigners, Sarah. We're sitting ducks. We're anyone's enemy."

She stared at him. "You mean the people shooting at us from across the river had nothing to do with the soldiers who attacked the clinic?"

"Probably not."

"Then where are the soldiers?"

"Probably tracking us."

She shuddered, clutched her arms over her knees. "And you really think going through the forest will be safer than along the river?"

"Tougher, and slower. But yeah, it'll be safer, and the sooner we manage to reach the Blacklands, the better."

"Blacklands?"

"The dense jungle swamp of the interior. Locals believe the area is cursed. No one ventures in there apart from Pygmy tribes and wild animals. It's unlikely anyone will follow us in there."

"Cursed? You *are* toying with me…right?"

He smiled. "It's a local superstition born out of an Ebola outbreak several years ago. Villagers who'd been hunting in the swamp region brought the disease out with them. Anyone who came in contact with them got sick, started dying. As is the custom, the village elders consulted with their sorcerer, who told them the area had been cursed by evil spirits and that anyone who ventured into the region should be banished from the tribe, or killed. This helped control the spread of Ebola, and the belief in the curse became entrenched in local culture. No one ever goes in there now. Superstition in this place is supremely powerful, and it's not a force to be ignored. Out here, it's the law of life, and there's a reason for it. It preserves life."

"Well, I'm not going in there, either," she said. "I'd rather take my chances along the river."

He snorted softly. "You have less chance of stumbling over the Ebola virus in the Blacklands, Sarah, than you have of running into hostile militia along the Shilongwe."

"It's…it's not just Ebola. It's…" She glanced at the forest fringe. "There has *got* to be another way, Hunter. Please understand…I just can't do it. I can't spend another night stumbling blind through the jungle."

He studied her at length, his eyes growing cool. He looked suddenly distant, dangerous again. It made her nervous.

"I…I mean it," she said, her voice wobbling. "I just don't have it left in me. I—I can't."

The muscle at his jaw began to pulse softly. She could see he was thinking, trying to figure out what to do with her. And she didn't like how it made her feel a liability.

"Sarah," he said finally, "I can't force you to do it." He rose to his feet. "Stay here on the Shilongwe if you want. I'll take the pathogen, make better time without you. It's your choice." His eyes bored down into hers. *"It has to be."* He turned, strode down the beach, seated himself on the rock and resumed cleaning his gun in silence.

Her jaw dropped. He wouldn't leave her alone, would he? Could he really be so coldhearted?

She couldn't be sure. She didn't know Hunter McBride at all. She had no idea what he might be capable of. A mad terror began to nip at her brain, skewing her logic. Josh would do it. He'd leave her here. Sarah had learned the hard way just how cruel a man could be. She'd seen Josh walk out on six years of marriage without blinking an eye, and then send in his lawyer to pick the rest of her bones clean. Tears pricked at her eyes.

"You…you really don't care, do you?" she called out to him.

He lifted his dark head, studied her in silence. "No, Sarah, I don't." He turned his attention back to his weapon.

She jerked herself to her feet, swayed under a wave of dizziness, grabbed at a tree branch to steady herself. "Damn you and all men like you, Hunter McBride!" She yelled at him out of hurt and frustration and the sheer fear of going back into the nightmarish jungle. *Damn Josh.* This was his fault. She'd never have come here if it hadn't been for him.

Hunter ignored her, continued cleaning his gun.

She wanted to scream. She felt utterly powerless. She spun around and began to march blindly down the beach, barely noticing the burning heat of the sand under her bare feet, barely registering the wall of foliage next to her. Tears pooled in her eyes. She had no idea where she was going, she just had to move, do something. And above all, she didn't want him to see her crying, didn't want to give the brute the satisfaction of having pushed her over the edge.

"Stop!" His voice barked through the air.

Hesitation rippled through her, but she continued stumbling

along the small strip of sand. She had no intention of listening to him, of jumping at his each and every command.

"Now, Sarah! Stop!"

This time she did stop. This time she could not ignore the urgent bite in his voice. She started to turn around, but as she did, her breath congealed in her throat.

Everything moved into slow, sick motion. She saw him raise his arm, saw him flick the machete. She heard it whopping through the air, saw the blur of motion as it whipped toward her face....

Chapter 6

The machete sunk into the trunk of a tree with a dull *thuck* and quivered from the impact. The head of a snake fell to her feet, followed by a writhing, brown body. Sarah screamed.

"Don't move!" Hunter growled as he strode over the sand. He jabbed at the snake's head with a stick and the decapitated head bit down viciously on the wood. "Survival instinct lives longer than the snake," he said, tossing the head and stick into the bush. He stalked over to the tree, yanked his machete out of the trunk, used the blade to lift the snake's limp body. He held it up for her to see. "Black mamba. Gets its name from the color of its mouth," he said. "Shy bugger, but incredibly fast and very lethal if disturbed."

He tossed the snake's body into the forest, turned, pointed his machete at her face. "Next time, listen. If you're interested in living, that is." He stepped closer, his eyes drilling into hers. "I'm giving you the choice, Sarah. You have to *want* to live." He pointed his blade to the green abyss behind him. "You have to choose to tackle that jungle with me, or you won't survive." He watched her face, allowing his words to sink in. "It's that simple."

He turned abruptly, strode back down the beach.

Sarah sank to the sand in a heap. She was at his mercy. Completely. She was dependent on this brute of a man for every aspect of her existence. She felt sick. She reached for the comfort of her cross at her throat…and felt nothing.

Her heart stopped.

She fingered her neck wildly, searching for the delicate gold chain.

It wasn't there.

The little crucifix she'd worn every single day since she was fourteen years old was gone. It must've been ripped from her throat in the river.

Her brain went numb. She clutched her naked neck with both hands. The Congo had stolen her last link to civilization, the last vestige that helped her define her notion of self, of who she was as a human being in this primitive environment, of where she'd come from.

And now this man had stripped her to her very core.

Hunter glanced at the sky. It would be dark within fifteen minutes. Working mechanically, he started packing his gear.

Sarah was sitting in the lengthening shadows at the edge of the beach, silent, watching the river. She had barely moved since he'd told her to get out of the sun and to eat and drink something. She'd obeyed like a zombie. At least she *had* eaten.

And she'd rested. But she hadn't uttered a word. And the blank look in her eyes bothered him.

He tried to shut out thoughts of her as he worked. But as he scooped his stiff, dry shirt off the rock, he caught sight of the pair of white socks with their little yellow pompoms. His heart gave an odd spasm. He felt terrible. No matter how he tried to shut himself down, he hated the way he'd handled her. But the truth was, he didn't have a clue how to deal with this woman. Or how to cope with the things she was making him feel.

But Hunter did know one thing. He wanted to bring Sarah Burdett out alive. And for them to succeed, it was absolutely imperative that she obey his orders. And it was essential that she *wanted* to succeed. Because the journey was going to physically challenge every molecule in her body and test the limits of her mind. Without willpower at this point, she quite simply wasn't going to make it. And if his actions and his words had belied his intent, if they'd spooked her and made her think, so much the better.

Hunter cinched his backpack closed. Gear packed, he scooped up her socks along with her cotton pants. He strode along the beach, held her clothes out to her.

She lifted her eyes slowly. The bruised look in them almost choked him but he said nothing. Neither did she. She just took her clothes, and that's when he noticed the delicate gold cross that had nestled in the hollow of her throat was missing. He crouched down beside her. "Sarah," he said gently. "Where's your crucifix?"

She swallowed and blinked a little too fast. But other than that, she showed no emotion. "Lost it in the river, I guess." Her voice was flat.

Hunter's chest tightened. He'd seen what that little gold symbol had meant to her. And he knew the power of symbols, especially in a place like this. In losing her icon, she'd lost a basic belief in herself. He reached for her hand, covered it with his own. "I'm sorry."

Her eyes cut sharply to his. "Why? What's it to you, anyway?"

"I understand," he said simply.

Her brown eyes probed his. "How could a man like you possibly understand?"

Her question forced him momentarily to seek an answer within himself. It pushed him, once again, toward the slippery murk of his past, but he pulled himself back. It would serve no purpose. The answer, his reason for understanding, was not going to help her. She'd lost a trinket that had linked her to her psyche, to who she was as a person, and with it she'd lost her motivation to survive. He knew the signs well. And in this state, she wouldn't last another day.

What Sarah needed most was a vivid mental picture of herself making it out of the Congo. She had to *believe* she would. She needed faith in herself. And he alone had to give that to her.

He looked away, studied the river, trying to come up with something. It was tougher than he'd thought. He turned back to her. "When you get home, Sarah, what's the first thing you're going to do?"

Her eyes widened. Good, he'd elicited some kind of emotion, even if it was surprise. It bolstered him. He flashed her the warmest smile he could muster and settled back onto the sand beside her, his hand still covering hers. "Think about it, Sarah. Picture it."

She stared blankly at him.

"I hear Seattle has great coffee," he offered. "Personally, I could do with an espresso. But I wouldn't mind trying one of those—what do they call those things—lattes?"

Anger sparked in her eyes. "Don't patronize me, McBride. How the hell do you know I'm from Seattle, anyway?"

He blinked. "Jeez, Sarah, I'm not trying to patronize. And

I've seen your Aid Africa file. They gave it to us after we'd intercepted your distress call."

Her eyes flickered sharply. "So you know everything about me?"

"Hardly everything."

She pulled her hand out from under his and looked away.

He raked his fingers through his hair. "Okay, you want it straight?"

"Darn right I do. It's not like you've tried to coddle me or anything. And it's not like I have anything left to lose now."

He winced. "Ouch. You don't play fair."

"And you do?"

He studied her carefully. This woman wasn't just lost. Something elemental had shifted in her. There was a new rawness, a hint of lost innocence. "Look, Sarah, whatever I've done up until now has been purely in the interests of your physical survival. And I'm sorry if I hurt you. I truly am. I'm sorry you've lost your crucifix. I think I know what it meant to you—"

She opened her mouth to protest.

He held up his hand. "Hear me out. All I'm trying to do right now is to give you a goal to hang on to, something that'll pull you through emotionally. You can handle the physical side of this, I don't doubt that, but not without the right mind-set."

Her mouth opened slightly. She stared at him, a range of emotions pulling at her features. At least he'd knocked her out of the zombie state. It was a start.

"It's plain old survival psychology," he explained. "When people are lost in the wilderness, I mean truly lost with zero hope of rescue, more often than not it's the thought of home, the memory of a loved one, their children, something like that that pulls them through. People who have survived against ridiculous odds often say they did it *for* someone. For someone

waiting back home. *Home,* Sarah." He purposefully empha-
sized the word. "I want you think about Seattle, about home."

Her jaw tensed. She looked away from him and stared at the
river. "I'm not going back to Seattle. It's not my home anymore."

"Why not?"

She shook her head, still not looking at him. "A man like you
wouldn't understand."

A man like him? There, she'd said it again. What man "like
him" had hurt this woman, wrecked her notions of home?
Hunter wanted to touch her. He picked up a twig instead,
cracked it between his fingers. "Why don't you try me, Sarah?"

She spun back to face him, her eyes luminous. "It's none of
your damn business, McBride." She grabbed her socks, started
to ram her feet into them. "If you want me to voice a reason to
get out of this…" She swiped angrily at a tear that escaped and
looked him straight in the eye. "It won't be for *you.* Or for me.
It'll be for Dr. Regnaud. A man with integrity. A self-sacrificing
healer. A man you could *never* match, McBride. And it'll be for
all the staff at the Ishonga clinic. Warm and generous people.
People who *care.*" She lifted her chin, but couldn't hide the
husky catch of emotion in her voice. "And in spite of what *you*
think, I don't want the disease in that canister—" she pointed to
the biohazard container "—to hurt anyone else like I saw it hurt
the patients at the clinic." She grabbed her runners, shook them
out viciously, checking for scorpions. She yanked her shoes
over those ridiculous socks and pushed herself to her feet.

She stood over him, legs braced, the sinking sun lighting her
from behind, showing the curvy outline of her hips and the lean
lines of her legs through the thin cotton of her skirt. The orange
glow of the sinking Congo sun spun a halo of burnished fire
around curls that had dried into a wild and springy mass. In
spite of the situation, in spite of what she was saying, all Hunter

could think at this instant was that she looked unbelievably attractive. And the fire now flashing in her eyes and in her voice lit his soul.

Sarah Burdett had come back to life—and so had his body.

"Believe it or not, McBride, I actually *do* want to stop this thing you told me about."

Part of him wanted to smile. But he controlled the impulse, leery of making her feel patronized. Because that was the furthest thing from his mind. This woman had just earned his respect. Some people, when you knocked them down, just got up tougher than before. He was beginning to see she was one of them. And it forced him to realize he may have been wrong.

Maybe, despite her naiveté, Sarah Burdett *did* have the goods to take on this jungle.

He got to his feet, came close to her, hooked a knuckle under her jaw, tilted her face so that the setting sun caught the gold flecks in her eyes. "Touché, Sarah," he said softly. "You're more woman than meets the eye, do you know that?"

She shivered slightly but didn't back away, didn't break eye contact. Her physical reaction to his touch, to him, sparked a shot of unwanted heat into his belly. And this time Hunter didn't pull away, either. He kept his fingers against her skin, enjoying the softness, the closeness of the contact.

For a second, they just stood like that, embraced by the warm orange light of the sinking sun, separated momentarily from their environment, aware only of each other. It was as if an invisible and tenuous bond was being spun around them, a new level of unspoken understanding.

Sarah's lips parted slightly as she looked up at him, and Hunter could see a sensual awareness darkening her eyes. A thrill rippled through him and he wanted to pull her into him, feel her curves against him. He wanted to press his mouth over those warm, soft lips—lips he'd breathed life into only hours ago. But it would be flat-out wrong. This woman was vulnerable. She was also completely dependent on him. And if she was at all attracted to him physically, there was a good chance it was desire born out of the wrong kind of need. He pulled away slightly and a sudden look of nervousness skittered over her features.

"I…I'm not dumb enough to think I don't need you right now, McBride," she said softly, her voice layered with a husky thickness that made his stomach swoop. Just the thought of her needing him on *any* level was making him too hot, too hard.

"I'm dependent on you for every aspect of my existence. I know that. I haven't got a clue how to get myself out of here. But it doesn't mean I have to like it…and it doesn't mean you have to be an ass about it."

He raised a brow.

"And it doesn't mean you have to try and prove it to me at every opportunity."

A grin tugged at his lips. Look who was giving it straight now.

"But…" Her eyes flicked away for an instant. "Do we *really* have to go back into the forest tonight? Can't we wait until morning?" She glanced at the wall of jungle, then at the bio-hazard container sitting under the palm tree. "We'd move faster in daylight, wouldn't we? And maybe your people will come looking for us. If we stay out here on the beach, on the river, they'll have a better chance of finding us. They'll see us." A pleading hopefulness lit her eyes. Hope he had to crush.

He sucked in a deep breath. "Sarah, no one is coming. Forget about being rescued. The FDS is not going risk flying a search party around Congo airspace now. They don't even know if we're alive. All they do know is that *if* we're okay, we'll head for the border. And they'll be ready and waiting for us there, in Cameroon." He allowed his hand to drop from her face and trace down the column of her neck and along the smooth, taut skin of her arm. He encircled her wrist and pulled her gently closer, his body acting separate from his mind.

"We're on our own. We have to do this ourselves, you and me. There is no other way out."

She swallowed, her eyes still searching his, as if looking for a lie.

The sun was now a deep blood-orange and dipping behind the trees. The clock was ticking. Time was running out on them, on President Elliot, on the American people. Hunter cupped her cheek. "We *have* to go. Now."

She stared at him in silence for a long while. "Okay," she said softly. "Let's go, then. Let's get that canister to a lab." She paused. "I owe it to some very good people."

And in that instant Hunter felt a stab of something a whole lot different from lust, and with it a primal male urge swelled in him, an urge to protect a woman he was beginning to care about. There was just no way he could think of Sarah as a package anymore. And that, more than anything, unnerved him.

Because it could end up costing them both.

21:00 Alpha. Congo jungle.
Monday, September 22

Hunter adjusted his night-vision gear and swiped away the perspiration on his forehead. They'd been moving uphill along a narrow ridge for the last two hours. There was a sharp drop to the left, and it was hot, hard and careful work. Sarah was panting heavily behind him. She'd lost her footing twice in the last fifteen minutes, taking her shockingly close to the cliff edge. She was tiring and she needed a break.

Hunter stopped at the top of the ridge. He had a good vantage point from here. In the distance, the Shilongwe snaked between walls of dense vegetation, the water a gleaming silver ribbon under a narrow sliver of moon. And beyond it, the forest canopy mushroomed as far as his eye could see, spiked occasionally with raffia palms and multitiered emergent giants. The ground up here was dry and rocky. It was a good place to give her some rest.

"We'll stop here awhile," he said softly, as he took her wrist and guided her down to the ground.

"Thank God," she whispered.

Hunter sat beside her and handed her water. She took it, drank, handed the canteen back and moved right up against him. He smiled into the dark. Whether her contact was driven by fear or affection, it didn't matter. It just felt damn good to have her so close. Hesitatingly, he wrapped his arm around her. She snuggled even closer, and something achingly sweet and hot blossomed through his chest.

Hunter closed his eyes and sucked in air. Not since Kathleen had he felt this sensation. How could he not have realized he'd been missing this over the last fifteen years? How could he have been so empty as to not even know how hollow he'd become?

He sat quietly, content in the moment, enjoying the sensation of Sarah's body folded into his. He listened to her soft exhalations as she slept, and he watched the shimmering, twisting snake of a river far below.

Then something caught his eye. He tensed, stared hard at the river.

Coming round a distant bend in the Shilongwe was a boat, moving slowly, silently, flowing with the current, engines turned off, a searchlight panning the beaches as it moved.

Every muscle in his body snapped tight. He watched as the boat came closer. He could make out six men, soldiers with berets and guns. His gut twisted. The soldiers must have traced them to the banks of the Shilongwe, heard reports of the aborted rescue attempt, and come downriver after them. They probably didn't know if he and Sarah were alive or dead. But that could change as soon as their searchlight hit the beach they'd left at nightfall.

Hunter had done his best to erase their tracks in the sand with palm fronds. And because it was night, there was a chance the soldiers might miss the signs. But he wasn't going to bet on it. And he sure as hell wasn't going to tell Sarah. This would be more than she could handle right now. Her newfound resolve was still too fragile. She was still too exhausted. Knowing the militia were on their tail could break her completely. He had to find a way to keep her moving—*fast*—until they reached the Eikona River and crossed into the Blacklands, where there was a chance they wouldn't be pursued.

He nudged her awake. "Sarah," he whispered. "We need to move."

"Already?"

"Right now."

23:59. Venturion Tower penthouse, Manhattan.
Monday, September 22

Low autumn clouds swallowed the lights of the Manhattan skyline, and a sharp wind flicked rain against the glass. He paced the length of his windows, conscious of his reflection against the dark panes.

His point man in the Congo, Andries Du Toit, had told him their militia had picked up the nurse's tracks. That was the good news. The bad news was that someone was helping her run.

He cursed softly, swiveled on his heels, paced back along the length of the windows. Someone else had to know the importance of what was in that biohazard container; someone who had access to a helicopter, a bigger network. A real uneasiness bit into his usual steely calm.

He needed the woman alive. They had to make her talk. He had to find out who else knew about the pathogen, who was helping her. Because if whoever was with her was even remotely connected to the U.S. president, he had no choice but to launch the attack immediately. He checked the green glow of his watch. It was almost six in the evening, almost Tuesday in the Congo. He needed to meet with the others as soon as possible.

The phone rang, startling him. He jumped and grabbed the receiver. "Yes?" he barked.

"Dad? You okay?"

"Olivia, darling." Warmth flooded through him as he greeted his daughter. "I'm fine, just…planning my day tomorrow."

She hesitated. "You sure you're all right?"

He smiled broadly. "Of course I am. Just a small business glitch. I'll have it sorted out by morning."

Chapter 7

The day dawned to the high-pitched shrieks of African grays and a troop of gray-cheeked mangabeys proclaiming their territory with wild staccato barks and obscene deep chuckles.

Sarah winced at the monkeys' discordant sounds. They scraped against nerves already raw from stress and exhaustion. She'd been on her feet for almost a full twelve hours now, stumbling blindly behind Hunter with invisible things tearing at her clothes and skin. The night had taken a severe toll on both her mind and her body, and as a nurse, she knew she'd pushed herself to her limit. She was about to collapse physically, and snap psychologically.

And once again, with daybreak came oppressive heat and

humidity. Perspiration oozed a steady trail between her breasts and down her belly, plastering her camisole to her skin. Plus Hunter had made her wear her long-sleeved shirt overtop. She stumbled to a stop, wiped the back of her sleeve over her wet forehead. "Hunter," she said. "I need a rest."

"Not now." He didn't break his stride.

"I mean it!" she called after him.

He halted in his tracks. For a second he stood stock-still, as if trying to control his irritation before facing her. Then he turned around slowly, his face glistening with moisture and his eyes sparking with what she could only imagine was frustration. "You have got to keep moving, Sarah."

"No." She refused to budge. "I need rest. I know my limits."

Impatience flickered over his face. It made her feel like a tiresome piece of baggage. And that made her want to lash out at him.

He took a step toward her. "Sarah." His voice was low, firm. "We'll rest when we get into the Blacklands."

"Right." She slapped at a bug biting her neck. "The cursed land, the land that time forgot, where no one will find us." She bent over, rested her hands on her knees, trying to catch her breath. "Could I at least have some water?"

"Not until we find another source."

She knew he was right. She'd drunk most of his water while they'd waited for their rescue chopper, thinking they'd be out of the Congo soon. But she was dehydrated and was going to collapse soon if she didn't get some liquid into her system.

He must have seen the desperation in her face because his voice softened ever so slightly. "Sarah, I know this is tough, but we should reach Eikona Falls within the hour, and that means drinking water. And once we cross the Eikona, we'll be heading into some very dense primary stuff. It'll be darker, just a little cooler, and we can risk making a fire, which means dry clothes." He smiled slightly in encouragement.

She stared at the curve of his mouth, and the exhausted and rebellious part of her brain wondered if his smile was false, if it was just a pretense at camaraderie designed to fuel her hope. Because just a second ago she'd seen the raw impatience in his features. He was doing a damn fine job of hiding it now, behind that smile.

Josh used to play that game.

"Come, let's go." Hunter turned, slashed at a liana thick as a python.

But she could not go on. The muscles in her legs were ready to give out. She desperately needed to lie down. Even the dank carpet of slippery, rotting leaves and lurid-colored fungi was beginning to look appealing.

But Hunter kept moving forward, away from her, the thick curtain of foliage swallowing him as she watched. Panic licked at her stomach. "Damn it, McBride, stop!" She yelled after him. *"Please!"*

Hunter jerked around. "You have *got* to keep moving, Sarah."

"Just a few minutes? How can a few minutes hurt?" She slapped at another bug and began to peel her long-sleeved shirt off. She was desperate to get cool, to feel air on her arms.

"Don't do that," he warned.

She paused midmotion and glared at him. If she heard one more brusque command come out of Hunter McBride's mouth she was going to scream. *Don't do this. Don't do that. Do this. Do that.* It was all she'd heard through the black night as he'd dragged her at a breakneck pace through the forest. "Why not?" she snapped. "I'm dying of heatstroke here, in case you hadn't noticed." She swatted at a cloud of irritating black insects hanging around her face.

A look of strained patience tightened his features. "Better than being chewed to mincemeat by bugs." He fished into one of the many pockets in his flak jacket, handed her a small bottle of repellent. "They go for the wettest parts of your body—armpits, groin. They want the salt. Best you keep that shirt on, keep covered."

"It's sopping wet," she protested, and hated herself the minute the words came out of her mouth. But she'd completely lost the ability to be cooperative.

A muscle pulsed dangerously along his jawline. "Put the bug juice on, Sarah."

She smeared the insect repellent over the exposed areas of her skin, the chemical fumes nauseating to her empty and already queasy stomach. She handed the bottle back to him and watched as he carefully secured the flap over the repellent. Sarah wasn't able to stop what came out of her mouth next. "I wish you'd lost the damn bug juice instead of the phone. At least we could've gotten help."

His hand stilled. His brows lowered and a quiet, dark thunder crept over his features. He took a step toward her.

Sarah cringed, instinctively backing up against the trunk of a tree. Oh God, had she pushed one of his buttons again? She'd called his skill, *him,* into question. And he didn't like it. Not one bit. When was she going to learn to keep her stupid mouth shut?

"Sarah," he said ominously. "We're on the same team, and don't you forget it. I want to get you *and* this canister out." He clapped his huge hand over the biohazard container he'd secured to his belt with a piece of cord. *Her* container.

"I'm…I'm just stating the obvious. If we had the phone—"

"Did you not hear me? The phone would make no difference. No one is going to fly into Congo airspace. Not unless they want to die. Do you want that, Sarah? Do you want to make people die?"

She bit her lip. This man did not play fair. And she was a fool for pushing him. She'd seen he had low flash points, and she had no idea what could—or would—make him snap. She didn't want to find out. She did not want to be on the wrong side of Hunter McBride in a dangerous mood.

He came even closer, his breath mingling with hers in the moist jungle air. And for an insane moment she thought he was going to kiss her. She thought he was going to force his mouth down hard over hers and savage her right there on the jungle floor.

The thought both terrified and excited her. A mad part of her even wanted, needed him to. She needed to physically tap into his strength even while she was lashing out at him, pushing him away. Maybe this was what Stockholm syndrome was all about. Maybe she had developed an unnatural and deep attraction to her intoxicatingly powerful captor for fear of the alternative—certain death.

His mouth came even closer, his lips almost brushing over hers. Her breathing faltered and her world telescoped in on itself. She closed her eyes.

He traced her jaw very gently with his fingers. "And maybe, Sarah, just maybe, the phone is gone *because* of you."

She flashed her eyes open. "What? Oh, I get it. You lost it because you were too busy looking after me, is that it? I'm a pain in your butt. You think I'm holding you up—"

"You *are* holding me up," he said simply.

Anger bubbled up through the strange mix of sensations swimming through her. She glared into his eyes. "Well, let me tell *you* something, Hunter McBride. Without me you wouldn't have your precious pathogen all boxed and ready to go. You'd still be running around looking for it somewhere in central Africa."

He didn't move a muscle; not even a flicker ran through his strangely colored eyes. His mouth, his body were still just as close.

Sarah's knees started to wobble, but she forced herself to meet his smoldering intensity head-on. "Think about *that,* McBride. Count the days I've saved *you,* and you'll see that dragging me along is a pretty damn small price to pay. So I'd really appreciate it if you'd cut me some slack and let me rest for a damn minute."

Light glimmered in his eyes and a smile tugged at his lips. "Now *there's* the spirit I want to see."

Her jaw dropped. Oh, she saw what he was doing! He was finding hot buttons to make her angry, to feed her energy, anything to kick her in the mental butt and keep her moving through the damn jungle. He was manipulating her emotionally.

Her heart went stone-cold.

That's exactly what Josh used to do. He'd toy with her emotions to get her to react the way he wanted her to. And it had taken her years of psychological and emotional manipulation before she'd even recognized it for the abuse it was, before she'd seen how Josh had been twisting her mind to first blind her to his affairs, and then to make her accept them, as if she were somehow to blame, as if it was *her* fault that her husband needed to look elsewhere for sex. And the fact that she was unable to bear children had played right into his manipulative hands. He'd used it to make her feel worthless as a woman.

Sarah suddenly felt embarrassed. She covered her face with her hands. In her exhausted, dehydrated state she was confusing things, coupling old pathological reactions with the present. She was allowing Josh to get to her even now, a continent and an ocean away. She was seeing him in Hunter McBride. That wasn't fair. But she was too tired. Too tired to think, to stand… She sagged back against the tree and allowed herself to slide down to the spongy ground.

Hunter crouched down beside her. "Sarah?"

For an instant she thought he was going to touch her, and she braced herself. But he didn't. Her heart swooped even lower with hurt, rejection. When was Josh going to stop haunting her? She burrowed her face into her arms.

"Sarah?"

She gritted her teeth, refused to look at him.

"Sarah, *look at me.*"

"I know what you're doing, McBride," she mumbled into her arms. "You *wanted* to make me angry." A dry sob shuddered through her body. "You're doing what Josh used to do to me."

"Josh?" Hunter's brain spun. The Aid Africa file had indicated she was recently divorced. "Is he your ex?"

"Just forget about it!" she muttered.

Hunter frowned. What had her ex-husband done to her to make her feel like this so many thousands of miles away?

But he didn't have time to ask, to coddle. Not if he wanted to save her life. Those soldiers couldn't be far behind. He placed his hand on her shoulder. "Sarah, honey, listen to me, I'm just trying to help get you moving. I want to get you out of here, alive—"

She jerked her head up, brown eyes glistening. "Don't you *honey* me. I'm just a job. You said so yourself. That's it, so quit messing with my head."

"Sarah, that's not—"

"Not what? Tell me it's not true. Tell me you weren't manipulating me."

"Jesus." He dragged his hand through his damp hair. He was at a complete loss for words. "Of course I'm trying to give you motivation. Your mind is the most important survival tool you've got out here. But you're misinterpreting things. You're fatigued." He grasped both her shoulders, forced her to look up into his eyes. "Listen, Sarah, the militia picked up our tracks last night. Six men are coming after us, and you can bet your life they're moving much faster than we are right now."

Her eyes widened in shock. "How…how do you know?"

"I saw them on the river last night, and there's a good chance they picked up our tracks on the beach."

Her eyes flicked wildly around. "Why didn't you tell me?"

"Because you can't afford to panic, like you're doing now. It drains physical resources. You use too many calories, need too much water, can't focus, you make mistakes. Panic is a deadly emotion out here." He paused. "This is not about mind games, Sarah. This is not about you or me or your ex. This is about pure survival."

She stared at him, visibly trying to tamp down her fear. She was struggling both emotionally and physically—and it ate at him. But he *had* to get her moving. He reached for her arm, helped her up.

She hesitated, then looked deep into his eyes. "Tell me one thing, Hunter," she said, very, very softly. "If you are forced to choose between me and that container, which will you pick?"

"Sarah, that's not fair, and you know it."

"Tell me."

His mouth tightened with bitterness. He would have no alternative but to choose the container. That was his job. Those were his orders. "Sarah, you're tired—"

"See? I'm right." She shoved her damp tangle of curls off her forehead. "At least I know where I stand, what I'm worth in this game."

"Sarah…" He reached for her.

She jerked away from him, held up both hands. "Please don't touch me. Don't mess with my head anymore."

His jaw clenched. There was no time for this. And even if there was, there was zip he could do about it. She was twisting everything, making him feel about as lost and confused as a water buffalo in New York City. "Fine," he said. "Whatever. You win, now let's go." He turned and swung viciously at a liana with his machete, dislodging a bunch of epiphytic orchids as he did so. His boots stomped over them as he pushed his way into the forest.

Sarah stared at the crushed blooms in his wake. Oh God, what had she just done? Because of her obsession with her past, with Josh, with her own failures, she'd pushed away the one man who *could* give her the strength to get through this.

She put her fingers to her temples, trying to gather herself. She'd made the mistake of thinking she could put her past behind her by just packing up her life and getting on a plane. But instead, she'd dragged her baggage all the way over the ocean to Africa, into the very heart of the Congo. And it was chasing her down right now, just like those soldiers coming after her.

Sarah could see now that no amount of running was going to help distance her from the effects of Josh's emotional abuse, her past mistakes. They were going to haunt her right into the Blacklands and beyond, unless she found a way to tackle her own ghosts.

Hunter was right. It had to be *her* choice. She had to want to survive. She had to find a way to do this. She had to look into herself, figure out how to sever the past and move forward with only the good memories, not the bad ones. She needed to envision a future for herself, just as he'd said back on the beach—a future beyond the jungle, beyond Josh. She had to try and picture it. Trouble was, she couldn't.

"Sarah!"

She forced her exhausted limbs to move. "Coming…coming." She stepped around the bruised petals and followed him deeper into the jungle.

* * *

They broke through the tangle of foliage so suddenly Sarah thought they were going to pitch straight over the cliff and tumble down into it. She groped instinctively for a branch—anything to help hold her back from the hungry, churning maw below.

The Eikona River.

The ground literally fell away at her toes, where a rocky chasm yawned. Tens of feet below, to her right, a torrent of white water raged through a tight gorge and boiled angrily out the other side, rising in violent waves several feet high that fell back on themselves with a booming sound. The explosive action sent a plume of white mist right up the cliff face on which they stood. It formed tiny droplets on her eyelashes that flashed with rainbows of color when she blinked.

To her left, about five hundred yards downriver, the raging froth calmed and settled into a startling glasslike sheen of emerald-green, broken only by rocks that sliced through the surface.

The water then disappeared into space, under another cloud of white mist churned up by what sounded like a thundering waterfall.

The sight was so awesome, so spectacular, that if she wasn't so exhausted and sore, and her brain so numb, Sarah knew she'd find it heavenly. But right now she had a sick feeling that this was going to be just one more terrifying obstacle she'd have to overcome.

Her eyes cut to Hunter. He was surveying the cliffs as if looking for a way across. *Please, God, no! Don't tell me we have to cross this.*

"That's the Blacklands on the other side," he said. "Once we get across, we'll be safer. And closer to Cameroon—maybe only two days from the border if we keep moving."

Sarah gulped. "How do we cross *that?*"

"See that ledge down there?"

The blood drained from her face as she saw where he was pointing—to a rocky outcrop that hung above the point where the river narrowed into an angry, frothing mass and licked at a monstrous fallen log balanced precariously across the gorge.

"We need to work our way down there, to where that old Bombax has fallen over the gorge. We can use it as a bridge. I'll go first, test it, draw a rope across, secure it, and then you can edge over, using the rope for support."

Her mouth went bone-dry. She didn't think she could do it. But she wasn't going to whine. Not now. Never again. She'd come to Africa to prove she could be strong once more. And she was going to. Exhaustion and fear had almost gotten the better of her, but she wasn't going to let it happen again. She was going tackle her fears head-on—even if it killed her. Because what did she have left? She reached for her crucifix before remembering that even that wasn't there. Then she heard something else, a pulsing sound rising faintly over the hollow boom and thunder of the Eikona River.

It was a thudding so vague and strangely omnipresent she thought at first it might be the beat of her own heart or the blood in her ears. But it swelled around her, grew louder, faster, rising to a panicked rhythm that seemed to grip her heart and make it race along with the sound.

Her eyes flashed nervously to Hunter's. "What's that?"

"War drums."

She listened, trying to identify the direction of the noise. Was she imagining it, or was one set of beats being answered by others? The drumming seemed to be coming from all around her, from everywhere, emanating from the booming river, echoing through the core of every tree. It was the heartbeat of the very Congo itself.

Goose bumps crawled over her skin. She could feel the primeval beat right through her core, talking to the rhythm of her pulse.

"Sarah…" A cool edginess sparked in Hunter's eyes. "We need to get into the Blacklands now. Those drums—the dissention is everywhere."

She looked at him, then the river. The sound of the drums swelled, echoed. She shivered. "You're sure we won't…won't be followed?"

"Not by anyone local." He unslung his pack, removed a length of bound black rope. Talons of fear ripped through Sarah's heart as she stared at the rope. He meant it. She had to cross the Eikona. Her resolve wavered.

She glanced in desperation at the jungle, then back at the river, then at him. He was unraveling the rope. "I'm going to fashion a crude harness to help you down to that ledge," he said as he worked. "You go down first, I'll belay you from above. Once you get to the ledge, wait and I'll follow." He looked up. "Got it?"

She stared at him, unable to move.

He reached out, cupped her face. "Sarah, it's not a tough climb. You can do this." His eyes drilled into hers.

"I know," she whispered. "I know." This was her test. This was where she made her ultimate choice. If she lost her willpower now, she would die. She knew that. And she wanted to live, even if she couldn't yet picture a life for herself beyond this jungle.

Hunter studied her face for a moment, then nodded as if in approval. "Hold out your arms for me."

She did, and he looped the rope under them and around her back. She watched as he knotted the rope carefully above her breastbone.

"Ready?"

She slid her eyes up to meet his. This man was the most solid thing in her world right now. "Yes," she said quietly. "Yes, I'm ready." *In more ways than one.*

Hunter could see that something profound had changed in Sarah. The jungle hadn't broken her yet. She'd tapped into some well of inner strength, and she was doing her damnedest to hold on to that. It made him ridiculously proud of her.

He helped her edge over the first rocky outcrop, and began to feed the rope out gradually as she worked her way down to the ledge, bits of rock and sand kicking out from under her feet as she moved. She slipped suddenly, and the rope jerked taut. Hunter's heart stalled. But she found her footing again, dislodging a small shower of stones as she did. They tumbled down to the river and she turned her head to watch them go.

Don't look at the water, Sarah.

But she stared at the raging torrent below, unable to get going again. His throat went tight. "You're doing great, Sarah," he yelled over the roar of water. "Keep going. You can do it." He willed her to get moving.

Relief washed through his chest as she began once again to inch her way down. She finally found her footing on the ledge, and looked up.

Hunter blew out the breath he'd been holding, gave a thumbs-up and quickly climbed down after her. He reached the ledge and couldn't help what he did next. He yanked her into his arms and held her tightly, too tightly, for just a moment. He told himself it was to feed her resolve, but deep down he knew it was more. *He* needed to hold her. In more ways than one. And that meant he was in serious trouble. "You did great, sweetheart," he whispered into her hair. "Just one more leg and we're over."

She said nothing, just nodded, but he could see that her face was porcelain with fear.

He quickly untied the harness and secured his polypropylene rope to a solid piece of rock jutting from the cliff face. He looped the other end around himself, then glanced up at the jungle fringe along the top of the cliff. Still no sign of the militia. The quicker he and Sarah got over the river and into deep cover on the other side, the better.

"Okay, Sarah, hang ten here. I'm going to draw the rope across the log, secure it at the other end and come back for you. Got it?"

She nodded. Her lips had gone thin and white and she was trembling. He had to move fast, before she lost it.

He edged out onto the thick log and his boot slipped almost immediately. He caught himself, hesitated. The wood was rotting under the constant spume of mist, and covered with a slick layer of black detritus. He steadied himself, bounced lightly, testing his weight. The fallen log was solid enough to hold them both and seemed securely planted against the opposite rock face. He edged sideways along it, feeding the rope out as he went, testing resistance with small bounces. The awkward cylindrical shape of the biohazard container tied to his belt threw his balance off. The thing weighed maybe eighteen pounds, and he had to concentrate on compensating.

River mist saturated his hair and droplets began to drip into his eyes. The rope was also wet now. But Hunter made it to the narrow ledge on the opposite side, and again looked up at the rock face. It wasn't that steep on this end. It would be a fairly easy scramble up into the forest cover. He just had to get Sarah across. He drew the rope taut and secured it to the trunk of a sapling that grew out the rock face. Grasping the rope, he made his way quickly back over the log to Sarah.

He held his hand out to her. "Your turn."

She stared at his hand, unable to move.

"Sarah, you *want* to survive. Make it happen."

She clasped his fingers, a little too tightly, a little too desperately. Worry pinged through him. He told himself he had to exude calm. He had to show that he had confidence in her. He guided her hand toward the rope as she edged her feet onto the log.

"It's slippery, but solid. Just work your way along slowly. Hold the rope with both hands, but don't lean into it. Don't think about the water. Don't even look at it."

She let go of his hand and grabbed the rope, immediately putting too much of her weight into it, and swaying out over the water. Hunter's heart kicked. He jerked the rope back so that her weight was once again centered over the log, almost losing his own balance in the process. The biohazard container lurched around his thigh, threatening to topple him.

"Easy, Sarah. Easy does it. Keep your weight over your feet. Just use the rope as a guide."

She swallowed hard and began to shuffle sideways, making little moaning noises as she went. He moved slowly alongside her, muttering words of encouragement, ready to grab her if she slipped.

They were completely drenched now, Sarah's hair plastered to her face and her knuckles white on the rope. Her movements grew jerky as she neared the center of the gorge. Hunter could literally see her losing her nerve. She made it to the middle, where the boom of the water was loudest, echoing between the rock walls of the canyon. Waves licked up toward the log. She faltered, then froze. "Just a few more steps and you're more than halfway," he yelled over the roar.

She glanced nervously at the opposite bank, subconsciously leaning toward it as she did. The motion shot her left foot out from under her, and she went down onto log with a scream, just managing to hold onto the rope with one hand. The movement knocked Hunter off balance. He flailed backward and the canister swung wildly out behind him. He grabbed for the rope, catching himself, but his added weight jerked it from Sarah's hand. She screamed as she clutched at a small bit of branch, just managing to halt her slide off the log and into the river. Her feet dangled precariously over the churning white water as she stared, wild-eyed, up at Hunter.

He dropped flat onto the log. "Sarah! Give me your hand!"

But she couldn't seem to make herself let go of the small, rotting branch she was hanging on to for dear life. He could literally see it tearing loose. It was going to go at any second.

He lunged for her, grabbing her arm just as the branch gave way. The canister swung out over the water, threatening to pull him over, too.

Hunter hung on to Sarah desperately as she swung over the gorge. He could feel his grip on the log slipping as the black detritus began to slough off. Her arm was also slick with river mist, and he could feel he was losing his grip there, too, gravity and her weight conspiring to fight him, the river hungry and waiting below.

She began to slide from his grasp, and the waves licked at her shoes. She flailed wildly with her free hand, trying to grasp the canister hanging almost within her reach. She grabbed it just as her arm slid free of Hunter's hold.

The fresh weight on his belt yanked him sideways around the log. Hunter swore as he dug his fingers into the rotting wood, knowing that if he lost his grip, they would both go down.

He clung with all his might, but the thin cord on his belt gave, snapping free with a jerk.

His heart lurched. He scrambled up onto the log, and the last thing he saw was Sarah's hair churning like brown streamers in the white water before the foam swallowed her completely.

Then he saw her head pop up downriver, the canister lolling

in the waves beside her—both heading inexorably toward the smooth, glassy sheen of water racing toward the falls.

He could never reach both before one went over.

He faced the choice. Sarah or the canister.

Her life, or the lives of millions?

Hunter plunged feetfirst into the roiling maw.

Chapter 8

08:22 Alpha. Eikona Falls.
Tuesday, September 23

Sarah thrashed against the roiling current, but the powerful Eikona sucked her under, whirling her along.

She forced her eyes open, trying to figure out which way was up and which was down, but all she could see was a milky-green blur. She was running out of breath, and she didn't even know which way to push for the surface! Terror squeezed her lungs. She knew she was being hurtled toward the falls, could already feel the change in the water… *She was going over.* But just as the knowledge slammed into her, she felt something grab at her.

Hunter!

Hope kicked at her heart. She began to fight harder against the current, struggling to find the surface. She felt the iron strength in his arms as he pulled her toward him, hooked his arm around her chest and dragged her up through the water until they popped to the surface like corks. She gasped for air as he towed her diagonally across the ribbed sheen of water that surged toward the falls, and into the calm of an eddy. He hauled her roughly up a slope of rock, dumped his pack with a thud beside her. His gun and machete clattered down beside it. "Use them if you need them!" he yelled over the roar of the falls.

And he was gone, back into the river, cutting across the glassy, swollen surface with smooth, powerful strokes. Sarah's heart stalled as she saw him heading for the biohazard container bobbing dangerously close to the brink of the falls.

It was impossible. He'd never reach it in time. She watched in numb horror as Hunter was swept sideways faster than he could close the distance between himself and the canister.

She saw him near the container, grab it. Her heart jerked against her ribs. He turned, began to swim toward her. But he was moving backward even faster. She caught her breath.

He wasn't going to make it!

Sarah leaped to her feet, pressed her hands over her mouth as everything began to unfold in sickening slow motion.

Hunter was pulled to the edge of the falls, and for a second he seemed to hang there, poised in the mist on the knife edge of the swollen, glassy river. Then the Eikona sucked him over and he disappeared into the steaming sky.

"No!" she screamed. "Oh, God, no! Hunter!" She spun around, hysterical. She didn't know what to do! Then she spotted his pack, his gun, his machete. He'd left all his equipment. *He'd known all along he wasn't going to make it.* She was on her own. He'd left her all the tools he could for her to try to survive without him.

For a second sheer terror paralyzed her. She wouldn't believe it. She could *not* believe he was gone. He was invincible. He was her lifeline. She choked with emotion. No, he wasn't invincible. Hunter McBride was only human in spite of everything she'd learned and thought about him. He'd saved *her* first. Her life *had* meant more to him than his mission.

Tears streamed from her eyes. Oh God, she had to find him! She pressed her hands to her temples, trying to think. She'd need his pack if she found him. She'd need the first aid gear, food, whatever else he had in it. She grabbed it, hefted it up to her back, but it swung violently, throwing her off balance. Her wet runners slithered out from under her on the slick surface. She crashed down onto the rock, landing hard on her hip. But she barely registered the explosive spark of pain. She scrambled back onto her feet, repositioned the pack on her back. It felt incredibly heavy in her weakened state. Bowing under the weight of Hunter's gear, she grabbed his assault rifle and machete, slung them over her shoulders.

How in heaven had he carried all this stuff, and hacked through the bush at the same time? How could he have possibly looked so relaxed under all this hot and cumbersome gear? Sarah clenched her jaw against the strain, staggered awkwardly over the rocks in her sodden runners. She reached the muddy bank, grabbed a fistful of coarse grass, dragged herself up off the rock slab. On hands and knees she clambered up the steep slope toward what looked like a narrow path along the ridge.

Breath rasping in her throat, fear slamming her heart into her ribs, she reached the path. She bent over to catch her breath, saw animal tracks in the red soil. She lifted her eyes. It was a narrow game path leading toward the falls, where it disappeared alongside the booming curtain of water. She suspected the trail led all the way down to a big calm watering hole at the bottom of the falls. She'd seen something just like this on a nature program.

Sarah staggered along the path, fatigue and panic making her sway wildly under the weight of Hunter's pack and gun and machete. Her hair was plastered to her face, her wet clothes chafed her skin and her feet skidded and squelched in her drenched shoes. But she was blind to it. All she wanted was to get down that path and find Hunter.

But the jungle fought her every step of the way. She tried to run, making it to the edge of the falls before the weight of the pack swung her sideways and she skidded on vegetation slick from the heavy, constant mist churned up by the thunderous falls. Sarah landed hard on her butt and began to slide downhill alongside the crashing curtain of water. She held the gun tight at her side, worried it would go off as she tried to control her hectic tumble down the steep path. She hit a rock, lurched head over heels, came to a dead stop. Blood thudded loudly against her eardrums.

She had to focus. What had Hunter said? Panic could kill you. She forced herself to breathe, and peered nervously through the mist and rainbows.

She could see something down below. A dark, limp shape lay at the edge of a tranquil, turquoise-green pool at the base of the falls. She froze. The shape was unmistakably human. It was him, had to be, lying facedown in the mud, sprawled out, unmoving. Her heart stalled. A part of her didn't want to believe it was Hunter. She willed him to move, to show some sign of life. But he didn't.

"Oh God, Hunter," she whispered. "Please be alive. Please be alive. Please be alive…." She repeated the words over and over like a mantra as she scrambled down the path to the rim of slippery, rust-colored mud.

She stopped at the bottom, afraid to go up to the water's edge, petrified of what she might find. She began to shake violently, and tears made her blind.

She swiped them brutally out of her eyes. *Control yourself, Sarah. He needs you now.*

God, she hoped he *did* need her, that she would find some sign of life in her invincible mercenary, the hardened man who had touched her so tenderly, helped give her willpower. The man who—she choked on a sob—the man who had chosen *her* life over everything he'd been trained to do.

She began to squelch toward his limp form, swallowing her trepidation and forcing herself into clinical mode as she got closer.

He was lying on his stomach, his right arm twisted at a strange angle, his fist still clutched around the handle of the bio-hazard container. One side of his face was in the mud. His eyes were closed and his skin was gray. Sarah's heart plummeted. She'd seen that look before.

She knelt at his side, her heart beating light and fast. "Hunter?" she whispered as she touched his face. His skin was ice-cold. "Hunter!" She grabbed his shoulders and shook him. She could not, would not, lose someone else to this jungle. Not him, not Hunter. He had to be alive. "Hunter!"

She felt him move. Her heart pounded against her ribs. "Hunter?"

He lifted his head slightly out of the mud and his eyelids fluttered open. He stared at her, slowly registering his surroundings. Then he grimaced. "Hello, angel."

A wave of emotion surged through Sarah, so strong it stole her breath and ability to form words. Hot tears of relief filled her eyes. She smiled and placed her hand against his muddy cheek. "Thank God, oh thank God you're alive."

He closed his eyes briefly and his body shuddered.

"How…how badly are you hurt?"

He tried to lift his head again, groaned, let it fall back into the mud. She winced and a new set of fears crept into her heart.

He tried to move again. "Help…help me up, Sarah." He ground out the words through clenched teeth. "I need to get up there…by the trees. Less mud there." He maneuvered himself onto his good elbow, his eyes bright with pain. "And we…must…stay…near cover." He swallowed a bark of pain as he tried to sit up.

"Maybe…maybe you shouldn't move. Maybe you should lie still until—"

His eyes cut to hers. "Until what? The ambulance comes?"

It hit her then, the implications of being hurt in the wilderness. There was zero hope of help, no civilized system to come to their aid. They had only themselves, two humans against a deadly jungle where only the fittest survived. And now the balance of power between her and Hunter had shifted squarely onto her shoulders. *He needed her.* And she had the skills to help him. She could no longer be a victim in any way. It was up to her now.

The realization shot a jolt of determined fire through her body. She couldn't afford raw fear now. She had to focus and fight—for him.

She sucked in a steadying breath. "Hunter, before I help you move, you have to tell me exactly where you hurt, so that I—"

He was feeling his left shoulder with his good hand. "Anterior dislocation of the sternoclavicular joint."

Surprise rippled through her. "What?"

"My left shoulder—" he groaned as he forced himself onto his knees "—it's dislocated."

"How do you know?"

"I know. I can feel it."

She stared at him, momentarily stunned. "It…I mean, it could be broken, or—"

"No." He staggered to his feet, gasped as pain punched through him. "I…felt it go…when I tried to keep hold of the container as I went under at the base of the falls."

"You're sure?"

"Of course I'm sure! The muscles are already going into spasm. You've got to help me reduce it immediately, Sarah." His eyes pierced hers. "I need my arm. We *both* do if we want to get out of here."

He was right on that count. And if his diagnosis was correct, the top of his left humerus had been forced forward out of the shoulder socket. The longer it stayed that way, the less likely it was they'd manage to get it back into place without surgery. And that was impossible. If left untreated, he'd be seriously disabled and in constant and debilitating pain.

He started to stumble through the mud, holding his injured arm steady with his good hand. "Bring the container," he called back to her as he made his way up to the trees.

Sarah grabbed the handle of the biohazard canister and got to her feet. She squished through the mud after him, the gear on her back weighing her down.

He sagged under a tree where the red laterite was packed hard. She removed the rifle and machete slings, shrugged out of his pack and dumped it on the ground. He gave her a grin twisted with pain. "You *are* an angel. You brought all the gear."

A wedge of pride jammed into her. She smiled. "Yeah, I did."

His eyes trailed over her. "You got a bit messed up, though."

She glanced down at her clothing and a crazy giggle rippled through her. She looked like an urchin out of a Dickens novel. "Guess I was in a bit of a hurry."

He nodded, and his tacit approval warmed her. She felt suddenly as if he respected her, as if they were part of a team now. And she couldn't begin to articulate what that meant to her.

He slid his hunting knife out of the sheath on his thigh, held it out to her. "Here."

She stared at it. That knife had killed her pursuers.

"Take it, Sarah. Cut my sleeve off."

She swallowed her mix of feelings and clasped her fingers around the hilt, felt its weight in her hand. She needed this knife to help heal him now. This was her present reality. And in some strange way, in taking hold of that knife, she felt as if she'd just become part of this strange system, this living organism of a jungle that was probably the most competitive natural arena on earth.

She lifted the fabric of his camouflage shirt away from his shoulder, poked a hole through it with the hooked tip of the blade and jerked her hand back. The blade sliced neatly through the strong material. She pulled the sleeve loose and maneuvered it carefully down over his injured arm.

She recognized the profile of a dislocated shoulder instantly. The next thing that struck her was that his muscles were rock-hard and in serious spasm.

She placed her hands on his shoulder. His skin was hot. She fingered along his joint, locating the position of the bones. "You're right," she said. "I can feel the medial end of the clavicle here—" she moved her hand over his skin "—and the head of the humerus here. It's an anterior dislocation."

He said nothing, just watched her intently.

She checked the pulse at his wrist and compared it with the strength of the pulse at his elbow. She let out a silent sigh of relief. The major blood vessels that passed through the shoulder area were undamaged. "Pulse is fine." She pinched the back of his hand. "You feel that?"

"Yeah, I felt a nibble."

She smiled. His muscles were so tense and his skin so taut it was impossible to grab enough flesh between her fingers to give a real bite. But the fact he'd felt it at all showed his nerves were in working order. She pinched his rock-hard deltoid muscle, just below his shoulder on the top of his arm. "And that?"

He nodded. "That, too."

Relief surged through her. His axillary nerve, one of the most vulnerable in this sort of injury, was undamaged. This was looking to be a straightforward dislocation. All she had to do now was manipulate the joint back into place without damaging any nerves in the process. That was easier said than done. His muscle tone, strength and size were phenomenal, while she was slight in stature and in a weakened state. She was no match for his body. His muscles were going to fight her every step of the way.

She rocked back on her heels, pushed her wet hair off her forehead. How in heavens was she going to do this?

He was watching her, reading her mind. "You have to fix it, Sarah."

"I…I know. It's just—"

"Do it, Sarah. *Now*. We don't have time to waste. The longer we leave it the more my muscles are going to fight you."

She began to remove her shoe. "Lie back."

Hunter lowered himself slowly down onto the packed earth. The pain in his left shoulder was excruciating, and his muscles had tightened to fight against the injury. This was going to take time—time they could ill afford. They needed to get well into the cover of the jungle before the soldiers arrived and sighted them from the opposite bank of the river.

Sarah positioned her butt in the dirt at his side, one shoe off. "Ready?"

Hunter stared at the little yellow pompom on her wet sock, and in spite of his pain, he felt a smile in his heart. This woman was something else. "Yeah, I'm ready."

She positioned her socked foot in his armpit, wrapped both

her hands around his wrist and leaned back, exerting pressure
with her foot as she began to pull his arm.

His nerves screeched in pain and his muscles contracted in
resistance. But she kept the pressure steady, consistent, fighting
his body. He knew Sarah had been running on empty before her
plunge into the river, and she had to be even more drained now.
But she kept at it, color beginning to rise in her cheeks.

He felt his muscles begin to give, and a groan of pain
escaped him. Shock flared in her eyes and he felt her
release the pressure slightly. "No." He ground out the word.
"Keep…pulling." This could take upward of twenty minutes,
the way his muscles were protesting.

Perspiration began to bead on her brow and glow on her face.
Her limbs started to tremble with the effort. "This…this isn't
working, Hunter," she gasped.

"Pull, damn it!"

She gritted her teeth, scrunched her eyes tight, held the
pressure. Hunter used every ounce of mental strength to force
relaxation into his spasming muscles. And finally he felt them
begin to release. "Hold…hold it now!"

Sweat poured down her brow and she steadied the pressure.
He could feel the muscles in her leg quivering with the sus-
tained tension. But she was good. Damn good. A pro. He could
feel her twist his arm, maneuver his bone ever so slightly,
timing herself, releasing movement when she could sense give.
She eased, waited. Eased. Waited again. Then suddenly he felt
the telltale bump as his shoulder jerked back into place. The
intensity of pain subsided almost immediately.

Hunter released a huge breath of air, and his body went
limp. He laughed out loud in sheer relief, couldn't help himself.
"God, you really are an angel, you know that?"

She kept her eyes closed. She just sat there, hunched over,

her face streaked with mud, her hair a wet tangle, one shoe on, one shoe off, her wet sock with the pompom now streaked with bloodred dirt. And in that instant, Hunter had never seen anything more endearing, more appealing, than this woman.

He pushed himself to a sitting position. "Sarah?"

She still didn't open her eyes. Tears began to leak out from under her lashes and drip silently down her cheeks, tracking crooked trails through the dirt. A sensation washed through his body, a feeling for her so deep and so explosive he couldn't begin to articulate what it was. He'd done the right thing going after her. He knew it in his heart. He would never have been able to live with himself otherwise.

She opened her eyes and looked right into him, into his soul. "Thank you," she whispered. "Thank you for coming after me." She leaned forward, cupped her hands around his face and brushed her lips softly over his. "I didn't believe in you. I'm so sorry."

He closed his eyes, shuddered. How could a simple touch be so sweet, words so achingly painful? It was as if she'd just ripped a yawning chasm of need right through the very center of his heart, an empty void so deep and vast that he knew he was going to spend the rest of his life trying to fill it. *Damn this woman.* The rawness, the explosive clout of the unexpected emotion was almost too powerful.

"Hunter?"

He couldn't talk to her. Not now. He had to get control of himself. He climbed to his feet and reached for his gun. They needed to fill the canteens and get into jungle cover ASAP.

"Hunter—"

"My knife, hand me my knife," he barked. He knew his words were clipped, but he couldn't stop himself, couldn't handle his feelings.

Her mouth dropped open slightly. Confusion knitted her brow. She reached for the hunting knife at her side, handed it to him. "What about your arm? We should splint it. I should check the pulse again to see that we didn't—"

"Later. We move now!" he snapped. He turned his back on her, angrily blinking back the hot burn in his eyes. Christ, he hadn't shed a tear in fifteen goddamn years. He wasn't about to go soft now.

Chapter 9

Sarah's triumph in having helped Hunter—a man she'd viewed as invincible—had fired her with a fierce new determination to survive. It also gave her a deep sense of her own value, something she'd been lacking for a long, long time. The old Sarah, the person she'd been before Josh, was finally poking through, and in her heart she was feeling strength again. But the nurse in her was still worried about the mercenary.

She watched Hunter carefully as he led the way along the narrow, rutted game path. The going was relatively easy here, the ground drier, the trees tall and covered with white lichen. But the two of them had been walking for almost four hours since he'd gone over Eikona Falls, and she could see he was beginning to weaken. He'd given her the biohazard container so that he could keep his left arm immobile, but he insisted on carrying the rest of his gear himself. She wished he'd allowed her to splint his arm. If he fell, it could pop out again.

"Hunter," she called to him.

He stopped, turned around. The strained tightness of his features, the bright sheen in his dark eyes startled her. She hoped he didn't have some internal damage he wasn't telling her about.

"Could we take a rest?" This time she wasn't asking for herself, she was asking for him. She knew he wasn't going to stop because *he* was tired.

"Not yet." He began to turn back.

"Hunter! I insist."

He glanced over his shoulder, cocked an eyebrow.

"I need to splint that arm, and I need to check your pulse again. The nerves could've been pinched when the bone went back into the socket."

A grin twitched along one corner of his mouth. "That the nurse I hear talking?"

"Damn right. You have *got* to take a break. You said we'd be safe here in the Blacklands, once we got into the trees."

He studied her.

"Well? Are we safe now?" She angled her head. "Or were you lying just to mess with my mind again?" And with a little spark of surprise, she realized she'd just joked about something that up until this second had been dead serious to her.

That smile tugged at his mouth again. "Another hour," he said. "Then we rest."

She scowled at him and put her hands on her hips.

His grin broadened. "I promise."

"Okay, but I'm going to hold you to that promise, soldier."

* * *

The day grew hotter as they moved deeper into the Blacklands, and her clothes, still damp from the river, chafed against her skin. The sound of a bird—*tok tok-boo, tok-tok-boo*—seemed to follow them constantly.

"What *is* that?"

"Red-crested cuckoo. Each bird calls to the one in the next territory as we move."

It made her feel creepy, as if they were being watched, their progress being telegraphed from one cuckoo camp to another in some kind of jungle code. A chill of foreboding crept over her skin. She hoped Hunter was right when he said no one would follow them into this place.

They broke into a clearing and were hit with such a fierce wave of sunlight and heat that it stole her breath. A narrow corridor of grassland stretched out in front of them, perhaps half a mile long, bounded by thick shrubs and low forest. Golden grasses swayed gently in the hot breeze. She could see blue sky, huge cotton candy clouds scudding across it, driven by an invisible wind high up in the stratosphere.

Sarah stepped forward into the grass, and a cloud of butterflies the size of small birds fluttered up into the air. They were scarlet and yellow, some spotted and dashed with streaks and whorls of iridescent blue. Others were speckled with orange and brown, like autumn leaves that had come alive and taken flight. Sarah gasped. "It's…it's so beautiful," she whispered. "I never expected to see anything like this in the middle of the jungle."

"Edaphic savannah," said Hunter. "Little natural savannahs entirely enclosed by forests, pockets of grassland on soil too run-down to support even the smallest trees." He scanned the area with narrowed eyes as he spoke. "Usually you find them along sandy riverbeds that dry out when the stream changes course. Almost nothing is known about them...." He glanced at her. "What you're seeing is damn rare. This ecosystem is unique to this region of the Congo basin, and it's protected because few people dare venture in here."

She moved her hand slowly through the cloud of dancing butterflies. "A slice of pure Eden," she whispered to herself. "Cursed by the spirits or protected by the gods, it's a matter of perspective."

Hunter looked at her, a mix of interest and surprise crossing his features. "Exactly."

"We can rest here," she said. And it wasn't a question.

He consulted his watch.

She glowered at him. "You promised, Hunter. We can dry our clothes here, and I *must* splint your arm."

"Anyone ever tell you that you're bossy?"

"Anyone ever told you that you're insufferably pigheaded?"

He smiled again and the sunlight caught his eyes. Something cracked in her heart. She hadn't seen him smile like that. Genuine, gentle almost. It was as if he'd let his guard slip momentarily, and she was seeing the true man inside, the man behind the mercenary.

She reached for his pack. "Here, let me help you off-load this." He didn't argue, which vaguely surprised—and concerned—her. He turned around, allowing her to help him shrug out of his gear without putting pressure on his shoulder joint.

"You really should've let me carry more stuff."

"I'm fine." He crouched down, untied the roll of canvas and nylon that was secured at the bottom of his pack. "Hammock," he said as he flicked the roll with his good arm, sending it unraveling, the ropes flying. "Doubles as a decent ground cover." He handed her a corner and she helped him spread it near the roots of a tree at the edge of the clearing. The shade here was dappled, the sunlight not too harsh.

"Give me your shirt." She held out her hand. "I'll hang it in the sun."

He arched a brow, studied her. "This how you treated the kids in your ward?"

"Kids were more cooperative."

He shrugged out of his flak jacket and undid his shirt buttons with one hand. "What made you become a pediatric nurse anyway, Sarah?"

"How'd you know I was a pediatric nurse?"

"It was in your file."

Reality intruded and with it a twinge of unease. She nodded. "I see. Well, I love children, always have." She lifted her eyes, met his.

He studied her carefully as he shrugged out of his one-sleeved shirt. "Something tells me you're a sucker for the vulnerable, Sarah." He handed her his damp gear. "You're a born nurturer. It's your strength."

"And weakness," she muttered as she took his clothes. She hesitated, looking at his pants.

A grin ghosted his lips. "I keep the pants. For now." He sank down onto the hammock, leaned back heavily against the tree trunk and closed his eyes with a sigh.

Sarah removed her own long-sleeved blouse and the thin cotton pants from under her skirt. She ventured out into the long gold grass and draped their clothes over a scrubby bush in direct sunlight. She was surprised to feel how dry his high-tech gear felt compared to her stuff. The heat burned down on the top of her head, her shoulders and the bare skin on her arms as she made her way back to him and the shade. She sat on the tarp next to him and removed her socks and shoes. She wiggled her toes in the warm air and sighed. "Feels good," she said. "What about you, your boots?"

"I'm good. Jungle gear. Breathable."

She frowned. He wasn't relaxed enough to take his shoes off. He was still on guard. A niggle of unease skittered through her. She shrugged it off, pulled the first aid kit to her side, extracted a roll of bandages. "Okay, soldier, sit up and get that arm into position."

He did, his eyes locking on to hers. Up close they were the color of an evening sky slipping into velvet night. His breath was warm against her face, his scent masculine. Her heart skipped a beat, then kicked into a fast, light pace. She was suddenly very conscious of being so close to his naked chest, the dark hair that covered his powerful pecs, the glorious way it nestled between ridges of honed muscle and disappeared into the belt of his pants. Warmth unfurled low in her belly. She felt a little giddy.

She told herself it was fatigue, dehydration, lack of food, oppressive heat. Or maybe it was just the dizzying, life-affirming thrill of having once again cheated death.

Whatever it was, she hadn't expected to feel wild sexual attraction out here in the jungle. She swallowed against the dryness in her mouth, looked away from his eyes and began to wrap the bandage around him. She noticed her hands were trembling slightly as she worked, and it had nothing to do with fear.

"There. That'll help keep it still." She blew out the breath she hadn't realized she'd been holding, and made the mistake of looking back up into his eyes.

They smoldered with a dangerous, dark electricity, and the air seemed to suddenly pulse with the heat of it. Sarah couldn't speak. The mutual attraction was undeniable. And for a dizzying instant she felt as if they were poised on the knife edge of a torrent, just like he'd hung for a second at the brink of Eikona Falls. She feared what would happen if they were plunged into the depths of what swirled between them. In truth, she was flat-out terrified of feeling anything like this for a man as powerful as Hunter. She'd made that mistake before.

And it had cost her everything.

"Thank you," he said, his voice low and husky.

She jerked her mind back, swallowed once more. Then pinched his deltoid muscle. Hard.

"Hey, I felt that."

"Good," she said, and pinched him again, harder, this time on the back of his hand.

"That, too. I'm beginning to think I wouldn't want to get into a heavy tussle with you over taking my medicine."

She shook off the sensuous image that leaped into her mind, cleared her throat and checked his pulse at his wrist, and then at his elbow. "Looks like you'll live another day."

He studied her, a wickedly playful light beginning to twinkle in his eyes. "So, nurse, just how am I going to get my shirt back on?"

"What?"

He jerked his chin toward the bandage she'd used to carefully strap his arm to his chest.

She clapped her hand to her head and sank back against the tree, the heat of embarrassment warming her cheeks. "I wasn't thinking."

"Where did you say you went to nursing school?"

She began to laugh. It felt damn good. It released all the pent-up tension, the sexual heat.

He touched her jaw. She stilled instantly. He traced her profile lightly with his fingertips. "Do you have any idea how gorgeous you are when you laugh like that?"

She bit her lip, suddenly nervous. He'd put his attraction into words. It made it too real, something to be dealt with. She was afraid, not ready. And yet she was. She wanted him to touch her—wanted it with such a sudden deep and desperate need it overwhelmed her.

It was as if he read her mind. He smiled, a genuine, warm, caring smile, and dropped his hand from her face, reached for his pack, fished in an outside pocket, took something out. "Here." He held it toward her. "Reward for saving my ass back there."

She gaped. "Oh. My. God. *Chocolate!*"

"Want some?"

"Are you kidding?" She lunged for it.

He jerked it just out of her reach, wiggled the chocolate bar in temptation. "What's it worth to you?"

"Saving your butt again."

"That'll do." He handed it to her.

She tore it open. "Oh, my God, I can't believe you have chocolate. Hunter…I think I love you."

He stilled.

Oops. What had she just said? She looked slowly up into his eyes.

His face was dark. Unreadable. "You mean that?"

Her heart began to palpitate, her palms grow moist. "I… I—" Lord, what was it she felt for him?

His face cracked into a grin. "I'm kidding. You gonna share that? I want at least a third."

She moistened her lips and broke the soft chocolate bar in two, thankful for the task. She handed him half and popped a squishy square into her mouth.

She closed her eyes, leaned back against the trunk and let it melt over her tongue. It tasted like heaven. "Mmm, this is so good. It's the best chocolate ever." She opened her eyes as sugar surged through her depleted system. "You know, the night I escaped the clinic, I was hunched up in the roots of that Bombax tree, in pitch darkness, petrified, not knowing what on earth to do next, and you know what I was thinking?"

"What?"

She broke off another square. "I was thinking about buying chocolate, in a mall. I was thinking the stores in Seattle would be getting in Halloween stuff by now. Can you believe that? I was staring death in the face, and all I could do was think about candy."

"The mind seeks comfort in strange ways." He looked away from her over the gently swaying gold savannah grass, and his eyes grew distant. "Sometimes you have no control." He snapped back from wherever his thoughts had taken him. "And now? What're you thinking now?"

She stopped munching. "Now?"

"Yeah, now."

"I…I'm just happy to be alive right now. I'm not really thinking about anything," she lied. She could feel her face flush as she said it. She was a pathetic liar. But there was no way she was going to go near telling him what she was really thinking, about how damn attractive she found him, about how the way his hair disappeared into the belt of his pants made her want to melt from the inside out.

"You're not thinking about home now?"

"I told you, I don't have a home anymore." She forced a smile and held up her last piece of chocolate. "Besides, I have everything I need right here."

"Everything?" The muscle at his jaw pulsed softly.

She watched it, feeling her own pulse match his rhythm. She swallowed hard. He was doing the damnedest things to her body with a few words. She had to talk about something else, so she switched tables on him. "What're *you* thinking?"

"You don't want to know what I'm thinking, Sarah." His voice was husky as he said it.

Her cheeks went hot. She flicked her eyes away but something delicious tingled low in her stomach.

"Tell me about your ex," he said suddenly.

"What?"

"What happened? What did he do to you?"

She stared at him. Her marital failure was none of his business. Or maybe it was. Maybe she'd made it so by her ridiculous outburst back near the Eikona River.

He waited for her to answer. A bird called in the distant treetops, a long series of hoots, descending in scale and dying away to a single pitiful *hoo*. It was an eerie, lonely cry. A shiver chased over her hot skin. Maybe she needed to tell him, to share. Maybe she had to get this off her chest. Perhaps it would give her some sense of closure.

She sucked in a breath. "Josh left me for another woman." There, she'd said it. So why did it make her feel as if she'd just stripped off her clothes in front of Hunter and bared her body and soul? She waited, nervous, for his judgment, and at the same time hated herself for feeling this way. *This* was what Josh had done to her. His leaving her should *not* be a reflection on her worth as a woman. She shouldn't feel that she would be somehow judged lacking by his actions.

She knew all of that, but just couldn't shed it. That sense of failure, of inferiority had become a part of who she was. And not being able to bear children hadn't helped. Josh had used that against her, too. He'd abused her caring nature, used her every weakness to undermine her. And he'd done it so insidiously, and over so many years, that she'd finally integrated a sense of worthlessness.

It had become a part of her psyche. *This* was what she had

to shake. This was what she had to find a way to face down. She just wasn't sure how. But she had a sense she'd begun. Finally. And it was this jungle and Hunter that were, in a perverse way, showing her she really did have the courage and strength inside to do it.

He was studying her intently. She glanced self-consciously down at the chocolate wrapper in her hand, fiddled with the foil edges.

"Why did he leave you?" he asked, the words so simple.

"It's…it's complicated."

"Try me."

She looked up into Hunter's eyes. How could she tell him the real reason? How could she tell this übermale that she was pathetic enough to have allowed this to happen to her? It was humiliating. It made her furious with herself.

He hooked a knuckle under her jaw, made her look at him. "Sarah, talk to me."

"It…it was my fault. I should've walked out on him when he first started having affairs."

"Why didn't you?"

"You have to know Josh to understand. He's…he's powerful. He had a way of controlling my emotions. He…made me feel…inadequate."

Flint hardened Hunter's eyes. "Did he hurt you?"

She tensed at the overt aggression in his tone. "No, not in the way you think. Not physically. Just emotionally." She steeled herself. "Josh was…*is* a sociopath. He's charismatic, incredibly charming when he wants to be, but he's completely manipulative, ruthless in getting exactly what he wants out of a person." She hesitated. "Now that I have some distance, I can see that he'd been abusing, manipulating me emotionally for years. I should've seen it coming. I should never have allowed it to get as far as it did."

The muscles in Hunter's neck went stiff. She could almost feel the anger begin to vibrate off him. She had a sudden vision of Josh squaring off with Hunter, and there was no doubt in her mind who would win. Hunter McBride was a better man than her ex in every possible way.

"Why did you marry him, Sarah?"

Her chest went tight. Her eyes began to moisten. She didn't want to think about Josh. She wanted to forget the past. "Hunter...I—I don't really want to talk about it. I want to forget. I *came* here to forget."

He leaned forward. "But you can't forget, can you, Sarah? It's followed you. You can't even talk about it without feeling shame. I can see it in your eyes."

She bit her lip, fiddled with the wrapper in her lap. "I know. You're right." She lifted her eyes to his. "How did a soldier become so deep?"

"By making his own mistakes." He covered her fidgeting hand with his. "So why did you marry him?"

She sucked in another breath. "I told you, he can be a real charmer. We met soon after I got my first job at the children's hospital. He'd just been transferred to Seattle and was in line for a big promotion." She looked at the chocolate wrapper in her hand. "He's a mergers and acquisitions giant. He literally swallows people and businesses for a living without blinking an eye, and I didn't even see it, how mercenary he was, even back then. I totally fell for him. I loved him with all my heart, but now that I look back, I see that he probably never did love me. I simply fitted his needs at the time. Having a young, obedient trophy wife was just the kind of image he needed to cinch his big promotion. He got it, and he never looked back, just kept right on climbing. That...that was six years ago." She hesitated. "Now he doesn't need me anymore. He's moved on to a beautiful younger woman with a famous name—a model who's carrying his twins. It's gotten him into the papers, the tabloids…just what he wanted." Sarah paused, stared at the gold grass waving in the warm wind. "It's really quite shocking to realize you've wasted so much of your life on someone who never once gave a damn. Men like him can't care."

"Ah, I see. You were comparing him to me."

She whipped her eyes to his. "It's not true, Hunter. You're *not* the same. Josh would never have saved me over that canister. He would have let me die. *You didn't.*" She looked right into his eyes. "I am so sorry I judged you. I…I've been burned, and that makes me…careful. I just don't trust myself to make good judgments anymore."

He sat silent, his eyes glimmering, a powerful current pulsing through him—one she couldn't identify.

"What gave you the courage to finally leave him?"

She liked the way he said that. It implied he believed she'd found some inner strength. But she hadn't. "Josh left *me,* Hunter. He walked out the door the night I confronted him about his latest affair. He wasn't even bothering to be discreet about it anymore."

"His affair with the model?"

Sarah angrily sniffed back her emotion. "Yes. And you know how I found out about it? My friends didn't tell me. They were embarrassed for me. They didn't want to hurt me. But nothing could have hurt or humiliated me more than standing in that checkout line at the grocery store and seeing my husband's face staring at me from the magazine racks—my husband with his arms around another woman, a very pregnant woman."

Bitter tears blurred her vision. Sarah scrunched the chocolate wrapper into a tight little ball in the palm of her hand. "I actually put my sunglasses on before I got to the register. What a fool. I mean, who was I kidding?" She gave a light, nervous laugh. "I bought the magazine and went straight to the store bathroom. I locked myself in and read about my husband and his lover and the babies they were having. I sat there until the store manager banged on the door. I…I went straight home, waited for Josh. I sat in a chair, watching the front door, numb, just waiting. He came in after 2:00 a.m., and when I confronted him, he looked at me as if I was a pathetic stray animal. And— and he told me I was an idiot for not having seen that our marriage was over long ago." She stared at the balled chocolate wrapper in her hand. "My husband just turned and walked out that door, and I never saw him again. He sent his lawyer instead. I…I was such a fool, Hunter."

He grabbed her jaw, jerked her face to his. "Don't you *ever* say that." The ferocity in his voice startled her.

"It's *not* your fault, Sarah."

She wanted to thank him for saying that. She wanted to lean into him, to fold herself into his arms, to feel the radiating warmth of his solid chest, but she held back.

"That man is a sick bastard who took advantage of your most generous quality, Sarah. People like him prey on people like you." A raw anger glittered in Hunter's eyes. "Any man, Sarah, *any* man who walks out on a woman like you knows zip about life."

That did it. She couldn't hold it in anymore. Tears erupted and spilled in a curtain down her face. He gathered her to his chest and held her firmly against him and she sobbed, until his bandage was wet with her tears.

"Let it out," he said softly, stroking her hair. "Let it go, Sarah. Let it *all* go."

She felt herself begin to relax. But just as she did, every muscle in his body stiffened.

She shot her eyes up to his.

They'd gone ice-cold, dangerous. His face had completely changed. He'd become the fearsome man she'd first seen back at the Shilongwe.

Her heart began to pound. "What is it?"

He lifted a finger to his lips. "Put your shoes on," he whispered. "We've got company coming."

"What?"

He shifted his eyes to the trees at their right. "From over here. Listen, the cuckoo."

She heard it, *tok tok-boo, tok-tok-boo, tok tok-boo, tok-tok-boo,* the same sound that had followed them all the way from the Eikona River. Someone was coming. Someone had crossed the river into the Blacklands. Fear rose in her throat.

"I thought you said we'd be safe here," she whispered.

He pushed his AK-47 into her hands. "Take this."

Shock flared in her chest. "Why? Where…where are you going?"

"Just take it. I'll surprise them from the back," he whispered. "Make as if you're going to fetch the clothes. Get away from the trees here, out into the open. Keep the AK slung over your shoulder, ready at your side. If you see anyone, use it."

Her body went icy. "I…I can't. I've never used a rifle."

"Here's the trigger. All you have to do is aim and pull it. And Sarah…" he paused, looked deep into her eyes "…shoot to kill."

"I…I *can't.*"

"If you don't, they'll kill you first." He touched her face, then vanished like a ghost into the forest behind her.

Her mouth went dry. Her heart jackhammered against her ribs. And she heard it again.

Tok tok-boo, tok-tok-boo…

Chapter 10

Sweat dampened Sarah's torso as she edged away from the protective cover of the jungle and out into the clearing, toward their clothes drying over a bush. The heat of the sun was violent on her head; her palms were moist.

She kept her back to the clothes and faced the wall of green foliage, squinting against the white-hot glare, searching for a sign of movement, anything that might show her where the men were.

A twig exploded with a crack. She gasped, jerked around to the source of the sound, waited. Nothing moved. Blood thudded in her ears. She tightened her grip on the gun, curling her finger around the trigger. She tried to swallow. She stared at the shades of green in the forest fringe, trying to separate one dark shape from another. Another crack and a rustle sounded, to her right this time. She spun to face it. Oh God, how many were there? She was surrounded. She was a sitting duck in the clearing. Where was Hunter?

She heard another sound to her left. She swallowed her scream and spun around just as a massive soldier materialized at the edge of the trees.

Her heart stopped.

How long had he been standing there? How long had he been watching her from mere yards away? Her breath congealed in her throat. She couldn't move. Time warped in the heat, and sound slowed to the consistency of glue. Mesmerized, Sarah stared at the man's face.

His skin was glistening ebony, his cheekbones impossibly high. He wore a maroon beret cocked at an angle over his shining brow. But it was his eyes that held her. The whites of the soldier's eyes were almost yellow against his dark skin. And they were looking straight at her.

He moved slightly, and she noticed his sleeves were rolled up high against gleaming black biceps. He wore a red armband. His hands were massive. They held a rifle, just like the one in her own hands, and it was aimed right at her. Sarah stared at the muzzle of his gun. Why couldn't she make herself move? Why was everything happening so slowly? Why hadn't he killed her?

He took a step toward her. Sound coalesced into a dull, ringing buzz in her ears, and her vision narrowed to a tunnel of blurred color until all she could see was the end of the rifle aimed at her. Where was Hunter?

"Shoot to kill, Sarah...or they will kill you first." But she couldn't make herself move.

Then a noise, a strange sound, like one animal attacking

another, caused the man to jerk his head and his gun to his left. He raised his rifle, aimed at the source of the sound.

The sudden movement snapped Sarah back to life. Hunter! Oh God, the man was going to shoot Hunter! Sarah didn't think. She pointed the assault rifle out from waist level, closed her eyes and squeezed the trigger.

It all happened at once, in strangely slow time. Her gun exploded, kicking back into her stomach. She hadn't anticipated the thrust. She stumbled backward, tripped and flailed wildly. As she fell, she could see the soldier spin to face her. Sitting on her butt in the grass, she raised the gun again, squinted, aimed at his chest, fired. She heard a simultaneous crack as he shot at her. She heard, felt, a hot blur against her ear as the bullet whizzed past her head and shattered the bark of a tree behind her.

For a second everything stood dead still. She could feel the burning heat of the sun on her face, could smell the grass, like warm hay from the stables she'd worked at the summer she was fifteen. She could smell the acrid residue from the gun in her lap, feel the heat from the barrel against her skin. She could feel sharp bits of scrub cutting into her bare legs. Tiny insects darted in a soft cloud about her face, and grasshoppers clicked. Her heart banged against her eardrums.

Slowly, she pushed herself to a kneeling position so she could see over the grass.

The man's yellow eyes were wide. They looked right at her. He was holding his stomach, just below the diaphragm, and he was sinking slowly to his knees as blood oozed thick and shiny through his fingers.

Sarah couldn't breathe. Had she killed the man? She couldn't make herself look away from his eyes. They pleaded with her as he fought for life. Then he slumped forward into the long grass with a soft thud. She wobbled onto her feet, gun hanging in her hand. All she could see was the rounded hillock of his back, covered in drab olive camouflage, sticking up out of the long grass.

Her stomach heaved. Dizziness spiraled. She felt a heavy touch on her shoulder, and screamed. A flock of birds scattered, squawking, from trees across the clearing.

"Sarah, Sarah, it's okay, it's me."

She spun around, looked up into his eyes. Cold, hard eyes. His hunting knife was in his hand, blood on the blade.

"Looks like there were only two. I took care of the other one."

She began to shake.

"It's okay, hey, you're going to be okay." He touched her hair. "You did good."

She jerked out from under his touch, threw the gun to the ground, faced him squarely. "I thought you said they wouldn't follow us here! You said we'd be safe! You said—"

He tried to take her into his arms.

She backed away, shaking her head.

"Sarah, we *will* be safe. There were at least six men on the river that night, six men following us to the Eikona. It looks like these were the only two who dared to cross the river into the Blacklands. These were the only two who had the courage to defy the superstition. They're not locals. They're probably from the south. We should be okay from here."

"I don't believe you! I don't believe anything you say! What if they send more from the south?"

"We'll be gone by then."

"You're…you're lying!" She spun around, began to stumble through the grass to the man she'd shot. Hunter grabbed her arm, held her back. She fought against his hold. "He's injured. I shot him…I—I need to help him…."

"Leave him, Sarah."

"I can't…. I hurt him!"

"Sarah, he was going to shoot me. *You saved me.*"

"Let me go!"

"Sarah," Hunter growled. "He was going to shoot me and then kill you."

"He wasn't!" Tears flooded her eyes. "He *didn't* shoot me. He had the chance, but he *didn't.*" Hysteria began to cloud her brain, spin her logic dizzyingly out of control.

"Sarah, if he didn't kill you right away, he was going to do it later. Believe me. And it would've been far worse than anything you might imagine. If they wanted you alive, it was for a reason—information. They would have made you give it to them, Sarah. Then you would have died. Painfully. Brutally."

She yanked free of his grip, shoved at his chest with both hands, pushing him away from her. She glared at him. He was a complete stranger to her. What on earth had made her think she had a connection to this man?

He tried to touch her again.

"Don't! Don't touch me. Ever!" She whirled around and waded through the sharp blades of waist-high grass toward the fallen soldier. She crouched down next to his limp form, felt his neck for a pulse. There was none. His skin was still warm.

Remorse choked her. She jerked up to her feet. She had to get away. From Hunter. From this place. She had to get away from what she'd just done, from herself…hide from the fact that she, Sarah Burdett, had just killed a man. She'd looked right into his eyes and shot him dead.

She stumbled toward the cover of the thick jungle.

Hunter let her go. She wouldn't get far without him. She'd come to her senses soon. But right now she needed time. Space. This was a woman born to heal. The need to nurture and sustain life ran through the very fiber of her being. And she'd been forced to kill a man.

His heart ached for her. He knew…he knew firsthand how much it cut a healer's soul to take a life. How he'd felt the first time.

He watched her move through the golden grass in her white camisole and cotton skirt, the sun on her hair burning like auburn fire. And for an odd moment she looked like one of those bright shampoo commercials where the world smells like apples and strawberries and lemons.

He chewed on his cheek as he watched her near the trees. Hell, not even time was going to help this woman forget this. Nothing would. He knew how hard these things were to bury. And he also knew that she would forever associate him with this horror in her mind. If she was having trouble ridding herself of the specter of her ex-husband, there was no hope of redemption for Hunter. Not now.

His heart felt heavy as he crouched down next to the man she'd shot and rolled him over onto his back. Hunter checked the man's pulse, then searched his pockets for some kind of ID. He'd found nothing on the guy he'd killed in the forest, but Hunter knew already that both men belonged to the People's Militia. The red armbands and maroon berets told him that. It was the same red armband they'd glimpsed in the digitally enhanced footage sent to warn President Elliot. It was the armband, along with the equatorial vegetation, that had clued them in to the general location of the pathogen. Sarah's Mayday had pinpointed it.

Hunter took the soldier's handgun and his knife. He found cigarettes in his breast pocket. American cigarettes. He flipped the pack over, read the surgeon general's warning. They'd been packaged for sale to a U.S. market, not an African one. Nothing new about that. Stuff was smuggled into the Congo for bribes on a daily basis. Hunter went through the other pockets, found nothing but a book of matches from a bar in Brazzaville. If that's where this man came from, it would explain his disregard for the Blacklands curse. Not that it had done him much good.

Hunter patted the pockets on the guy's thigh, felt something, took out a corticosteroid nasal spray, for allergies. He turned the cylindrical container over in his palm, read the logo on the label. It was manufactured by BioMed Pharmaceutical. He read the prescription stuck across the cap of the spray. The man's name was Manou Ndinga and his nasal steroid had been prescribed by a Dr. Andries Du Toit.

Hunter glanced up, keeping an eye on Sarah, who was pacing up and down along the jungle fringe. He chewed his inner cheek. BioMed was a major U.S. pharmaceutical company based in New Jersey. But to his knowledge, they hadn't been supplying any central African clinics. They didn't have any kind of contract that he knew about, unless they were working through a subsidiary to market to Africa. But then the steroid wouldn't be bearing the BioMed logo. Still, that didn't necessarily mean a thing. Medicines were in short supply in the Congo and were sold on the black market daily. Long transparent plastic sheets of brightly colored antibiotics alone were hawked on each ferry crossing between Brazzaville and Kinshasa.

But now he had names, and that was a start. Dr. Du Toit might be a nongovernmental organization doctor with some rural clinic, or he could be working more closely with the military, perhaps even a militia doctor on staff. Once Hunter made it back to the FDS base, December could check into Du Toit's background along with his link to BioMed and to Ndinga here.

Hunter slipped the nasal spray into his pocket. He tucked the knife into a sheath at his ankle and the gun into his flak jacket. He removed the soldier's satellite phone. It was new, sophisticated technology. Most of the Congo militia cadres he'd come across were ill-supplied and used mostly radios, not high-end equipment like this. This guy even had a high-tech, fold-up solar charging device to go with his phone. That meant whoever was supplying these men had access to cash—and was going to be looking for results.

A phone like this could be tracked. Hunter looked up. Whoever was paying these soldiers probably had a position on them right now. But it would take time for them to round up men from the south, men who knew jungle warfare and who would be prepared to defy the powerful local superstition of the Blacklands territory. Hunter removed the batteries, disabling any tracking device. He tossed the phone into the grass next to the slain man and made his way to Sarah.

She was pale as a ghost. Her fists were bunched at her side, and the muscles in her neck stood out in narrow cords. Her mouth was strained and her lips flat.

"You okay?" He could see she wasn't.

She glared at him.

He wasn't sure what to say, either. She'd need to decompress, he knew that much. They were going to have to debrief her properly when he got her to São Diogo. He fingered the nasal spray in his pocket. Now was probably not the time. Hell, there was never a right time in a game like this. He took the spray out, held the canister out in the palm of his hand so that she could get a good look at it. "Do you recognize this logo, Sarah?"

Her jaw tightened. She refused to even glance at his hand.

"Sarah, this is a corticosteroid supplied by a U.S. pharmaceutical company. To the best of my knowledge, they have no Congo business connections. I need to know if BioMed supplied your clinic with medications, equipment, vaccines, samples, anything you can tell me."

She slowly lowered her eyes to his hand and stared at the medicine. "Yes."

"You mean BioMed *did* supply the Ishonga clinic?"

"No. But yes, I've seen that triangle logo."

"In Seattle?"

"Ishonga." Her voice was toneless. She looked up at him. Those lovely brown eyes were empty, as if part of her had died with that soldier. Hunter felt oddly deserted. It was as if she'd left *him* on some elemental level.

"I saw it on one of the hazmat suits," she said. "I saw it when I was looking out the window…when they started shooting the nuns…before Dr. Regnaud hid me in a hole in the floor."

His heart kicked. "Why didn't you tell me this?"

"I…I hadn't realized I'd seen it." He could hear emotion creeping back into her voice as she began to relive her horror. Color was also seeping back into her cheeks. "I…I was in a panic at the time."

"Are you positive this is the same logo?"

She turned away from him, clutched her arms against her waist. "I can see it," she whispered. "If I close my eyes I can see it exactly like a picture. It's burned into my brain. All of it." Her voice caught. "I…I guess I just hadn't wanted to look at it…again. If I look, I can see…" Her voice wobbled, then faded. She squeezed her arms tighter around her waist, her knuckles going white as she tried to hold herself together.

A pang of remorse stabbed Hunter. He hated pushing her back into those memories. But he had to ask her for more. He had to make her look back and think about what else she might have seen or known that could possibly be relevant.

He cleared his throat. "And this doctor—" he read the prescription "—Dr. Andries Du Toit, you ever heard of him?"

She nodded. "Dr. Regnaud was asking all the patients

about him," she said. "One of the women who died of the disease had told him that Dr. Du Toit was heading up some medical program in the interior for the army. Her boyfriend was in the militia, and he'd apparently told her about it." Sarah turned slowly to face Hunter. "I didn't think too much about it. Everything was going so crazy with the patients coming in."

He thought for a moment, processing what she had just told him. "Sarah, if Du Toit was working on clinical trials for the pathogen, that woman's link to her boyfriend in the militia could've been how the disease got out of the control group. And Regnaud's questioning everyone is probably what tipped the Cabal off and got him—and everyone else at the clinic—killed."

He stepped closer to her, took her arm, tried to draw her nearer. She resisted, her eyes hostile. He dropped his hand, feeling helpless. "This is a huge breakthrough, Sarah." But even as he said it, he felt defeated.

"Sure." She turned her back on him.

Hunter stared at the rip in her camisole, at the bandage he'd placed over her cut. In spite of this new lead, his heart felt incredibly heavy. He had a weird need to share this little triumph with her, but she wasn't interested. She was preoccupied with the fact she'd killed a man, and that wasn't just going to go away. How was he ever going to make this right for her?

He rolled the medicine tightly between his palm and fingers. It was probably a good thing. He'd lost sight of his reason for being here when he'd plunged into the river to save her over the biohazard canister.

It was the wrong decision to have made for his mission, for his team. But he knew he'd do it again in a heartbeat. He just wasn't capable of doing otherwise. And *that* was his problem.

That's what he *did* regret.

She'd gotten in under his skin, and he'd lost his edge. She'd made him *care*. And a man who cared had something to lose.

He wasn't prepared to lose anything again. Not in that way. Ever. He tightened his fist around the spray container. Yeah, it was better this way. If she needed this distance right now, so did he.

And it would be in the interest of both of them to keep it this way.

He turned away from her in silence and began to pack his gear. The sling she'd strapped over his injured arm had come undone in his struggle with the soldier, and having his arm bound up like that in the first place had just about cost him that tussle. The only real risk in not having it splinted was the possibility of dislocating it again. And if that hadn't happened in hand-to-hand combat, it wasn't going to happen now.

Hell, the only reason he'd allowed her to bandage it at all was because he'd sensed she needed to do it. *That* was the kind of mistake you made when you cared.

The kind that could cost a life.

He hefted his pack onto his back and reached for the biohazard container. He had to get this new intel into the hands of his men ASAP, so that December could start digging into BioMed's pharmaceutical business—and into Dr. Andries Du Toit.

14:13 Alpha. Congo.
Tuesday, September 23

"We lost them east of the Eikona River." He paused, deeply uneasy over how this latest development was going to go down in Manhattan. They were already blaming him for the infected patients outside the trial group. Silence stretched, crackled over the distance. He cleared his throat, spoke again. "It looks like they're going to make a run for the Cameroonian border."

"How did you lose them?" The man's voice was dangerously calm. "You had a visual, you had coordinates. How can one woman possibly lead a trained army on a wild-goose chase through equatorial jungle?"

Tension whipped across Du Toit's chest. This didn't sit easy with him, either. The woman was definitely being helped by a professional, but he wasn't going to say that; it would only inflame things further.

"Even if they do make it out of the Blacklands, they'll be calling for backup at some point. If they so much as touch a radio frequency, we'll be ready. They will *not* make it out of the Congo alive."

Chapter 11

They traveled in increasingly oppressive silence, the biohazard container clunking annoyingly, rhythmically against Hunter's thigh as they made their way deeper into the heart of the Blacklands. Heat pressed down on them and the air turned the consistency of pea soup. The ground became swamplike, the muck sucking at their feet. Each breath, each step, each swipe of the machete was becoming an increasingly laborious effort.

Hunter saw a set of giant leopard prints tracking through deep black mud. He looked up into the low branches, searching for signs that they were being stalked by the silent jungle predator. He couldn't see the creature, but that didn't mean it couldn't see them. He slapped at a tsetse fly that had stuck itself to his neck.

Damn. Insect repellent was useless against the bloody persistent creatures. The sluggish things were twice the size of a housefly and caused deadly forms of African sleeping sickness. He swatted another one on his arm, stopped and wiped the back of his wrist over his forehead. His body was drenched and the salt of exertion stung his lips. This was by far the worst terrain they had traveled through, and Sarah was not doing at all well.

He turned to look at her. Her skin was pale, her cheeks sunken. Flies and tiny bees buzzed around her. She was making zero effort to swat them away.

"You okay?"

She said nothing.

Worry tightened his chest. He took some twine from his pocket, crouched down and tied the cuffs of her pants around her ankles in an effort to keep the bugs out. Damn flies were biting right through his army pants, and her thin cotton was not a whole lot of protection.

He looked up at her. Still no response. He handed her some water and she drank in silence as he crouched again and checked his topo map and compass. She needed sleep. Food. He had to get her to higher terrain before nightfall, find somewhere to camp. This swamp was no place for humans.

He traced his finger along the contour lines of his map and breathed a hot sigh of relief. There was a chance they could make it out of swampland before dark. They could set up camp for the night, and if they got going by first light tomorrow, they could potentially make it to an abandoned rubber plantation on the banks of the Sangé and be out of the Blacklands and crossing into Cameroon by Thursday.

He got to his feet, pocketed his map. "Had enough water?"

She handed him the canteen.

His chest knotted. No amount of food, rest or water was

going to fix what he saw in her eyes. She'd been forced to go against absolutely everything that defined her, and she was dealing with it in a real bad way. He was going to have to do something about it or she wasn't going to make it out of here, but he had a sinking feeling that it would be no use trying to talk to her.

He was part of her problem.

21:03 Alpha. Blacklands.
Tuesday, September 23

Sarah watched as Hunter tossed another branch onto the fire and glowing sparks showered into the night.

She clutched both hands tight around his tin mug and sipped her tea. He'd made it strong and black, with lots of sugar to disguise the chemical taste of the water purifiers. The sweet, strong flavor reminded her of her grandmother's brew. Her gran believed tea was a remedy for the soul. She'd pushed a big mug of strong, sweet Irish breakfast blend into Sarah's hands the day her mom finally succumbed to her battle with cancer.

The fire cast a ring of flickering light around them, holding the encroaching blackness at bay. Smoke lay heavy in the air and burned her eyes, but it was keeping the bugs away and that suited her fine. She didn't have the energy to swat at them.

She watched Hunter over the rim of her mug as she sipped. He sat on a stump on the other side of the fire, keeping his distance.

She wanted to hate him, but couldn't. She wanted to talk, but couldn't. It was as if she'd been imprisoned inside her own body by the heinous thing she'd done.

He glanced up, caught her watching, but she couldn't even react. She'd gone physically numb, some neural connection severed in her brain to save her from her own mental anguish.

He picked up a stick, jabbed it angrily into the flames. His jaw was set. His skin glowed in the copper light, and a dark lock of hair hung over his brow. Sometime between the clearing and now, he'd cut off his other sleeve, matching the one she'd sliced off to reduce his dislocated shoulder. He'd probably done it for comfort. It accentuated his biceps, and in a distant part of her brain he looked beautiful, in a wild and dangerous way. The way you might think of a jaguar—an animal that killed to live.

She wasn't like him, could never be. She didn't understand how he could do what he did and live with himself. All she wanted was to get away from him, from this nightmare.

He jerked suddenly to his feet, stalked around the fire and sat on the log at her side. "Sarah, we *have* to deal with this."

She tightened her fingers around the mug, stared into the flames.

"I keep thinking I might be able to pull you through as long as you hold up physically, but…it won't work. You won't make it." He paused. "I want you to make it, Sarah."

She felt her pulse increase. But he was still at the other end of a tunnel, not quite reaching her. She knew he was trying. She just couldn't respond.

"What you did was the right thing. You need to understand that. You have to know what a vital role you're playing." He leaned forward, arms on his knees, the firelight catching his eyes. "So I'm going to tell you. And what I'm going to tell you is highly classified."

Interest flickered through her, but she stared intently at the flames. She didn't want to look into his eyes. They would suck her in again. She *wanted* to stay numb.

"This is not just about a biological attack, Sarah. It's far worse. If the Cabal—the group I mentioned to you—is success-ful in what they're ultimately planning, they will change the course of global politics, of history. If we don't stop them within the next—" he checked his watch "—nineteen days, twenty hours and fifty-seven minutes, democracy as we know it will be dead. And the world will be a very different place."

She turned her head, slowly lifted her eyes to his. "What do you mean?"

His shoulders relaxed almost imperceptibly, as if an invisible burden had been lightened just a little. He raised his hand to touch her, but took hold of another stick instead, used it to poke tentatively at the fire. "The Cabal plans to take control of the U.S. government by midnight October 13—exactly three weeks before the presidential election."

Sarah felt light-headed. She couldn't quite make sense of his words. "What do you mean, 'take control of the government'? Like a coup?"

"In a manner of speaking."

"Is…is that possible?"

"Yes. Very. It's been in the works for decades, and the Cabal is only days away from succeeding. All that stands between them now, Sarah, is you and me, and a few good men."

She lowered the tin mug to her lap. "I don't understand. How would they do this?"

"Like I told you, the Cabal is a clandestine group of inordinately powerful men. We don't yet know who they are or exactly what they control, but we do know their influence is vast, and it's global. Their goal is power, the ultimate power—control of the most influential government in the world."

"But *why?*"

He snorted softly. "Why does anyone want power or control?" He placed his hand over her knee. "I'm sorry, Sarah, but when you were handed that biohazard container, you instantly became a pivotal pawn in a deadly global power game.

It's not fair, you don't deserve this. And I'm going to do what it takes to get you through it." He paused. "But I need you to stay strong. You have to understand that what you did back there in that clearing was the right thing."

She stared at him. "How," she said slowly, "how does the Cabal plan on overthrowing the U.S. government?"

He chewed on his cheek and studied the fire for a while. "President Elliot is dying. He's being slowly assassinated by an unidentified stealth disease that appears to be eating away at his brain—a biological bullet administered by his own Secret Service, just one of the organizations the Cabal has managed to infiltrate. It's a disease very similar to the one in that canister, except this one moves much, much more slowly."

She felt the blood rush from her head. She glanced at the canister. The orange-and-black biohazard symbol emblazoned on the side flickered in the firelight with a life and warning of its own. *A container of death.* "How…how long does the president have?"

"Months, maybe. But his mental faculties are expected to deteriorate sooner." Hunter's eyes pierced hers. "No one knows this, Sarah. Only his personal physician, the FDS, and now you. And it must stay secret. Elliot is trying to hold on to his health just long enough to secure a second term in the November 4 election. At the moment, there is no doubt he'll win. News of a terminal illness will scuttle that."

"But why is he even running if he knows he's going to die as soon as he takes office? It doesn't make sense."

"If he bows out now due to ill health, Vice President Grayson Forbes will become the next president of the United States. Elliot can't let that happen because Forbes is the Cabal's man."

Sarah's brain spun. "But if President Elliot dies *after* winning the election," she continued, "Michael J. Taylor becomes the next U.S. president, because Taylor is Elliot's new running mate."

"Exactly. The Elliot camp denied Forbes a place on the ticket. An unusual move, but not unprecedented, and a serious blow to a faction that has been trying to maneuver Forbes into the Oval Office for years."

"A Cabal faction? *Within* the party?"

Hunter nodded. "Grayson Forbes has been groomed by this Cabal faction for years, and they made their big move when they threw his hat into the ring in the lead-up to the last presidential election. Elliot, however, narrowly beat out their man for the presidential ticket at the party convention, and Elliot's camp picked Charles Landon over Forbes for a running mate—a real slap in the face to Forbes and his people. It cost them both the presidency *and* the vice presidency."

"But then why did Elliot make Forbes vice president when Landon died of cancer last year?"

Hunter jabbed at the flames with his stick and sparks spattered into the night. "Landon didn't die naturally, Sarah. He was assassinated."

A chill ran up her spine. "By the Cabal?"

"Yes. Elliot was then informed via his own bodyguards that he, too, had been inflicted with a biological bullet, but his death would be slower than Landon's. It would resemble a rapid form of Alzheimer's, leading first to dementia, and then death within six months—giving him just enough time to name Forbes as replacement vice president. If he failed to do so by the appointed date, they told him a deadly pathogen would be released over Los Angeles, New York and Chicago."

"Why didn't President Elliot tell everyone what was happening? Why didn't he get help?"

"The Cabal told him the virus would be released instantly

if he so much as even *thought* of engaging any of the traditional agencies available to him. The president became a virtual hostage in the White House, his every move, his every communication monitored by his own Secret Service. He was trapped by the very security system designed to protect him. The only man he knew he could trust for certain was his personal physician, Dr. Sebastian Ruger. He's been communicating with him in secret, in writing, in the White House medical suite."

Sarah blew out a stream of air. "So President Elliot did the Cabal's bidding and named Forbes vice president."

"Only in order to buy time to come up with a plan. The Cabal, however, expected him to become incapacitated and die shortly after the nomination, or at least well before the November election."

"But he didn't…he *hasn't*."

Hunter smiled wryly. "He's a very determined man, Sarah. Whether he's still alive because of that, or because the biological bullet is not functioning exactly as anticipated, it's forced the Cabal's hand. If they lose this last little window of opportunity to get their man into power now, it will destroy decades of positioning. They won't get another opportunity like this. So they've issued the president an ultimatum—step down from power by midnight October 13, citing health reasons, or they will release the pathogen."

Sarah shivered in spite of the warmth. "I can't believe I'm even asking this, but why don't they just kill him before the election?"

"An overt assassination, especially days before the election, would spin the country and the global economy out of their control, and it would send the world on a witch hunt. That kind of economic disaster and scrutiny is something a bunch of imperialistic capitalists is *very* keen to avoid. They need this to look completely natural if they are to stay anonymously in control behind the scenes, and they can't afford to implicate Forbes in any way. He has to appear a strong and *rightful* leader. He has to be respected and trusted by the American people for them to be able to launch the next phase of their plan."

Sarah could barely begin to comprehend the scope of this, or the fact that she was slam-bang in the middle of it, playing a key role in an American nightmare in the middle of the Congo jungle. "I can't believe these men would actually kill millions of their own people to get into power."

"These guys make Machiavelli look like the fairy godmother. They'll do anything to justify their end, and they've shown us they have the biotechnology to do it—*and* the will to use it."

She fiddled with the handle of the tin cup. "What *is* the next phase, Hunter?"

He took the mug from her hands, tossed the dregs onto the fire with a sizzle. "Once the Cabal gets Forbes into power, they're going to want to keep him there. They're going to use their arsenal of high-tech bioweapons, like your pathogen there—" he jerked his chin to the container "—to launch a series of contained attacks in the U.S. The Forbes government will maintain the attacks are being perpetrated by terrorists or rogue nations, and he'll declare the country at war. Congress will in turn grant Forbes broad powers to manage the national economy and protect the interests of the nation. We suspect he'll declare martial law, call in the National Guard, curtail civil liberties and declare another election impossible for the foreseeable future."

Sarah stared at him. Who was Hunter, really? What had brought this powerful man to this point in his life, to this intersection with her? What had made him a mercenary? There was something deeper in him, something gentle buried beneath his armor—a kindness. She'd felt it in his healing touch, seen it in his eyes. And she had a sudden burning need to know him. Totally.

"What about the election next month?" she asked, her eyes fixed on his.

He shook his head. "I don't think there will be one—not if this Cabal gets their way. We believe the continued well-timed 'attacks' will put the Forbes government in a position to 'retaliate' by launching preemptive military strikes against foreign states that allegedly harbor the so-called terrorists or philosophies. And in doing so, the Cabal will be covertly launching a new era of aggressive imperialism designed to feed the pockets of the major transnationals that we suspect are controlled by Cabal elite."

"Some of this is conjecture, isn't it?"

"Only some of it. And it's the president's conjecture, not ours. He believes that if Forbes gets into power he'll immediately start the slow process of appointing Cabal puppets into key judicial, military, intelligence and economic positions. The long-term goal will be to effect the kind of legislative and constitutional change that will enshrine Cabal power for decades to come." Hunter threw another log onto the fire. "And he'll start by naming a new vice president to replace himself."

Sarah watched the flames gobble at the fresh piece of wood, and the hunger to know Hunter more intimately burned deeper in her. She studied his stark profile in the flickering light. He might be a mercenary, he might kill people with his bare hands, he might exist in the shadows of civilization, but he helped people sleep at night—whole populations who would probably never find out what he'd done for them.

"Hunter," she said softly. "How did you—how did the FDS get involved in all this?"

"The president's physician, Dr. Ruger, was at a U.N. conference in Brussels two weeks ago. So was my colleague

Jacques Sauvage. Sauvage handles FDS operations and was at the conference to lobby for an international standardized code of conduct for private military companies. Ruger managed to get to him in the washroom. He used the opportunity to covertly enlist us on behalf of President Elliot." Hunter paused. "It's a close to impossible mission, Sarah. But we took the job. Someone had to."

"The president *personally* hired you guys?"

"Everything else has failed him, and we were the one opportunity that presented itself. Besides, he knows our work, our reputation. We've contracted to the States before through a covert arm of the CIA."

It dawned on her suddenly. "Hunter, even if we *do* find the antidote to the disease in that container, it's not going to stop them...is it?"

"No. It won't. But if we can identify the pathogen within the next two weeks and find an antidote, we could save many lives. But most importantly, we hope to find some kind of biological fingerprint in the pathogen that will lead us to the lab that created it, and in turn that could lead us to whoever is pulling the Cabal strings."

The fire was dwindling, the jungle night creeping closer. She rubbed her arms. "So this is why they want to kill me," she said softly.

"Sarah, they don't know that you know any of this. If they thought you did, and if they knew that I'd been engaged to try and help the president, they'd launch the attack immediately. You're just a loose end right now."

He placed his hand on her knee. "And that's another reason you *had* to shoot that man. If they'd captured and tortured you—and they would have tortured you—you'd have been forced to disclose your connection to the FDS and by extension, the president. They would have launched the attack. You saved millions of lives by taking that one."

She bit her lip, trying not to see the dead man's eyes in the yellow of the flames, trying to understand what she'd gotten herself into. "But they'd prefer to avoid launching the attack before Forbes got into power, wouldn't they?"

"Yes. However, they *will* risk it rather than lose their last shot at getting their man into the Oval Office." Hunter took her hand. It was warm, comforting. "You did the right thing, Sarah. And…and I'm proud of you."

Her heart kicked at his words. "I used to think that taking a life was *never* justified. Now…now I just don't know." She didn't know anything anymore. There was no more black-and-white, just shades of gray.

He didn't answer. And they sat in silence, watching the flames die. Something screeched in the forest and she moved a little closer to Hunter. He put his arm around her. "We should get in the hammock."

"How do you do it, Hunter? How do you do this kind of thing over and over again, and still live with yourself?"

He stared at the coals for a while. "I'm really not that different from you, Sarah. At heart I think you and I are pretty much motivated by the same thing."

"How so?"

"We both want to help people who can't help themselves. And in places like this, people like you—nurses and doctors— need people like me so that you can continue to do your jobs. Whether we like or not, we're two halves of an uneasy partnership."

He drew her closer. "Besides, who else is going to come to

the aid of a lone American nurse who calls 9-1-1 from the heart of the jungle?"

That made her smile. "I wasn't thinking."

He gave her a squeeze. "Come on, it's bedtime."

01:03 Alpha. Blacklands.
Wednesday, September 24

Hunter could feel every soft curve of Sarah's body against his as gravity forced them together in the center of the hammock. It was strong enough for two, but made for one, with a cover over the top and mosquito netting around the sides. He lay there, zipped into the tiny cocoon with her, breathing the same air as her, fingering his gun and listening to the sounds of the jungle and the bump of bugs against the fabric. He was almost afraid to breathe too deeply. Each inhalation seemed to push yet another part of his body against hers, and he didn't want her to know that the contact had made him as hard as a rock.

Sarah moaned softly in her sleep and stirred, the movement pushing her breasts against his chest. Heat spurted to his groin. It didn't help that he was already stiff and aching with need. Hunter closed his eyes. This was pure torture. So much for maintaining distance, he thought wryly. Because right at this minute he was being squeezed as close to this woman physically as he was emotionally. He wondered just what it would take to finally tip him completely over the edge of control.

The hours ticked by interminably as he listened to her breathe, his own rhythm falling in time with hers. As dawn crept into the sky, he began to wonder what it might be like to sleep with her every night, wake up next to her each morning. Make sweet, hot love…. He caught his breath sharply. Not because of the pulsing ache in his belly, but because he'd thought of tomorrows. With her. How in hell had that one sneaked up on him? Hunter McBride couldn't offer a woman like Sarah Burdett anything, let alone the promise of a new day. And that's why he couldn't touch her.

She moaned softly and moved again. Hunter groaned. This mission was testing him in ways he'd never dreamed possible.

Chapter 12

They'd been on the move for two hours when a rumbling roar resonated through the forest, so loud it froze every molecule in Sarah's body.

Hunter's hand shot up. "Don't move!" he growled.

A crash of breaking brush sounded to her left. Sarah's heart leaped to her throat. Hunter made a quick motion, as if he were patting a basketball. *"Down!"*

She dropped to the ground, heart crashing against her chest wall. He crouched next to her. "If he comes at us," Hunter said in a hushed voice, "don't look in his eyes. Look at the earth."

"If *what* comes?"

"Gorilla."

She stared very hard at the forest floor, trying to make her body still.

They waited. A small cloud of bugs flitted about her face, but she didn't dare flinch. Her muscles began to ache. But there was nothing, no more sound. The beast was somewhere just out sight, watching them, waiting. She could sense it.

Hunter reached for a bush, pulled down a thin branch and began to strip the fat, shiny leaves off with his hand, crushing them in his palm, making a crackling noise.

"Do it," he whispered. "Make as if you're grazing. The sounds are familiar to him. If he hasn't seen us yet, this *will* alert him, but at least we won't take him by surprise."

Sarah swallowed against the dryness in her mouth. She didn't dare look up from the ground. She groped for the bush, pulled at the leaves, scrunched them furiously in her fingers.

"Over there," Hunter whispered. "Look."

Sarah raised her eyes slowly. Just beyond the bushes, partially obscured by leaves and brush, was the biggest wild beast she had ever seen uncaged. He was a mass of muscle on all fours, facing away from them. A shock of silver hair coated his impossibly broad back. The gorilla slowly turned his leathery face toward them, and gazed right into her eyes. Sarah's heart clean stopped. Everything about the animal screamed danger, but beneath his thick domed brow, his round eyes were liquid brown, gentle, full of intelligent curiosity. Looking into the eyes of the silverback, she felt as if she were staring right into the living heart of the jungle, a place as old as time. Her heart pumped back to life at the strange primal connection. A sense of awe overcame her, and for a moment she forgot her fear.

But all of a sudden, the silverback lurched up onto his back legs, pounded his chest and barreled at them with a gut-rumbling roar. Sarah gasped, jumped back, falling onto her butt. The gorilla stopped just short of them, reared up and beat his chest again.

Hunter's hand clamped on her arm. "Don't move!" he murmured. "Stop looking into his eyes. He sees it as a challenge."

Sarah glared at her toes as hard as she could, heart palpitating, palms damp. She could barely breathe. Slowly, the big old male silverback turned, gave them a last glance over his massive shoulder and swaggered off into the forest. All she could hear as the sound of crunching undergrowth died down was the blood rushing in her ears.

She let out a soft and shaky whoosh of air.

"Are you all right?"

She turned to Hunter. "That's the most incredible thing I've ever seen in my entire life," she whispered. "Was he alone?"

Hunter's brows raised. An odd look crossed his face as he studied hers. "You're not afraid?"

She laughed. "Petrified."

His eyes narrowed slightly. "But in a different way."

It wasn't a question, it was an observation. And with a strange jolt, she realized he was right. Something had happened to her. She'd been pushed beyond panic, beyond blinding fear, and what was coursing through her blood now was raw survival instinct. It was empowering, not debilitating. It made her acutely aware of everything around her. Sarah realized with mild shock that she felt strangely centered and in control. She'd been stripped of everything and driven to rock bottom. She'd been forced to kill a man, and everything else paled in significance.

He nodded slightly, as if confirming to himself he was right. Then he smiled, a warm light twinkling in his eyes. "I think he was."

She jerked her mind back. "What?"

"Alone. Wait here, stay low."

Hunter edged forward, pushing leaves aside with his machete, creeping through the foliage like a wild animal himself. He paused, listened, waited. Moved forward again, waited. Then he flicked his hand up, calling her to his side.

She crept over to him. "Has he gone?"

"Looks like it." He placed his palm in the center of a wide and squashed-flat circle of leaves and twigs. "This was his nest."

"They make nests?"

"The old male does. He builds his nest on the ground. His family, wives, children—they build platforms to sleep on up in the trees. He protects them from below." Hunter glanced up, scanning branches up in the canopy. "I don't see any platforms up there. This old guy's probably too old for family, that part of his life over…" Hunter's voice faded as he squinted up into the trees, his hand resting on the flattened twigs.

Sarah studied his rugged profile. He seemed momentarily distant, as if he were seeing something beyond the branches, beyond the forest. As if he was trying to feel what the old gorilla might have been feeling.

"Did his troop just leave him?"

"He would've been challenged and beaten by a younger male for them to have done that. Survival of the fittest. The younger genes keep the troop strong." Hunter scanned the trees again as if searching for the proud old male.

A strange sense of sadness filled her heart. "Will he die, then…alone?"

Hunter's eyes cut to hers. "Yes. Alone." He stood abruptly, turned away from her and ran his fingers through the straggly leaves of a plant that grew almost as high as her shoulders. "This is what he was here for. See the red fruits at the base of the stems? That's wild ginger. Gorillas love it. Look." He pointed out fruits that had been peeled, sucked dry and cast aside. She hadn't noticed them. She hadn't even known to look.

"And what's that?" She pointed to broken clumps of dried, dark brown mud near the bases of several trees.

He raised a brow, studied her face, and a smile ghosted his lips. "Termite nests. Gorillas smash them open and eat the grubs. Good protein." With the muzzle of his AK he poked at a lost little grub wriggling on the ground. A wicked playfulness lit his eyes. "Hungry?"

She pulled a face. "Not *that* hungry."

He laughed, held out his hand and helped her to her feet, drawing her close to his chest as he did. Sarah stilled at the look in his eyes.

For a second, silence hung thick, and a hot current pulsed between them, an invisible but tangible connection. The light in his eyes faded, darkening to something more feral. Sarah swallowed. She found herself looking at his mouth, becoming conscious of her own. She wasn't afraid he might kiss her, she *wanted* him to. A hot thrill of anticipation zinged through her, and for a fleeting second she thought she might act, might just lean up to him and put her lips to his. Because she could see he wanted her.

But he looked abruptly away. "We should get moving."

Disappointment spread through her, but the residual hum of desire remained, making her cheeks warm as she followed him into the forest.

As they moved deeper into primary jungle the air grew cooler, richer, more full of oxygen, the scent somehow greener. Sarah felt as if they were working their way slowly back in time. The tree trunks here were massive in size and spaced farther apart, giving the area a cathedral-like quality. She stopped, looked up in wonder. Branches knitted in a dizzying architectural puzzle all the way up to a translucent dome of green that quivered high in a wind she couldn't feel down on the forest floor. These trees had to be hundreds upon hundreds of years old. How could she have been blind to all this incredible beauty around her?

She felt Hunter watching her. Cautiously, she lowered her eyes and met his. That elemental wariness was back in them, a dark, predatory hunger. Heat rippled through her. She blinked, a little self-conscious under the intensity of his gaze and her instant physical reaction to it. "This place…it's incredibly beautiful," she said, her voice husky.

"Yes." He didn't break his gaze. "Very beautiful."

Warmth flushed her face. She glanced away, cleared her throat. "It's…so natural, yet it reminds me of the architecture of an ancient cathedral I visited in Barcelona. There's a similar ethereal quality to the light, the space. I don't really know how to put it into words…it has a timeless, almost sacred feel." She looked up at him. "That cathedral was probably built around the time some of these trees started to grow."

"When were you in Spain?"

She tensed at the blunt delivery of his question. "Six years ago…for my honeymoon."

His eyes narrowed. He adjusted the rifle at his side. Was the mercenary actually showing possessiveness? Was he uncomfortable thinking about her and Josh together? A ridiculous warmth blossomed through her at the notion. It made her feel good…about *herself.*

And then she realized what had just happened. She'd thought about the beauty of that cathedral, not about Josh. Not the honeymoon. Not her failed marriage. Not all the dark feelings that always came when she remembered anything associated with her ex-husband.

Excitement bubbled in her heart and she couldn't contain it. "Hunter, this the first time I've been able to think back to a time I shared with Josh without actually thinking about *him.*"

Hunter's expression didn't change. His eyes remained dark, watchful.

She didn't care. She blew out a breath she felt as if she'd been holding for years. She almost wanted to cry with spontaneous relief. "It's... I feel free." She laughed lightly, tears pricking her eyes. "Here I am, on the run in the jungle, being chased by—by militia, a group bent on dominating the world, poisonous bugs, snakes, gorillas and...and all I feel is *exhilarated,* free of my ex, can you believe it? How weird is that! Am I going totally insane?"

A smile crept along Hunter's mouth. A dimple deepened in one cheek and creases fanned out around his eyes. "Not *totally.*"

She'd made the hard-ass soldier smile, really smile. She'd made him reveal a dimple she hadn't seen before. He was truly happy *for her.* Damn, it felt good. She grinned. His eyes sparkled in response, edging her over, and she did it. She gave a little spin, her arms held wide.

Hunter threw back his head and laughed—a laugh that vibrated right through her, filled her with happiness. She spun again, round and round under the trees, her arms out, her hair lifting around her. Monkeys cackled in response. She found it funny that even primates in the trees saw the humor in it all. She spun faster and the world spun with her, and then suddenly without her. The ground dipped one way, the branches the other in a kaleidoscopic blur of green and brown and yellow.... She teetered, tripped, flailed and fell. Hunter caught her, and her body slapped hard against his chest.

She held still, the world racing wildly around her, the sound of blood again rushing in her ears.

Then everything grew hushed, even the monkeys. It was as if the whole jungle was holding its breath. She slid her eyes slowly up to his, and swallowed. The mirth, all signs of happiness in his eyes, were gone, replaced instead by dark, blatant hunger and the raw stamp of arousal etched along the lines of his mouth.

She could feel the thud of his heart, hard and fast, against her breasts. She could smell his maleness, feel the dampness on his arms, his hair rough against her skin. Heat seeped into her belly. The world narrowed around her.

He clasped the back of her neck suddenly, threaded his fingers into her tangle of hair, tilted her head back and covered her mouth with his. Raw lust exploded instantly, buckling her knees. He caught her at the small of her back as she sagged, yanked her hard up against his torso and sank his tongue into her mouth. Sarah's vision swam. She opened her mouth to him, tasting his salt, feeling his teeth, his size, the rasp of his stubble against her cheek. His tongue slipped around hers, searched her mouth, forceful, rough, hungry. He slid his hand down to her butt, pulled her higher up into himself, and she felt the hardness in his groin press against her pelvis. Dizziness clouded her brain and she began to pulse with a hot ache, a desperate need to open herself to him.

Nothing in this world could have held him back. Nothing in this jungle could have made him stop. For some absurd reason, Sarah's joy, her newfound sense of freedom, made Hunter feel he suddenly had a right to do this. And the idea made him blind with hunger.

And now that his reins of control had snapped, his appetite was savage. He couldn't get enough. She moved invitingly against him, opening her mouth wider, challenging him, firing him with her own hunger. He grasped her breast, rasped his thumb over the thin fabric, found her nipple hard and tight. He groaned, moved his hand down over her stomach, cupped her between her legs. She slicked her tongue around his. She wanted him. Completely. And it made him wild with the need to consume her, totally, right now, right here, under the trees.

He began to draw her down to the ground, his body acting without his mind. But as he did, a flare of logic cut through the blinding curtain of his desire. He hesitated. This wasn't right. It had been wrong last night and it was still wrong, for all the same reasons. He pulled back, shocked at how his desire had blinded him, how it had completely consumed him like that.

Sarah felt stunned, as if something had been ripped right out of her. She opened her mouth to ask him what had happened to make him stop wanting her…but she couldn't. She couldn't face the rejection. Not from him. Not now. Hurt and confusion welled through her. She looked away. This was ridiculous. She was being way too emotional about everything. But she couldn't help it. Everything was coming out unfiltered. All her senses were heightened, everything coming straight from her gut and heart. *Dumb. Dumb. Dumb.* She was stupid for even acting on her impulses. She should know better. Hadn't she learned?

He placed his hand gently against her cheek, tilted her face, forcing her to look back into his eyes. "Sarah." His voice was hoarse, his lids thick, his breath heavy. "I…I'm sorry. I can't do this."

She nodded, tried to look away.

But he held her firm. "No, look at me, Sarah. I can't do this to you because…because—" He jerked away, turned his back on her, dragged both his hands through his dark mop of hair. He stood still for a minute, then turned again to face her. There was a strange light in his eyes, almost a vulnerability, and his mouth was twisted in a kind of pain, as if he was trying to hold a tidal wave of stuff inside.

It dawned on her slowly. This man hadn't rejected her. He was fighting with something inside himself. He was hurting. The notion tugged gently at the nurturer in her. She touched his arm. "Hunter, it's okay, really. I—"

"No, damn it!" He raked his hand viciously through his hair. "It's *not* okay." He sucked in a deep breath, forced it out. "You're special, Sarah, you're…too damn special for me. I can't do this to you. We…we're too different."

She shook her head, bemused. "You said we were the same at the core, Hunter."

"I lied, okay?"

She stared at him, speechless.

"Look, Sarah, I can't offer you anything. You were right, our lives are worlds apart. When we get out of here, I go on another mission. That's what I do. You…you need—"

She pressed her hand against his mouth. "Shut up," she said softly, gazing right into his eyes. "I said it's okay. And don't try to tell me what *I* need. I'm not asking for promises, Hunter. Right now I'm just figuring out how to be in the present. I'm only just getting rid of my past. The future is more than I can deal with right now." She paused. "You just do your job and get us out of here, okay?"

He covered her hand with his, pressed it hard against the stubble on his face and closed his eyes. He remained like that for a while, as if drinking her in, as if finding his center again.

When his eyes flashed open, the cold, controlled mercenary Hunter McBride was back. Sarah blinked. Had she even witnessed what she just thought she had? Had she actually seen through a chink in this man's hardened armor and glimpsed something inside—an old-school guy, a gentleman who wouldn't kiss her because he couldn't promise her tomorrow?

Something swelled so fast and sweetly sharp in her chest that in that instant, she thought she might just be in love with this man. He was everything she hadn't expected.

Hunter McBride was both a mercenary *and* a gentleman.

11:01 Alpha. Congo-Cameroon border.
Wednesday, September 24

Andries Du Toit studied the black clouds massing along the horizon. There was a thunderstorm brewing. The air had that thick, electrical feel about it. He turned his eyes to the red haze of dust being raised by his troops moving north along the Congolese side of the border, then turned his attention back to his map, smoothing it out over the hood of his Jeep.

"We should have this section of border covered by nightfall," he said. "If they try and make it out of the Blacklands, they'll have to cross somewhere between that point there on the Sangé and that point to the west." He jabbed his finger at the map. "They won't come around that way—that's razorback mountain terrain." He looked up at the militia leader in his employ. "Keep scanning all radio frequencies. The instant they try to make any kind of contact, we'll have them. They *do not* escape the Congo, *comprends*?"

"*Oui, je comprend.*"

"Alert the rest of the People's Militia and the rebel cadres in this entire region, lead them to believe you have reliable intel that President Samwetwe is being smuggled into Cameroon sometime within the next seventy-two hours. Suggest they capture anything that moves. What we don't have covered, they will." Du Toit glanced at the clouds again.

"If we're lucky, they'll be found before they even get close to the border."

Chapter 13

11:10 Alpha. Blacklands.
Wednesday, September 24

The forest canopy thinned and the vegetation turned to thick brush. The sun baked down on Sarah's hair, her skin began to burn and her throat grew parched. They needed to find another water source soon. Hunter whacked at the leaves with his machete, his arms glistening with perspiration, his black hair damp over his brow. The muscles in Sarah's forearm began to cramp from toting the awkward, heavy biohazard container. She tried to mesmerize herself with Hunter's slashing motion, tried to ignore the burn in her thighs and calves, the deep ache in her shoulders.

He stopped suddenly, breathing hard. "See that?" He pointed his machete blade at a strange pattern of herringbone scars cut into the bark of a tall, skinny tree. Below the scars the trunk had begun to grow over a rusted metal cup.

"And that?" He pointed to another tree, same size, same pattern in the bark. Sarah began to notice more trees, all similar in size, spaced the same distance apart.

"Rubber trees." He wiped his wrist over his brow. "We're about ten klicks farther north than I figured."

"And this is good?"

He grinned. "This, Sarah, is an abandoned rubber plantation." He waved his machete over the scrub. "Sangé River should be only a few hundred yards in that direction." He took out his map, crouched down, spread it over his knee. "See, we're here. The plantation runs up this way, along the banks of the Sangé. The farmers used the river to ship their product north—" he looked up at her "—right into Cameroon."

Nerves bit at her. "Are we still in the Blacklands?"

"Just. The plantation lies along the edge of the Blacklands border." He turned his attention back to the map. "From our most recent intel, there should be a mission station there—" he jabbed his finger on a bend in the Sangé "—run by two Italian priests." He glanced up at her. "If we can secure a canoe from that mission, we can float into Cameroon tomorrow night under the cover of darkness."

Sarah swallowed. She had a sinking sense that her time with Hunter was almost over.

He folded his map, slipped it back into his flak jacket and got to his feet. "We can rest up in the plantation buildings tonight. We should find food there—whatever they used to grow should still be growing wild. Then we move out of the Blacklands at dawn." His eyes grew serious. "They'll be expecting us to cross somewhere in this region, Sarah. Travel will be different, dangerous. Once we get to the Italian mission, we'll lie low until dark." He glanced up at a ridge of clouds massing along the distant horizon. "And if that cloud continues to move in from the north, it'll be in our favor. The night will be pitch-black."

They broke through coarse brush and moved onto the wide banks of the Sangé River just after noon. The water flowed slowly, cascading in places from rock pool to rock pool. Two hippos waded on the water's edge, and a huge black-and-white bird with a down-curved beak flew with swooping movements over the surface. The water was such a welcome and life-affirming sight that Sarah slipped her hand into Hunter's without thinking. He gave her fingers a squeeze.

They rinsed off in the pools, filled the canteens and walked north along the riverbank in silence. Two fish eagles soared high above them on thermals of air. Sarah stopped to watch them, and couldn't help noticing the bank of ominous clouds encroaching from the north, black and swollen with rain. It made her tense on some gut level. Even the air around her felt charged.

Hunter must have sensed her growing apprehension because he smiled and pressed his index finger under her chin. "Hey, it's just a thunderstorm, and it's not going to arrive before night-fall. We can take shelter in the old plantation mansion."

But it wasn't the rain she was worried about. It was more a sense of time leaking through her fingers, of reality creeping closer, of unspecified danger waiting for them beyond the Blacklands. Some weird part of her was not quite ready to leave this cursed region, to cross into Cameroon, to say goodbye to Hunter. They hadn't been together that long but it had been intense, and it had the feel of forever. Emotion choked her throat as they resumed their trek along the shimmering white-hot sand. She told herself it was nothing. She was just tired.

He stopped suddenly, drew her to his side, pointed down-river. "Look, there it is."

A large double-story structure rose out of a riot of glossy green vegetation at the curve of the riverbank. As they neared, Sarah could see black and red mold growing across what must have once been a white facade. Cerise bougainvillea scrambled up the walls, snaked along the lintels of glassless windows and exploded in a mass of color over the rusting tin roof. A stone veranda ran along the front of the house, and vines with white flowers tangled around stone columns. Banana palms and papayas grew in a thick grove along one side of the crumbling mansion in what must have once been a fruit and vegetable garden. Nature was devouring what had likely been an exotic home for some large colonial French family.

"What happened?" she whispered in awe. "Where did the people go?"

"Most colonialists fled the region when the Marxists took over," said Hunter, studying the mansion. "But I reckon this plantation was abandoned during the last Ebola outbreak."

"You think they got the disease?"

"My guess is they could no longer get people to come and work this massive plantation once the sorcerers declared the area cursed. They had no choice but to leave." He took her hand. "Come, let's go check it out."

Hunter led her up crumbling stone stairs flanked with clay pots bursting with weeds and flowers gone wild. The heady scent was almost overwhelming in the heat. Sarah could also smell the hot tin of the rusting roof and the underlying musk of decay.

They stepped onto the floor of the veranda. It was scattered with leaves and twigs and dead flowers. A stone fireplace and large oven had been built into a wall at the far end. Whoever had lived here must have enjoyed outdoor cooking and entertaining. Sarah could almost imagine the family sitting out here on cane chairs, sipping cocktails, watching animals come to water in the Sangé as the sun dipped behind the trees. She could almost hear their distant voices speaking in French, the echoes of children laughing in the house.

Hunter dumped his pack, and she jumped, her mind jerking back to the present. He carefully pulled open the creaking double doors that hung on rusted hinges. Sarah peered into the gloomy interior.

Vines draped across the windows, blocking out sunlight. Her eyes adjusted slowly and she began to discern the shapes of a sofa, chairs, a table, odd bits of furniture covered in sheets and left behind. She stepped inside and cobweb curtains billowed in her wake. There was an overpowering smell of mold and rotting wood inside. A snake slithered through the leaves on the floor on the far side the room. Sarah jumped, her heart quickening.

"Looks better out on the veranda, huh?"

She nodded, almost overwhelmed by the sense that a family had once lived here, laughed here, cried here, made love here, had children here. And now the place was simply a husk permeated with a hollow sense of abandonment. It was, she realized with a jolt, that same hollowness that Josh had left in her when he'd walked out the door. She turned back to Hunter, suddenly needing to touch him, to feel his vitality, the security of his strength.

A frown creased his brow. He lifted a strand of hair from her cheek. "Hey, you okay?"

"Yeah." She smiled. "I'm fine."

His features relaxed. "How about you try and clean up the deck a bit, maybe gather some fruit—"

"Excuse me?"

He grinned. "—while I go catch us some fish. Equal division of labor, no chauvinism intended."

She laughed, suddenly grateful to be focusing on the present. "And just how are you going to catch fish?"

A wicked gleam lit his eyes. He slipped his hunting knife out of its holster, pointed the blade toward the river. "See that tree hanging over the bank there, the one with the yellow fruit?"

She squinted into the haze.

"The locals call it a fishing tree. The fish wait under it until one of those yellow fruits drops off then…bam—" He crouched down in a blur of movement and lopped the pompoms off the back of her socks with his blade before she even realized what he was doing.

"Hunter! *What the*—"

He stood up, held the grubby yellow pompoms out in the palm of his hand, his eyes laughing. "Perfect lures once I get my hook into them." He angled his head. "I knew you'd come in handy at some point, Burdett."

She scowled at him.

He winked, closed his fist around her pompoms. And in that moment she had a warm sense of being part of a couple, the two of them at ease and comfortable with each other. It was a nice feeling—one she hadn't had in more years than she could recall.

Night had fallen thick and fast. The storm clouds had moved in, swallowed the stars and the small sliver of moon. Darkness was now complete, save for the roaring fire Hunter had built in the fireplace on the veranda. He'd lit it after the sun had gone down so no one would see their smoke, and he'd raked glowing coals over to one side to slowly roast the fish he'd cleaned by the river.

They'd both washed in sweet water he'd managed to crank up from the old well on the property, and Sarah had swept the veranda with palm fronds. She'd laid out his hammock as a tarp and taken great pleasure in personally lopping off banana leaves with his machete to serve as plates for the fresh fruit and fish. She'd found fat candles in what was once the kitchen area of the mansion, and positioned them around the deck in a circle to ward off crawly things.

A velvet breeze stirred as the storm closed in, making the candlelight quiver, and lifting the fragrance of the tropical night into the air. The smell of flowers mingled with the comforting scents of wood smoke and the coming rain.

Sarah sighed, feeling utterly content. This was the most delicious meal she could ever remember, and although the night sounds of the jungle rose in a raucous crescendo across the river, she felt safe on the covered deck of the old house, with the fire and candles and Hunter and his gun at her side.

She'd enjoyed cutting down the fruit, in spite of the snake she'd disturbed, and the spiders. Wielding the machete to provide for their dinner had empowered her in a way that had surprised her. And she'd taken great pleasure in cleaning off the veranda, arranging the candles and the slices of fruit on the banana leaves and putting a flower in her hair.

It made her realize that while she'd come to this wild place to do good, to offer her help to others, to challenge herself in a new environment, she still really loved the simple pleasure of creating a beautiful home. It was a pleasure Josh had stolen from her, and it was the last thing she'd expected to rediscover in the heart of the cursed Congo jungle.

"Fit for kings," Hunter said as he leaned back on his elbow next to her, eyes on the fire. He was relaxed enough to have taken his boots off, and he was naked from the waist up. She studied his rugged profile, the hardened and scarred muscles of his torso, and smiled sadly. He was right when he'd said they were different, that they needed different things. While she was coming to the realization that what she really wanted, *needed,* was a home—a real home, full of love and warmth— Hunter McBride was just about the furthest thing from it. There was nothing mainstream about this man. He existed on the fringes of society, and she had a sense it was something no woman could take from him. This man could not be put in a container behind a picket fence. He *belonged* in untamed places like this.

He caught her watching. He smiled, reached up and touched the flower tucked behind her ear. "Nice."

She smiled back, caught his hand in her own before he could move it away from her face. "This is your injured arm, Hunter."

He grinned. "Yeah. And it's doing good, thanks to you."

She made a mock frown. "You never put that sling back on after you…fought with that soldier. You think I didn't notice?"

He moved a little closer to her. "So?"

"You were just humoring me back in the clearing when you let me bandage you up, weren't you? You wanted to give me a sense of purpose, a job."

"And you did it so well." A mischievous light danced in his eyes. "Even though there was zero chance I could get my shirt back on."

She jabbed at him. "You're awfully smug in your medical knowledge, you know. How does a soldier know so much?"

He looked away, the play of firelight and shadow hiding his expression. A fat drop of rain hit the tin roof. The breeze shifted, intensified. Leaves rustled.

"Rain's coming."

"You're changing the subject, Hunter. Where *did* you get your medical knowledge? What did you used to do before you joined the FDS?"

His features hardened. He stared at the flames for a while. "I served with the Légion Étrangère—French Foreign Legion."

Surprise flared in her. "The Legion? It still exists?" She'd heard about it. Her father, an armchair military buff, had loved to tell her old war stories, and among them were tales of the famous and exotic French Legionnaires—men's men in a landscape of hot deserts, dense jungles and fierce combat. He'd told his stories with such passion and excitement, she'd often wondered how much of it was really true, but the notion he might've been embellishing hadn't bothered her one bit. She suspected her dad had fancied himself as one of the Legionnaires in his dreams of adventure. And she'd happily lived the dream with him on cold winter nights by the fire.

He'd stopped telling the stories, though, after her mother had died. And Sarah had missed that connection with him more than he could ever have imagined. If he'd known just how much it had hurt her, how desperately cut off he'd made her feel on top of losing her mother, it would have broken his heart.

"The Legion still exists, but apart from military experts, I guess not many people know that it does. The force currently has about 8,500 professional soldiers and 350 officers ready for rapid-action deployment anywhere in the world at extremely short notice." Hunter still wouldn't look at her. He stared instead into the crucible of flames he'd built in the stone oven.

Intrigued, she drew her knees into her chest and leaned forward. "How long did you spend with the Legion?"

"I fulfilled my five year contract." He grunted softly. "If you want to leave any earlier than that, you have to desert. And then they come hunting for you. It's not pretty when they find you. And they *do* find you."

Sarah looked at the flames, as if she might see what he was seeing in them, see into his past. From what history she knew from her father, if the French Foreign Legion had forged Hunter's character, it explained an awful lot about him.

Her dad had told her that the Légion Étrangère was often referred to as the Legion of the Damned. It was an army comprised completely of foreigners—hard men who were usually running from something back home, men who had to set aside cultural differences and learn quickly to communicate in French. Men who were prepared to give up their pasts, their countries, their families and their homes in order to fight and die for a country that wasn't their own.

It dawned on her then that the whole French Foreign Legion was a mercenary army, and it had been modeled on generations of private armies in Europe that went before it. So why should what Hunter did for a living now be so unpalatable to much of the world? Sarah suddenly felt like a hypocrite. As a young child she'd relished the exotic tales of combat, but she'd grown into a woman who abhorred war. Was it because her dad's stories had seemed so foreign, so fictional, so far removed from her reality that they had existed in a separate part of her psyche? Maybe it was because the time spent with her father was so special she just refused to see anything negative about it.

She studied Hunter's profile, a clearer picture of him emerging in her mind. Her father had told her that when a man joined the Legion he could take nothing of his past with him, no clothes, no cash, no trinkets or photos. Everything was confiscated, even passports. A man literally had to check his past at the gates. And *if* he survived his contract, he earned the right to become a French citizen. He was given a new passport, and if he wanted, a new name and new identity documents. It was the perfect place to officially bury a troubled history.

"My dad used to tell me stories about the Legion," she said softly.

His eyes flashed to hers. "He did?"

"He told me that if a man wanted to hide from something terrible he'd done, he could join, and after he'd served his contract, *if* he survived it, he could—"

"Be rectified, get a new identity."

"Yes. He said criminals did it to avoid the law."

Hunter gave a dry laugh. "Criminals, refugees, revolutionaries, paupers, poets and princes—all welcomed into the French Foreign Legion since King Louis Phillipe established the force in 1831. Yeah, I've heard those stories, too." His eyes held hers. "That's the romantic version, Sarah. It's not quite like that now. Not *that* easy for a criminal to get in."

Was he mocking her? She studied his eyes. "Why did *you* join, Hunter?"

He shrugged. "Must've read the same stories your dad did, got the same romantic notions in my head. You know, the promise of exotic adventure in a man's world. Hot sun, victorious combat, cool desert nights, cheap wine—" he cocked a brow "—and of course, compliant females."

Warmth tingled over her skin at the thought of sex with Hunter.

He looked away. "Or maybe it *was* the promise of a cloak of official anonymity, the promise of a new life."

Sarah had an uncomfortable and growing sense that this was the truth. His accent was Irish, yet he'd told her he was a French citizen. He had to have been rectified. But why? What had driven him to do it? What dark past was Hunter McBride hiding from?

"Is your name really Hunter McBride?"

The fire popped and cracked. The wind rustled in the trees and fat leaves clacked together. A few more drops of rain plopped on the tin roof. He sat up suddenly, reached over, took both her hands in his.

"Yes. I wouldn't hide that from you. Not now."

What are you hiding then? "You're Irish," she said. "At least you were before you became French."

"That was another lifetime."

"And you don't want to tell me about it?"

A darkness sifted into his features. His jaw hardened and his eyes turned cold. That look of danger was back. She wasn't sure she wanted to know the truth about Hunter McBride. "It's okay," she said, backpedaling. "Maybe…maybe some other time."

"Yeah." He picked up a twig blown in by the wind and tossed it at the fire. "Maybe another time."

But there wouldn't be one. The notion of a future hung unarticulated between them. The wind whipped a little harder and the fire wavered. Drops of rain began to bomb steadily against the tin roof, and the banana palms swished against the walls.

Hunter stared into the coals. His heart was thudding hard. He'd allowed Sarah to push him right up to the very edge of his past, but he was incapable of going further, incapable of giving her the whole truth.

Yet he'd crossed a line with her—in more ways than one—and he knew in his gut there was no turning back. He just didn't know if he could go all the way. Or why he should. She'd be out of his life within seventy-two hours.

If they were lucky, by this time tomorrow they'd be in Cameroon. He'd use his radio to contact the FDS. It would be risky, but not as risky as using it in the Congo. The FDS had an agreement with the Cameroonian government, and FDS soldiers were free to operate in the area. He could have Sarah on an FDS chopper within an hour or two of crossing the border.

Hunter would then move on to the next phase of his mission, which was to help "kidnap" Dr. Jan Meyer from his research station in Gabon. The man was a world-renowned expert in infectious diseases and affiliated with the Prince Leopold Institute of Tropical Medicine in Belgium, Europe's answer to the CDC. If anyone could identify the pathogen it was he. The FDS knew Meyer would come to the São Diogo lab willingly, but in the interests of secrecy, they couldn't let him know about the pathogen until they had him sequestered. They would make it look as if he'd been taken hostage by rebels for cash, and they'd set up a fake negotiating system in an effort to stay under Cabal radar. The next major challenge would be to find an antidote in time.

Time.

Hunter stared at the hot orange embers as the fire began to die down and rain drummed on the roof. Everyone was running out of time. Even him, for God's sake. He'd be forty-three in a few weeks. Jesus, what was his life all about, really? How often did a woman like Sarah come a man's way?

And what fool would honestly let her go?

He jerked to his feet and threw another log onto the fire. The rain came down even harder, waves of sound hammering over the roof with each gust of wind. A loose sheet of tin began to bang somewhere, and wind began to moan eerily through the old structure.

Sarah was watching him in silence, those beautiful warm brown eyes liquid with the reflected light of the flames, searching his face for answers. He sat down beside her, unable to talk.

"Hunter." She touched him, fingers soft on the skin of his arm. "I didn't mean to pry." Her eyes glimmered. "I care about you. I…I just want you know that."

Wind tore suddenly at the banana palms and rattled the leaves. Thunder rumbled in the distance and lightning flashed. The rain came down in a solid silver curtain, and water began to drip through rusted nail holes in the roof.

Hunter stared at her hand, pale and smooth against his sun-darkened skin. His throat tightened. Emotion began to burn in his chest. When had he last felt a touch like that? When had anyone *cared* about him?

He lifted his eyes slowly and his gaze meshed with hers. The warmth, the tacit permission, the invitation he saw in her eyes engulfed him in a dizzying wave.

She got to her knees, leaned forward, her lips slightly parted, her lids low and sultry over her eyes. And Hunter's heart clean stopped. Thunder crashed. His heart kicked back at twice the pace. She placed her hand against his face and brought her mouth closer to his.

She was going to kiss him.

His mind raced, scrambling again for all the reasons he shouldn't do this. Then her lips touched his, brushed over them, soft as butterfly wings. His stomach swooped and his mind went blank. He closed his eyes, tried to hold himself still, but his muscles began to tremble.

She brushed her mouth over his again and then he felt the tip of her tongue, wet, soft as velvet, run over his lips. Hunter groaned as he grew hard and his groin started pulsing with each beat of his heart. He could think of nothing beyond losing himself deep inside this woman.

But just as he reached up to cup her head, to pull her mouth down harder on his, she drew away.

His eyes flared open.

She sat back on her heels and was watching his face. Arousal flushed her features, and he could see that her nipples were pressed hard against the soft fabric of her thin camisole. Another wave of delirious heat swooped through his belly. But he didn't dare make a move. Not this time. This had to be her decision and hers alone. She had to be sure.

Lightning cracked again and thunder followed almost immediately. The storm was right over them now. The rain hammered and the piece of tin banged louder, faster.

She moved her hands to the hem of her camisole, and with her eyes holding his, drew it slowly up over her belly, then her breasts, then lifted it over her head.

Hunter's mouth went bone-dry.

She sat in front of him, naked from the waist up, breasts aroused, her burnished tangle of curls brushing her shoulders.

He shook his head mentally, thinking for a fleeting moment he was dreaming. But he wasn't.

She stood up, wriggled her skirt down over her hips, taking her panties with it. She stood absolutely naked in front of him, the firelight flickering gold over her creamy pale skin.

She wanted him, all right. He tried to swallow, couldn't. He stared at the dark delta between her thighs, and the hot, pulsing ache in his groin screamed for release. He lifted his eyes slowly, trailing them up from the insides of her thighs to her belly button, up slowly to her breasts. She was beautiful and there was nothing shy about her. Those facts sparked something dark and savage in him. He clenched his teeth. He wanted to haul her to the ground, plunge himself into her…but he didn't want to make it happen too fast. He wanted her to take him where *she* wanted. He had a sense she needed it that way. She needed to be in control. And a part of him found intense delirious pleasure in the notion.

She knelt down slowly, bringing her mouth close to his ear as she reached for his belt. Her hair fell across his chest as she whispered, "I want to see you naked, Hunter McBride."

His mind swooned. He moved his head around to kiss her, but she pressed her fingers to his mouth, holding him back. "Naked first," she murmured.

Hunter closed his eyes as she undid his belt buckle. This woman just didn't stop surprising him. How could a man have ever let her go? How could *he* let her go? He felt himself swell into her soft hands as she freed him from his zipper. He groaned with pleasure as she clasped her hand around him and began to caress him. He watched her face as she stroked him to an unbearable pitch. She smiled, her lids heavy, and began to tug his pants down over his hips. He lifted his body to help her.

Thunder crashed again and sheet lightning illuminated the sky. The world flickered like old movie. She sat back on her heels and ran her eyes brazenly over his body.

He leaned forward to grab her, to pull her down onto him. But she restrained him with the palm of her hand against his chest, slowly straddling his legs. The idea of her thighs parting over him nearly drove him wild. His heart began to palpitate and his vision swam. He placed his hands on her hips, ran them up along the contours of her waist to the swell of her breasts. He cupped them, squeezed, grazed his thumbs over her nipples. They grew even tighter. She lifted her chin, tilting her head back, and moaned softly. Her motion had the effect of opening her legs wider, slanting her pelvis toward him.

He slid his hands back down along her waist, down the outside of her thighs and then slipped one hand around her buttocks and moved the other to the inside. The skin here was unbelievably smooth and soft. With the hand on her behind, he tilted her pelvis even more, and cupped his other palm over her hair, his fingers seeking the soft folds within. He found them, slipped his fingers up inside her. She was wet, slick, hot. She moaned again, sinking some of her weight down onto him, and her eyelids fluttered in pleasure.

For a second Hunter couldn't breathe. And in the next second he couldn't hold on any longer. In a swift movement born of years of hand-to-hand combat, he had her flat on her back and was kneeling over her. With one hand he pinned her wrists to the floor up over her head, with the other he traced the line of her breasts. Shock—and desire—flared in her eyes.

He grinned. "My turn, Sarah."

Chapter 14

The savage look in his eyes shot a thrill through her. He had her hands trapped above her head, her body exposed, at his mercy. He knelt over her, phenomenal in his nakedness, pure male power and potent arousal. The wind gusted, blowing a fine mist of moisture over her hot skin. Sarah shivered.

He leaned down, caught the lobe of her ear between his teeth and whispered words in French she couldn't understand—and didn't need to. The seduction was rich enough in the way he said them. Waves of scarlet pleasure wheeled through her brain. He traced his mouth down the column of her neck, over her breast and down her stomach, tasting, teasing, flicking with his tongue as he moved along the length of her body. He reached her thighs and she felt his hands part her, then she felt his tongue. Hot. Wet. Her world narrowed to just the sensation. His tongue flickered, traced the part of her that throbbed with each pulse of blood through her body, then suddenly thrust hard and deep. She cried out in delicious shock. His tongue moved inside her and she arched her back, aching for release. But just as she thought she was going to explode, he withdrew.

She gave a crazy sob of relief, desperately eager to hang on to the painful pleasure of her need, not ready to let go yet.

He knelt between her thighs and used his knees to push her legs open wide, impossibly wide. He leaned over her, covering her body with his, and she felt the hot, smooth, rounded tip of him enter her. He watched her face as he slowly, rhythmically, dipped just the tip of himself into her, not once breaking visual contact. Sarah tilted her pelvis up in desperation, opening wider to him, aching for all of him. He smiled, dark and feral, and then plunged deep into her with a hard, guttural groan.

She gasped. He was incredibly hot. He moved inside her fast, hard, faster, the slippery heat of his friction against swollen nerve ends almost unbearable. Her eyelids fluttered. Crimson waves spiraled through her brain. She could control nothing that was happening in her body. He rocked his pelvis hard against hers, thrusting deeper each time. Her nerves screamed for release, and suddenly her muscles exploded around him. She dug her nails into his back and swallowed a cry as contractions shook her.

Her release pushed him to the edge. He took her jaw, made her look at him, and with a final hard thrust, he shuddered into her.

Sarah lay naked, enfolded in his arms, the tropical air soft on her skin. Rain still fell in a curtain around the veranda and clattered on the tin roof. The fire crackled as it died down to embers.

She could not have imagined anything like this in her life. She'd left a cold and dreary Seattle with a dead heart, and she'd come to the Congo to liberate herself. And she had, in just a few weeks—but she'd also stumbled into an adventure and met a man beyond her wildest dreams.

She closed her eyes, sighed softly. Whatever happened now didn't really matter, she told herself. She'd finally lived. She'd be okay. But she knew she was lying. She just didn't want to entertain the thought of never seeing him again.

She tried to force it from her mind. She told herself it wasn't worth worrying about a future when they might never make it to Cameroon alive. This might be all there was going to be for her, and at least she'd have found herself and found pleasure on the night before she died. She curled against him and drifted into a deep, contented sleep.

Hunter lay awake, holding her, feeling the softness of her bare skin against his, listening to the steady drum of rain on the tin roof, drinking in the musky scent of her sex. He felt himself stir again with a soft, pulsing need. He could have her all over again right now. Just the thought made him harder.

She shifted against him, her head nuzzling into the crook of his armpit, her messy curls tickling his face. He tangled his fingers through them, playing with the light spring in them as they curved around his hand. She began to make soft little snores and he smiled into the dark. Who would have thought a sound like that could make him feel so complete? Who'd have thought that lying naked with an American nurse in the ruins of a colonial French mansion, on an abandoned rubber planta-tion in the heart of equatorial Africa—with a lethal bioweapon at their side—could feel so absolutely right, so natural, so normal? A soft laugh escaped him. It sure beat a regular date.

A gust of wind swished the banana leaves against the building. The rain was dying down, the scent of wet soil was rich and the air felt cool. He reached for his shirt, pulled it over Sarah's shoulders, careful not to wake her. She needed her sleep. Tomorrow was going to be rough. The militia would be watching, waiting for them to try and make a run for the border.

He closed his eyes and said a silent prayer that he'd manage to get her through alive—and shock speared through him.

His eyes flashed open and he stared up at the rusted roof. Wow. A prayer? Hunter McBride hadn't treaded there in fifteen years.

The rain stopped shortly before dawn, and the whole jungle rustled with the sound of fat drops on thick leaves. As light seeped into the sky, he watched rainwater leak down through a rusty hole in the tin. He hadn't been able to sleep all night. This place, he thought as he stared at the roof, was like a symbol of the husk that was himself. Once solid, once full of love and the promise of life, but now in a cursed no-man's land, abandoned, empty, getting a little older, crustier, meaner each day, crumbling one piece at a time while the world passed him by.

Sarah stirred in his arms, her breast a soft warm weight against his chest. He stroked her hair. She filled this space. With her candles and beauty and nurturing warmth, she'd managed to create a sense of home in the middle of nowhere. She filled *him,* made him feel alive. She made him want to live. Really live. She made him want more than what he had right now.

He closed his eyes. Right now he was free. He had nothing to lose. And that's the way he'd wanted it since the day he'd lost everything. That's why he'd joined the French Foreign Legion. Falling for Sarah meant losing that freedom. It meant he once again *had* something to lose. And a man with something to lose had fear. It was not something he needed in his line of work. Part of his success as a warrior lay in his complete lack of fear, his willingness to take risks daily that could cost him his life.

She stirred again and her eyelids fluttered open. "Hey."

He stroked her cheek. "Hey to you, too."

A sleepy smile crept over her lips.

No. He was wrong. He wasn't free right now. That was forty-eight hours ago. He'd already crossed the line. He already had everything to lose. He just didn't know what in hell to do about it now.

Sarah propped herself up on her elbow, her breasts brushing against him, her hair wild and lustrous over her bare shoulders, her eyes sexy with sleep.

She traced his lips with her fingers. "Why are you smiling?" Her warm brown eyes were full of soft light. What would it be like to wake up to that beautiful face every morning? To lose himself in her each night, to make babies, to give her the children he knew she'd love? Could he make it happen? Did he want to?

Hesitation flickered through those eyes. "Hunter? Come on, tell me what you're thinking. What's making you smile like that?"

He filled his lungs. What the hell, why not just say what was on his mind this very second? It wouldn't kill him, would it? *Push yourself, you jackass. What have you got to lose? Nothing you haven't lost before.*

"I was thinking about you. And I was thinking about this house, about what it must have been like, full of life, laughter and…you know, children. I was thinking about how much you love kids." He rolled over, dragged his knuckle softly across her cheek. "I was thinking what a wonderful mother you'd make."

Her smiled faded. Hunter wavered. He had a sudden sinking feeling he was heading down a one-way street about to meet an oncoming bus he couldn't see.

"And?" she asked.

He noted in some part of his brain that his pulse rate had just increased. "And…and I was thinking what fun we could have making those babies." There, he'd hung his heart right out for the first time in fifteen years.

Her body tensed and something shuttered instantly in her eyes. She sat up, stared down at him, didn't say a word.

A pang of uneasiness speared through him. The wind stirred,

leaves clattered against each other. A cry echoed in the jungle. He knew it; he should never have spoken his mind. He didn't know how to do this stuff anymore. He should have stuck to what he knew best. "Sarah, what's the matter?"

She looked away. Something was wrong. Very wrong. He sat up. "Sarah—"

She grabbed for her shirt, shoved her arms into the sleeves and fumbled with the buttons. He noticed her hands were trembling.

"Sarah, talk to me."

She spun around, glared at him. "You're messing with me."

"Oh, sweetheart, I had no intention…" He reached for her, but she moved out from under his touch.

"You…you said we were different."

He frowned. He wasn't sure what he'd said. Different. The same. It didn't the hell matter to him anymore. "Where are you going with this, Sarah?"

"You—you said…" Her eyes glimmered. "You said you would go on to the next job. And now you're thinking of children…of…" A tear leaked out of the corner of one eye and trailed down her cheek.

He blinked. His mind reeled. He was confused as all hell. Here he was thinking *maybe* they could take a shot at a future. Just maybe he could make some changes, try to figure it out so that he could be with her…and she didn't want it. What was this? A one-night stand? Was *that* what she wanted? To prove something to herself? To validate herself as a woman, or something? Did she have *any* idea what she meant to him?

He dragged both his hands through his hair. This had been a mistake. A big mistake. He'd known in his gut it was the wrong move.

"Look, Sarah, you asked what I was thinking, so I told you." He got up, pulled his pants on. He was angry, no, *furious,* at himself. Afraid. Hurt by her odd rejection, the notion that she might really have meant it when she'd said that she didn't want anything from him, that she wanted to try and exist only in the now. He didn't want to believe that. It was out of character. There was something else going on here, and he'd be damned if he could see what it was. He cinched his belt tight, stared down at her. "I was thinking about how much I want to be with you. You wanted things from me straight, well, that's about as bloody well straight as it gets." He grabbed his shirt.

Her bottom lip began to wobble. Tears ran down her face, but the look in her eyes was angry. "Why have *you* never had kids, Hunter? Why didn't *you* get married and do it? Why don't you want to tell me about Ireland? *What the hell are you hiding from?*" She was shaking now.

He stared right into her eyes. "I *did* want to get married, Sarah," he said slowly, quietly, the cold mist of that memory circling his heart. "I was engaged. Things went wrong."

Uncertainty flickered across her features. "And…and you wanted kids?"

"I did, very much."

"And now?"

He felt a little ill. "Sarah, kids don't have anything to do with this—"

"And now?" she insisted.

Tension tightened the muscles around his throat. "I just told you I was dreaming about kids. I just spilled my guts, for chrissakes." The sun burst over the forest canopy, exploding yellow light onto the veranda.

"What happened in Ireland, Hunter? Why won't you tell me about it?"

He cursed softly. Ten seconds ago he would have. He'd finally been ready to go there. Now? He just couldn't do it. He'd read her wrong. He'd read *himself* wrong. He was better off the way he was. Past buried. Dead. Gone. Forever.

He tightened his jaw. "Ancient history, Sarah. It would serve no purpose now. Get yourself together while I scrounge up some breakfast. We leave ASAP."

He turned, stalked off the veranda, took two crumbling stairs at a time, his brain spinning sickeningly. He stopped for a second at the bottom of the steps and caught his breath. What in hell had just happened back there? He swore again. This was his fault. He should never have slept with her. He was all too aware of the uncharacteristic things people did under stress. Sleeping with him had probably been one of them, something she was already regretting.

Whatever was going on in Sarah's head, she was going to need time after this mission to decompress. There was no point in pushing her now. And he'd be better off focusing on getting out alive, and then just letting this whole thing go. Who had he been trying to kid, anyway? He'd been absent from mainstream life for way too long to even begin to think he could give Sarah what she needed.

He steeled himself.

He had a job. *Focus.* They'd be out of the Blacklands within two hours. Then he couldn't afford to think about another goddamn thing until he'd gotten her and the biohazard container over that border and into Cameroon.

His mind firmly back in the zone, Hunter stomped off into the bush to find breakfast.

Sarah stood at a broken window and watched Hunter stalk into the jungle. The dripping vegetation and haunting river mist seemed to swallow him whole. She looked up at the sky. It was clear above the shroud of fog, but in the distance, to the north over Cameroon, strange dust-orange clouds were mushrooming again. She shivered in spite of the steamy morning warmth and clutched her arms around herself. She was afraid. Afraid because she was falling for him. And her fear had pushed him away. She wasn't a fool. Sarah knew even as the stupid words had come out of her mouth that her subconscious was trying to sabotage her. Because deep down she knew it could never work. She'd already been through it all in her mind. You just didn't change a man like Hunter McBride. You couldn't take the mercenary out of a man. And she couldn't change who she was for him, either.

But that hadn't stopped her wanting him, and it didn't stop her wanting him now. God, she wished she'd never seen that look in his eyes when he'd told her his thoughts. It made her want his children in such a deep, primal way it hurt. She tried to tell herself it was the jungle, it was everything she'd been through, it was the fact she'd been stripped down to her raw emotional core.

Sarah shoved her hair back from her eyes with both hands and tried to force some logic into her brain. She still really knew nothing about Hunter's past, about why he'd joined the Legion, about what he was running from. And it was better that way. She needed a home in her future. A man on the run didn't.

She bent down, began to roll up the hammock. A scorpion scattered over the stone and disappeared into the cracks.

09:32 Alpha. Congo.
Thursday, September 25

Hunter's eyes had gone hard. Even his face seemed carved from granite. He was once again the fearsome and implacable man she'd first seen back on the banks of the Shilongwe River. It was as if the Hunter she'd come to know in the Blacklands had never existed.

He was leading her along a narrow path. The red dirt under her feet was packed hard and this alone was unnerving. It meant the path was well-traveled, and it meant they could encounter someone at any time.

He spun round suddenly, grabbed her arm and yanked her down into the thick bush along the trail. The movement was so harsh and quick she opened her mouth to cry out in surprise. He clamped his hand hard over her lips before she could, muffling her shock. His eyes bored into hers, fierce with warning. He waited for her to calm down before he removed his hand, then he lifted his finger to his lips and pointed into the trees. She saw and heard nothing at first. Then she caught snatches of voices growing louder, more distinct. Several men speaking Lingala were coming their way. She could hear the boots now, thudding along the trail of packed dirt, coming closer.

Sarah turned to look at Hunter. He glared at her, his eyes telling her not to move a muscle. She saw the hunting knife ready in his hands.

The sounds grew closer. A man spoke loudly and others laughed in response. They rounded the bend in the trail and came into view. Her heart began to palpitate as she recognized the uniform of the man she'd killed. There were seven, no, eight militia soldiers with maroon berets and red armbands marching right toward them.

They came so close she could smell them, and a panicked part of her brain wondered if they could smell her, too. She held herself motionless as the dust-covered boots thudded inches from Hunter's and her hiding spot. She could see them clearly, high black webbing around the ankles. Sarah could barely breathe. Then she saw the blood on one man's boots and gasped softly. The soldier stopped suddenly, listened. Hunter tensed instantly, moved the knife forward.

The soldier slowly scanned the trees behind him. Then he turned his attention to the bushes along the trail. He was so close Sarah could see the beads of perspiration on his brow under his beret, and she could see there was blood on his machete. Her heart went stone-cold. His eyes moved gradually toward them. One of his comrades called back to him. He paused, seeming to look right at her. Then he turned and answered loudly in Lingala. One of the men up ahead laughed and yelled something. The soldier chuckled quietly in response, turned on his heels and began to follow the others down the path.

Sarah started to shake. Oh God, she couldn't go through all this again. Hunter placed a hand on her shoulder. "Be strong," he whispered. "And Sarah, do *everything* I say and we may stand a chance of getting out of here."

She nodded. She'd heard it all before, back on the Shilongwe. She suddenly wanted to get as far away from him as she possibly could, and from everything he represented.

"You ready?"

She nodded fiercely. She was more ready, more determined to get out of this place than he could begin to imagine.

The trail wound back down to the banks of the Sangé. The river here was wide and sluggish, the sandbanks a deep ochre color. The heavy morning mist had burned off and the air was oppressively still. As they moved along the water, they heard drums, soft at first, then growing louder, beating faster until they matched the rhythm of Sarah's pounding heart. The sound echoed along the river and pulsated in the thick, hot air.

Sarah glanced at Hunter. There was no sign of emotion on his face, but she knew now the drums were not good. She recognized the unique rhythm of the beat from the Eikona River, the drumming that had sounded after the clinic and the village were burned, after news of the coup in the south. No matter how Sarah tried to calm herself, her heart kept beating harder, trying to match the rhythm of the drums. It made her body break out in a drenching sweat and it fed her fear.

When they reached a wide bend, Hunter motioned for her to move off the path and crouch down in the bushes. He left her like that while he crept along the bank, staying just under cover of the trees, his rifle ready in his hands. She had no idea what he was looking for, or what might have alerted him. He disappeared around the bend for what seemed like forever. Then all of sudden he was back, working his way along the bank. He made a motion for her to join him.

She edged over the sand. "What're the drums about?"

"Trouble." He pointed above the trees in the direction he'd just come. Faint wisps of black smoke snaked into the air and birds circled. Big birds. *Vultures.* Her chest constricted. Her eyes shot to Hunter.

"The Italian mission has been attacked."

No. She shook her head. No. She started to back toward the trees, tripped, stumbled. He shot his hand out, grabbed her wrist, his fingers curling around it like a metal cuff. "We have to go there, to see if they left a boat we can use."

"Hunter," she whispered, "please, I...I can't. I can't see anything like that again. Ever. Please." She tugged against his hold. "I beg of you."

His eyes remained fiercely cool, his grip firm. She glanced back at the jungle, a part of her wishing she could go back in there, go back in time, back to the Blacklands, just hide forever at the mansion on the white banks of the Sangé in lands protected by ghosts with the man she thought she'd met in there.

"Sarah." His voice was as hard as his hold on her wrist. "It's the *only* way."

12:13 Alpha. Italian Mission.
Thursday, September 25

Hunter wouldn't allow her to enter the riverside compound. He'd left her hiding among a cluster of straight-stemmed palms while he crept into the clearing to see if there was a canoe he could salvage.

Sarah crouched near the base of a palm and watched a snake slide through the leaves across the path from her. She didn't move. She didn't even feel any fear. In a part of her brain, she marveled at how much the snake's skin resembled the decaying leaves it moved through, at how the little cluster of tiny horns on its nose looked like bits of twig. Before she'd come to the Congo she'd gone to several Aid Africa briefings in Washington. Among other things, they'd shown the recruits pictures of the snakes, insects and plants that would kill people very quickly. She couldn't remember them all, so many things could kill humans in this area. The only reason she knew that she was looking at a Gaboon viper now was because of the funny rhinoceros cluster on its snout. *Their fangs deliver fifteen drops of venom a shot. Four drops will kill you….*

Funny the things one recalled. She'd never have noticed the viper if she hadn't been sitting stock-still. Concentrating on the lethal reptile took her mind off thinking about what had happened at the Italian mission. The soldiers they'd seen along the path earlier that morning had come from this direction. The blood on the man's shoe must have been shed at this mission…. She looked up, staring hard at the little weaver birds darting between woven nests that hung from the scruffy green-and-brown palm fronds. She focused on the nests to keep her mind from the vultures. She thought they looked like straw Christmas baubles, the way they hung in the trees. She tried to count how many weeks it was to Christmas, wondering where she would be—

Hunter suddenly materialized in front of her, making her catch her breath. The man moved as quietly as a snake when he wanted to.

She looked up into his eyes, trying to see what he might have seen. But his face was absolutely expressionless. "There are canoes," he said. "We can't wait until dark. We must take one now, try and get a ways down the river, find a place we can hole up until nightfall."

She began to rise to her feet. He stopped her, placing his palm on her shoulder. He crouched down to eye level and took her hands in his. "Sarah," he said quietly. "We have to go through the compound to get to where the canoes are beached."

She swallowed, nodded.

His eyes lanced hers. "I don't want you to look. I want you to focus on following me. Just move fast and keep looking at me."

Her heart began to pound. "Have…have they been killed?" she whispered.

"Yes."

"All of them?"

"Yes."

"Even the priests?"

He nodded.

Her stomach turned over and she stared at her toes.

"Come." He took her arm, pulling her to her feet. "We have to move quickly."

Sarah concentrated on the backs of Hunter's boots as he led her through the center of the mission compound. But she could smell the sickly sweet scent of spilled blood, the acrid scent of burned thatch. Sweat dampened her skin. In her head, she could see Dr. Regnaud's glazed eyes behind his goggles, could hear screams of the nuns back at the Ishonga clinic, could hear the moans. The moans seemed real…too real…. She faltered, suddenly unable to move, unable to discern memory from reality. She watched Hunter's boots moving away from her. Then she heard it again, a moan. Her heart skipped a beat. *It was real!* She glanced up. "Hunter! Stop!"

He halted, spun round.

"Someone…someone's hurt. I can hear them."

He took two strides toward her, grabbed her arm, digging his fingers into her skin. "Come," he growled.

"No!" She tried to yank free of his hold. "Listen."

She heard the low moan again. The sound was coming from the trees behind the wattle-and-daub hut to her left. Sarah turned to look, and bile heaved to her throat as the carnage around her filtered into her vision. Several bodies were scattered around the clearing. Massacred with machetes. She clamped her hand over her mouth.

Hunter flung his arm around her, protecting her from the sight with his body. He lowered his face to hers. "Sarah, just keep moving. Don't look."

She jerked free and ducked out of his hold. *"Someone's still alive."*

"Sarah—"

She spun and stumbled over the dirt, making her way around the hut with its partially burned thatch roof, trying not to absorb too much. But she was compelled to find the source of the sound.

She found it in the shade of a kapok tree.

A young woman lay sprawled on the red ground. Blood covered the side of her head and face, and her belly was round and swollen under her T-shirt. Her eyes were open and she stared right at Sarah and moaned softly.

"Oh my God!" Sarah rushed forward, dropped to her

knees at the woman's side. "Hunter…come quick, help me. She's pregnant!"

His hand gripped her shoulder hard. Her eyes shot up to his. "We've got to do something!"

"Sarah, we have to *leave. Now.* There's nothing we can do for her."

"How can you say that! How do you know?" Sarah turned to the woman, felt for a pulse at her neck. It was very weak and rapid. Her skin was cold to the touch, and Sarah's fingers came away covered in blood. She quickly lifted the woman's T-shirt and palpated her swollen belly. She felt a movement under her hands. Her heart stopped, then started racing. "Oh, God, the baby's alive." Sarah felt the woman's belly again. She could tell by the height of the woman's expanded uterus that the fetus was probably at thirty-eight weeks' gestation. "I—I think it's term," she whispered.

She glanced at the woman's face. Her eyes were rolling back, her lids fluttering. She was losing consciousness. Sarah felt quickly for her pulse again. It was thready, barely there. *They were losing her.*

Sarah felt utterly helpless and bewildered. She'd know how to help in a hospital situation. But out here? She reached up, grabbed the fabric of Hunter's army pants. "The baby—we've got to do something!"

He crouched down, looked into her eyes. "Sarah," he said softly, urgently. "You *can* help. You can help by staying alive yourself, by getting this pathogen out so that it can be identified. You can help by saving the lives of millions upon millions of innocent people. People just as innocent as this woman and her unborn child here."

She stared at him, speechless. How could he ignore this pregnant woman?

"Think of it as triage, Sarah. You have to help those with the most chance of survival first. Sometimes the decisions are tough."

"No." She shook her head, jerked away. "I can't. I can't leave this woman and her baby to die alone with the vultures circling up there. *I just can't.* I have to at least make them comfortable." She glared at him. "And don't try to make me leave. You made me shoot a man. Don't make me do this, too."

His eyes narrowed. He clenched his teeth and a muscle in his neck began to jump fast. He glanced at his watch and cursed viciously under his breath. Then he shrugged out of his pack, dropped to his knees beside her, felt for the woman's pulse, began to palpate her stomach.

Sarah's mouth dropped open. He moved like a professional.

He turned the woman's head to the side, exposing a thick, gelatinous puddle of blood and a clean machete gash that sliced right through her skull into gray brain tissue. Sarah's stomach bottomed out. Hunter was right. There was no hope for her. How she'd held on this far was incredible. She had to be doing it for her child.

Hunter glanced at Sarah. "She's going into cardiac arrest. We've got five minutes."

"What?"

"To save the fetus. Pass me my pack. Quick." He unbuttoned his shirt as he spoke, shrugged out of it.

Sarah stared at him.

Hunter reached over her, grabbed the pack himself, extracted the first aid pouch, rolled it open, began to snap on a pair of latex gloves. He hesitated for a millisecond, then closed his fingers around the scalpel. "Get the flashlight out, Sarah. Position it at the side of my head, shine it on her stomach as I work."

Her brain felt sluggish. She realized they were in the shade. He'd need light. How did he know what he was doing? She fumbled in the pack, her mind racing. She flicked the light on.

"Use one hand for the torch, Sarah. Take those gauze pads in the kit with your other hand, use them as laparotomy sponges, pack off the fluids as I work. I don't have clamps, I'll need to move fast. Use my shirt for the baby. You're going to have to be ready to do neonatal resuscitation if necessary, while I look for equipment in the huts. Mission should have antibiotics, blankets, formula, especially if they were caring for a young woman like this. They'd have been ready…." He lifted the scalpel as he spoke, performing a neat midline abdominal incision that would allow fast access to the uterus.

Sarah's chest clenched. Her mind reeled. By God, this man knew *exactly* what he was doing. He was a professional. There was no doubt in her mind.

Hunter McBride was a surgeon.

Chapter 15

She was small and coffee-brown with black hair, and she was the most exquisite and perfect little thing Sarah had ever laid eyes on. She hadn't been breathing when Hunter took her out, but Sarah had managed to resuscitate her while he went through the partially burned-out huts and found blankets, bottled water, antibiotics, disposable diapers and prepared formula.

They'd cleaned her tiny body, and Hunter had clamped and sterilized her umbilical cord and administered preventative antibiotics. The baby girl was an excellent weight—Sarah judged her to actually be on the higher end of the normal spectrum. Her mother had obviously received excellent care and nutrition at the mission, and all of this gave the child one hell of a fighting chance.

Sarah knew from experience that a healthy newborn of good weight could survive up to a week without any care as long as there was no umbilical stump infection, which could lead to systemic infection or tetanus within a couple of days. Plus they were more than lucky to have found formula. The gods had been looking out for this little girl, she thought as she stroked the infant's silky head.

Hunter had explained to her as he'd loaded the canoe that the missionaries would've been prepared for the young mother to leave the baby with them and return to her village once she'd given birth. If she was here to have her child, it was likely because she'd become pregnant through an act of violence and rape. It was all too common in this region, and in some tribes, a baby conceived in that manner was considered dirty and unwanted. It would have been discarded as soon as it was born. This young woman would have come to the Italian mission in a brave and desperate act to save her child. And she would likely have left it with the priests to be put up for adoption.

Sarah lifted her camisole and cuddled the newborn against her naked skin, a soft flannel blanket wrapped over the little back. This skin-to-skin contact was called kangaroo care, and it increased an infant's chances of survival tenfold. It also helped the child bond with the mother. She'd seen it done at the children's hospital when police had brought in a newborn found abandoned in a bus shelter. Sarah had taken a special interest in the care of that baby, helped nurse it back to health, and had been utterly heartbroken to see it leave.

"See?" she whispered as she stroked her hand over the soft spot on the newborn's skull. "Everything happens for a reason, little sweetheart. You've got a better chance with me and Hunter here than most kiddies born out in the jungle, you know."

The baby stirred slightly and made little suckling noises. Emotion welled sharply in Sarah's chest, and a soft, maternal warmth shot through her blood. What she was experiencing was indescribable, overwhelming. It made her feel as though she could take on the world, do *anything* to protect this innocent little life.

She looked up at Hunter. He sat in the stern of the canoe, facing her, still naked from the waist up, his chest muscles rippling under tanned skin as he maneuvered their craft into a dark and narrow tributary of the Sangé River. His face was still completely devoid of emotion. Not once during the entire operation had he showed any sign that he was feeling a thing. But she knew he had to have been. She'd glimpsed enough to know that whatever armor this man had managed to erect around himself, whatever iron-willed control he exerted over his emotions, there *was* someone under it all who cared deeply enough to have done the things she'd seen him do over the last few days. She wanted to talk to him, to ask him. But she sensed now was not the time.

Drums continued to thrum in the distance, echoing in faint waves of sound as his paddle dipped and splashed softly in the deep, black water. Trees began to crowd in, branches hanging low over the narrow waterway, muffling sound. Water hyacinths and orchids grew in thick reed beds along the shore. A fish plopped, startling Sarah, and she could see a monkey the size of a man standing in the fork of a tree, watching them. Nerves began to eat at her. She pressed the baby closer to her chest.

The canoe rocked gently as Hunter paddled. He scanned the encroaching bush constantly, his gun resting within instant reach of his fingers.

17:19 Alpha. Sangé River.
Thursday, September 25

They sat under trees on a slab of warm rock that jutted out into the small tributary. The cloud-filled sky turned a dirty orange as the sun began to sink toward the horizon. Hunter absently fingered his rifle, making sure it was at his side, ready. Cloud cover was good. It would mean complete blackness tonight and additional protection as they tried to cross the border into Cameroon. Rain, however, would not be good for the baby.

He turned to look at them. Sarah was trying to nurse the little infant with a bottle of prepared formula. She tapped the nipple against the baby's cheek, and her mouth instantly began to root around for it. She found the nipple and began to suckle, beetle-black eyes fixed intently on Sarah's face. His heart clenched tight, so tight it almost choked him. Hunter blinked back the weird hot surge of emotion and looked out over the river.

It was deserted here on the banks of the tributary, but they'd heard gunfire earlier, to the north, and it concerned him. There was way too much activity in the region. Something wasn't right.

"Hunter?"

He flicked his eyes to her.

"You're a surgeon."

It wasn't a question, and her voice was completely neutral. He studied her carefully. There was no judgment in her eyes, either. Sarah and he had both come to a point that went beyond judgment, and there was no use pretending now. He didn't even want to anymore. She'd forced him to pick up that scalpel and do what he'd been trained to do. He couldn't even begin to articulate what saving that little infant had done to his soul. He'd been outed. After all these years, the old Hunter McBride was back. Sarah had forced him be to the man he used to be, and there was no putting that past back into the bottle now. He just didn't know what the hell he was going to do about it.

"I *was* a surgeon," he said quietly. "In another lifetime. In Belfast."

"What happened?"

He moistened his lips, reached over and stroked the baby's hair. "We should name her."

"What happened, Hunter? What made you walk away?"

He sucked air in through his nose, scanned the trees across the water. It would be dark within the hour. They would have to move soon. He still had a job to finish.

"Hunter?"

He exhaled heavily. "It was more than fifteen years ago. I'd completed my surgical internship at the Catholic hospital in Belfast and taken a position on staff." Just thinking about it was rough. Making the words come out of his mouth was worse. He flashed his eyes to hers. "Sarah, it was a long time ago, and we really should—"

"I need to know, Hunter." Her gaze tunneled into his. "And I think you need to talk."

He gave a soft huff, nodded slowly. She was right. He couldn't bury this all again, not now. "I was connected. I was engaged to the hospital board director's daughter. Her name was Kathleen." He glanced at Sarah. "You remind me of her…a little." He paused, fingered his assault rifle. "No, that's not true. You did jolt my memory when I first saw you. You made me think about her, about the past. But…you're different." He smiled at her. "*Very* different. In the best possible ways."

The baby made a little noise. She'd had enough milk. Sarah set the bottle down and moved the infant up to her shoulder to burp her, all the time looking into Hunter's eyes, watching him, waiting for him to continue.

He said nothing for a while. The orange in the sky began to go purple. "Colin O'Brian," he said suddenly. "That was Kathleen's father's name. Big, big Catholic figure in the Belfast community, tons of cash, and major political clout. He first took me under his wing when my dad and two brothers blew themselves up in a bombing on his account. I was twelve at the time."

"What?"

"That's just how it was, Sarah. The region was deeply divided along political and religious lines, and each faction looked after their kind. Everyone accepted it. When my brothers and dad died they were considered heroes, martyrs for their cause, and my mother was well looked after by the community until she passed away—and she died a proud widow. But as a kid, I had this whole internal rebellious attitude to the conflict, to the death. It just seemed pointless to me, and when I saw my family blown up I got mad as all hell. But there was no place in my community for a fatherless kid to stand up to centuries worth of hatred. Instead, I developed this desperate need to mend the people that were broken by the violence. I wanted to become a doctor." He looked into her eyes. "Not just an ordinary doctor, Sarah, but a surgeon, someone who could sew people back together again. It was *my* survival mechanism, *my* way of fighting back."

He chewed on his cheek, trying to navigate the old memories, consolidate them into words. "Because of what my father and brothers had done for him and his cause, Colin supported me after they died. And he supported my ambition. He funded me through medical school and it saved me from being recruited by his underground factions. And I did the man proud,

Sarah—" he snorted "—so proud that the old guy was delighted to give me Kathleen's hand in marriage when I asked him."

A strange light flitted through Sarah's eyes. "Did you love her?"

He nodded. "Yeah, I did."

"What happened to Kathleen?"

He blew air out softly, tasting the bitterness in his mouth. "She cheated on me. She got pregnant."

Shock flared through Sarah's eyes and emotion skittered over her features. She reached for his hand, covered it with her own. Her touch made his chest hurt. It made his eyes hot.

"Who was the father?" she whispered.

"Son of the opposition. Kathleen cheated not only on me, but on her whole family. She slept with the eldest son of the leader of the Protestant faction, and she tried to hide her affair and her pregnancy from the whole community for fear of the potential political fallout." He turned to look out over the black river. "People have gone to war over lesser things, you know?"

"I know."

He sat still for a while. The sky began to darken and a hot breeze rippled the water. Sarah didn't ask any more questions. She was giving him time to go at his own pace.

Hunter ran his tongue over his teeth. "Kathleen went and got herself an abortion. In secret. She developed septicemia, and by the time she was admitted to hospital, it was too damn late to save her."

"Is that why you left Ireland to join the Legion?"

"No. I left because they blamed me for killing her."

"What!"

He nodded, slightly bemused at how easy it actually was to say these things to Sarah. It had been a secret bottled inside him for so long, he thought he'd never be able to talk about it, let alone feel this strange catharsis in doing so.

"I was Catholic, remember. In Colin's eyes that meant *no one* slept with his daughter until she was married. He immediately assumed I was the one who'd knocked her up, and he went blind with rage. He figured I was also the one who'd tried to take care of it. He thought I killed his daughter, my own fiancée, and he came after me with all the cash and power and fury he could muster. It started with my suspension from the hospital, and then the police came knocking. I was done for. Professionally. Emotionally. My life in Ireland was over."

She moved closer to him, just close enough so that her body lightly touched his. "I'm so sorry, Hunter."

He reached over and stroked the baby's head. "I would have looked after the baby, you know? I would have accepted her child as my own. That's the irony of it, Sarah. As much as her infidelity killed me, I would have protected her. She didn't trust my integrity enough to tell me."

"Betrayed in love…and in death," Sarah whispered. She lifted her eyes to his, as if seeing him—really seeing him—for the first time. "What did you do?"

"I wanted to die." He laughed softly. "The only thing that saved me was a book from my childhood library."

"*Beau Geste*…about the Légion Étrangère."

Startled, he stared at her. "How did you know?"

"Smart guess." She smiled. "It was one of my dad's boyhood favorites. It's the one that sparked his interest in the Legion." She looked into his eyes. "He'd like you, you know?"

"Your dad—he still around?"

She nodded. "Not my mum, though. She died when I was fourteen. Cancer. My gran kind of stepped in and looked after us both. She was Irish, too. She came from this huge Catholic family, lots of kids, tons of stories. It sounded such fun, and being an only child myself, I…I always felt I was missing out on something." She smoothed the blanket over the baby. "Maybe that's why I always wanted to have children, to fill some subconscious hole in my psyche. Goodness knows, perhaps that's even the reason I ended up working in a pediatric ward." She smiled a little self-consciously. "To tell you the truth, I don't think I really realized that until now."

"Can I hold her?"

Surprise, then delight rippled through Sarah's eyes. She leaned forward, moving the baby away from her chest, and wrapped the flannel blanket carefully around the tiny body. She handed the crinkled bundle to him.

He brought the small, soft, sleeping newborn up against the skin of his chest and studied the wrinkled face. The baby made a snuffling noise and her little mouth puckered and began to suckle at an imaginary breast. The sensation punched something so savagely primal through Hunter that for an instant, he couldn't breathe. His eyes turned moist. How could such violent potency coexist with such tenderness in one overwhelming sensation? Was that what it felt like to be paternal, to be a father? Holding this little life in his hands made him feel like a god. It made him feel as if he could conquer the world, made him *want* to.

He swallowed. "Sarah," he said, gazing at the child's face as it slept in his arms. "This is probably a really dumb question, given everything you've told me about your marriage, but why didn't you and Josh have kids, back in the beginning when you thought you were still okay together?"

She was silent for a while. "I can't have children."

He studied her face. "Medical reasons?"

She bit her lip and nodded.

He nodded in turn, saying nothing. He recalled her outburst at the plantation. It made sense now. Him telling her that he was dreaming of children, *her* children, must have cut her to the quick. He could only begin to imagine what it must be like for a woman who loved children with all her heart not to be able to bear them, and how a man like Sarah's ex-husband might have used that to undermine her.

Hunter turned his attention back to the coffee-skinned bundle in his arms. Her lashes were dark and silky, like her hair. She was so beautiful. So innocent, so very helpless. An orphan of war. "I always liked the name Branna," he said softly.

A mix of tenderness and unease crossed Sarah's features. She hesitated. "What's going to happen to her? She has no future."

He slanted his eyes to hers. "We can give her a future, Sarah."

Surprise flitted through her. She searched his face, looking for something, an answer to some unspoken question. Gunfire sounded in the distance, but her gaze remained steady, her eyes holding his, as if she desperately needed to know something. "Why did you join the FDS when you quit the Legion, Hunter? Why didn't you go back to medicine? What made you want to keep fighting…killing people?"

He could see where she was going with this. She didn't believe a man like him could give *anyone* a future, let alone this child.

"I was good at war. I excelled in the Legion. It became what I knew. And by that stage I was comfortably numb. I was with men who never talked about the past, never asked questions. I never had to think. I never had to *feel*. And that suited me fine. It *made* me good at what I do. And I didn't join the FDS, I formed it. Ten years ago."

"Formed it?"

"With three other guys who served in the Legion with me— Jacques Sauvage, Rafiq Zayed and December Ngomo. As our five-year contracts drew to an end, we began to look ahead. We saw a market for a small but highly efficient private force of professional soldiers modeled on the Legion's paramilitary regiment. We got contracts and began to build our business. Our reputation grew, and so did the bank accounts. We were based out of South Africa at first, but a change of legislation there put our business on the wrong side of the local law, so we had to find another location. We eventually signed a deal with the government of São Diogo. The island economy was dying, and moving our base and our business there was an ideal economic solution for the small nation. Our soldiers and their families now support the local economy, and the islanders support us."

"Those men, the ones you formed the FDS with, have they been rectified?"

He gave a wry grin. "We don't talk about the past, Sarah. Ever. They're men I will die for, and they will do the same for me. That's good enough."

She studied him in silence. It was almost dark now, the clouds low and the air thick with hot electrical energy. Gunfire sounded again, somewhere to the north. Hunter handed the little bundle in his arms back to Sarah. "It's time."

21:29 Alpha. Cameroon border.
Thursday, September 25

The night was pitch-black and hot. All Sarah could see was the oily shine of the rippling river and the dark shapes of trees along the shoreline. Water slapped lightly on the hull. She had no idea how long they'd been drifting northward. She figured they must be getting close to the border by now, and she thanked the Lord that she'd managed to stop Branna from crying. She liked the name Hunter had mentioned—Branna—

and that's who the baby had become in Sarah's mind. She stroked her little head, drawing comfort from the contact. The baby was sleeping now. Sarah just hoped she kept on sleeping while they crossed into Cameroon.

Hunter had helped her bind Branna to her chest using the blanket in the way the natives did. She'd be able to move faster this way.

She felt Hunter's hand on her knee, then his breath in her ear. "We're almost at the border," he whispered. "Don't let her cry. Be ready to move when I tell you."

Sarah swallowed. Perspiration prickled along her brow, the baby against her chest making her even hotter. She wished she could see what Hunter was seeing through his night-vision gear. She heard the slight splash and swoosh of his paddle, and she felt the canoe turn. They began to move faster, picking up a stronger current.

She heard another slight swoosh of his paddle and the canoe veered to her right. She felt a bump, then the brush of leaves over her face. He touched her arm, indicating that she stay still while he dragged the canoe higher onto the shore. She heard the slosh of water as his boots moved through it, felt the canoe jerk up onto the beach. He took her arm, helped her out.

Relief spurted through her. If they were getting out of the canoe, they must have made it over the border without incident. *They were safe.*

All they had to do now was move farther inland and Hunter would radio his contact. For the first time in days, Sarah actually began to think they might make it out alive.

But he grabbed her arm suddenly, held her motionless. She blinked into the dark, seeing nothing. Then she heard voices drifting in snatches over the water. Her heart started to thud. Lights flickered in the distance, as if people were moving through the trees with flashlights. Sarah's mouth went dry. Branna stirred against her body. She placed her hand over the infant's head, willing her to be still, but she began to cry. The lights up ahead stilled, as if the searchers were listening. A wild terror clawed through Sarah. She placed her pinkie in Branna's mouth and the baby began to suck. The flickering lights moved on and the voices began to fade.

Hot relief swooped through her.

They waited for what seemed like hours until they were sure the men were gone. "Looks like Congo militia crossed the border into Cameroon," Hunter whispered against her ear. "And it looks like they're hunting us. They know we're in the area. We need to get farther inland. Fast." He clasped his hand around hers, drew her deeper into the trees. They moved along what seemed like a winding path. Sarah tried hard not to stumble, worried she'd hurt Branna if she fell. The path widened and the surface under her feet began to feel much harder and smoother. The darkness was less complete here and she realized it was because trees had been cleared to make a dirt road.

They followed the road in silence for what must have been at least an hour until they heard the distant sound of an engine.

Hunter pulled her off the road and down into an overgrown ditch. She saw headlights flickering through the trees. Sweat trickled down her ribs. Branna moved against her and made a little noise. She was waking up again. The headlights came closer, the engine noise growing to a loud, rattling rumble. It was a truck, an old one. It clattered past them and Sarah's mouth filled with the taste of dust and diesel. They waited until all was silent and until the red taillights disappeared into the darkness.

"There's a clearing up ahead, Sarah, on the other side of this road. The chopper can land there. I'm going to radio in now."

She heard Hunter fiddling with his gear. Then she heard the whine and crackle of static as he adjusted the frequency. The sound was oddly comforting, a link to the rest of the world. And even though she could barely see a thing in the velvet blackness of the equatorial night, her mental horizons were immediately expanded by the sense of connection. She heard him speaking low, very low. "Bongani, this is Jongilanga, over. Bongani—"

The set crackled and a voice answered, the volume dropping as he turned it down. "Roger, Jongilanga. Coordinates? Over."

She heard him give their GPS coordinates. "We have hostiles in area, what's your ETA? Over."

"Twenty. Clear."

Hunter swore softly. Then all was silent. Sarah swatted blindly at a cloud of insects she could feel hovering near her face. He took her arm, helped her rise, led her back up the road. They began to walk briskly. He then guided her down what appeared to be another path toward more trees.

"I want you to lie low in the woods here until you see the chopper. Don't move until it's right over the clearing, then you run for your life, okay? There will be light, you'll be able to see where you're going."

A cold feeling of unease began to leach through her. "Where will *you* be?"

He guided her into a crouching position in the trees. "Wait here," he whispered. He took her wrist and wrapped her fingers around the handle of the biohazard canister. "And take this."

Panic ripped through her. "Why? Where are you going?"

He cupped her face in his palms, turned it to face him. "If the militia crossed the border into Cameroon and are looking for us, they will pick up my radio signal, and you can bet your life they're already on their way. I'm going to leave you and Branna here, and I'm going to try and engage them farther down the road, give the chopper a clear path in and you time to get out."

A cold dread took complete hold of her. "No, Hunter," she whispered. "You can't! You'll be outnumbered. They'll kill you!"

"I'll be fine. The FDS would've alerted the Cameroonian troops to hostiles in the area. With luck they'll arrive in time to do the real dirty work, but I must leave, *now,* or they'll be within shooting range of the chopper."

She opened her mouth to protest, but he muffled her words with a hard kiss. Then he pulled away, held her face, studied her quietly in the dark. "Wait for me on São Diogo, Sarah," he whispered. "I need to talk to you. We…have some things we need to work out." He hesitated. "I love you."

And he was gone, a shadow melting into the night, just the lingering, salty taste of him on her lips. Tears burned her eyes. Her heart thudded against her ribs. *He loved her.* And the notion that she might never see him again speared through her gut. She cradled Branna, rocking back and forth on her heels, trying not to let wild panic and desperation blind her.

She forced herself to calm down, tried to conjure up Hunter's comforting, grounding bass voice, imagine his eyes. Home. *He* was her sense of home. He'd said he loved her.

She was going to get out of this. She was going to do this for him. For Branna. For a chance at a future. The notion filled her mind, and suddenly she was no longer alone with a newborn in the dark. A quiet determination filled Sarah, and she waited in silence, Branna making hot little snuffling noises against her chest.

Then she heard it, a distant chop in the air, growing louder. Her pulse tripped into high gear. She could see the lights coming over the trees from the north.

Then an explosion rocked the air and orange light flashed in the distance, to the south. She heard gunfire. Another explosion.

Hunter!

The helicopter materialized over the tops of the trees, a massive black blot in the sky. It banked sharply and hovered over the clearing, the whir of lethal blades drowning out the sound of gunfire. As it lowered, a searchlight flashed on, illuminating the ground with a halo of white light, instantly bringing her world into focus. Long grass flattened under the downdraft. One side of the chopper was open, a man waving at her from the doorway. Sarah grasped the handle of the canister, hunkered low over Branna and ran for her life.

Somewhere beyond the trees she could see the faint orange explosions cutting through the blackness, but the sound of the chopper overpowered everything. She stumbled, almost fell, caught herself, ran a little more carefully, the blades of grass lashing at her legs. She couldn't afford to fall. She'd hurt Branna. The violent downdraft forced a stream of tears from her eyes and whipped her hair around her head. She was vaguely aware that Branna was screaming under chin.

As she reached the door, a giant of a man, in military gear with a pack on his back, jumped out, ran toward her. He took the biohazard container with one hand, her arm with the other. He guided her to the hovering craft, and another man reached down, hauled her up into it. She barely found her feet before the craft lifted sharply and veered up into the air and over the trees, leaving the first man on the ground.

A dark-skinned man with hooked brows guided her down onto a hard bench and began to strap her in. She realized she was shaking violently and Branna was screaming bloody murder.

"What about Hunter?" she yelled over the roar of the engine as the helicopter rose higher in the sky and banked again.

The man said something, but she couldn't hear him above the deafening din of the blades. The door was still wide-open. She leaned forward, could see the black trees fading into the distance. Terror clawed at her heart.

"You've got to get Hunter!" Hot tears streamed down her face. "He's down there! You've got to help him!"

The man motioned with his hand for her to calm down. She couldn't. Hysteria was overwhelming her. She just could not think of leaving him down there in that place.

The man leaned over her and she realized he was putting earphones and a mouthpiece over her head. She heard his voice in the set. "Sarah, I want you to stay calm. My name is Rafiq Zayed, I'm with the FDS—"

"Where's Hunter?"

He raised his hand. "He'll be all right." He had a rich Arabic accent and his voice was deep, smooth, strangely calming. A sense of rationality began to diffuse through her and she began to pull her surroundings into focus. She was in a big, hollow military craft equipped with the bare minimum. Rafiq Zayed sat on the bench opposite her. He was leaning forward, studying her with intense, piercing dark eyes. His face was angular and his glossy black hair was tied back in a ponytail.

Rafiq. That was one of the names Hunter had mentioned, one of the men he trusted with his life. The knowledge took the brunt off her panic. She began to rock Branna, trying to get her to suckle on her pinkie. Hunter had all the baby milk in his pack. "What's going to happen to Hunter?" she asked, much more calmly, speaking into the mouthpiece.

"December Ngomo—the man who helped you into the helo—he is with Hunter. They will be going into Gabon tonight. They will be picking up a doctor at a research station who will help us identify the pathogen you brought with you."

The hatchet of panic struck right back into her heart. "What do you mean? Do you know what he's been through? And what about the militia that came across the border—the fighting down there?"

A smile pulled at Rafiq's lips. "McBride has Cameroonian army support, and he and Ngomo will have air support into Gabon. It's a simple mission." He reached forward, placed a hand on her knee. "Don't worry. He'll be fine."

Sarah stared at him, barely able to absorb what he was saying. Hunter had hardly slept in days. What kind of men were these? She turned to look out the gaping doorway. She could see ocean below them now, shimmering like beaten black metal in the pale light of the small moon. She could see the pale purple hint of dawn along an endless horizon. She swallowed, turned back to Rafiq. "My baby needs milk. She…she needs medical attention. She's an orphan, a newborn." A sob of emotion choked her. "We rescued her. Her name is Branna."

Rafiq nodded calmly, as if this kind of thing was done daily. "We'll have her in the clinic on São Diogo in under two hours. I'll radio ahead and we'll have a physician waiting for both of you."

Sarah sank back against the cold metal and stared down at the sea. She could feel the steady, powerful throb of the machine vibrating through her. They were out of the cloud, and stars spattered the sky. She could see strips of land below, islands. She felt Branna sucking on her finger, her teeny little hands groping. And Sarah knew she could never, ever live with a man like Hunter. She just couldn't be with a man who got up every morning to do a job like this.

Tears burned behind her eyes. *He couldn't even get on the damn helicopter with them.* He had another job to do. He'd said it would be so, and he'd already moved on. That's how it would always be for him. Whether he loved her or not. She closed her eyes against the emotion that swelled though her. She'd known it would be like this. She'd known this feeling would come. She just didn't think it would hurt this badly.

If there was one thing she could take away from all of this, it was Branna. Sarah would adopt her. She would give her a future. She would nurture and cherish this innocent little life that had been born out of violence and chaos.

And even though she couldn't be with him, she would always cherish the man who'd saved them both and taught her how to be strong again.

Chapter 16

"Yes?"

Andries du Toit cleared his throat nervously. "We got them."

Silence.

It made him uncomfortable. "They were both killed in a shootout on the Cameroonian side of the border. The nitrogen in the biohazard canister ignited in a mortar blast. The pathogen has been destroyed," he lied.

Silence stretched again. Then the man in New York spoke, his voice dead calm. "What about the Cameroonians? What do they think happened?"

Du Toit mopped the sweat off his brow with his handkerchief. "They think it was rebels. We've done cleanup operations, taken care of their bodies. There's no sign we were ever there."

"Thank you," the man said simply. And the line went dead.

Du Toit swiped his handkerchief across his forehead again, then stuffed it into his breast pocket. He took another swig of his whiskey. He could *not* let New York know that he'd failed, that the nurse had escaped. Besides, it would all be over before anyone found out, anyway. Still, he'd play it safe. Once he'd collected final payment, he'd disappear—just slip into the wild of Africa. He'd done it before. He would do it again.

The man in New York replaced the receiver on his secure phone and ran his tongue slowly over his teeth. It appeared the glitch had finally been sorted out, thank God. Things could now proceed normally, just as soon as he'd taken care of the last loose end. He pulled open his desk drawer, withdrew a cell phone, the one he used only to contact his "caretaker." He pressed a button. He had to wait only one ring.

"Yes?"

"Kill Du Toit."

17:15 Alpha. FDS base, São Diogo Island.
Friday, September 26

Sarah followed the sandy path through the dune scrub, making her way down to the beach. The clinic doctors had tried to give her medication to help her sleep through the day, but she'd refused to take it. Perhaps she should have. She felt both overtired and edgy, as if there was too much caffeine buzzing through her system. But there was no way she could think of numbing herself and going to sleep while Hunter was still out there somewhere.

And this was exactly why she could never be with a man who did what he did for a living. It would kill her—waiting for days and nights for him to come home from his next mission, wondering *if* he'd come home. Wondering what he'd done, who he'd killed, knowing he'd never talk about it.

She sat on the highest dune, pulled her knees in close to her chest and stared out over the Atlantic. God, she hoped he was all right. She felt sick not knowing. At least Branna was fine. The doctors had put her in an incubator, just to be sure. She'd been a little dehydrated, but otherwise she was in perfect health.

Sarah watched the waves rolling relentlessly to shore, white spindrift blowing in the wind. Hunter had told her to wait for him. She gave a soft laugh. What a joke. She couldn't leave this little island paradise if she tried, at least not until she'd been fully debriefed and this whole mission of theirs was over. Rafiq had made that politely, yet perfectly clear last night. He'd said he'd debrief her himself tomorrow, once she'd rested a little.

A silver speck over the horizon caught her attention. Sarah shielded her eyes and watched as it came closer, the sound of chopper blades eventually reaching her over the crunch of the waves along the white beach. *Hunter?*

Her heart began to thud against her chest. She got to her feet, watched the helicopter near the island. The chopper buzzed right over her and came in to land on the helipad just behind the ridge of dunes.

She couldn't help herself; she raced along the ridge toward the area, then stopped and squinted against stinging sand as the helicopter settled onto the packed earth.

The door opened. December, the soldier who'd helped her into the chopper in Cameroon, hopped out and assisted an older man behind him. The man was stooped slightly, like a question mark. He had a shock of white hair, glasses and a lab coat that flapped about his knees in the downdraft. He must be the doctor from Gabon, the one who'd come to analyze the samples in Dr. Regnaud's container.

Sarah took a step toward the helipad, then froze as she saw Hunter jump down. He was still in military gear and his face was once again streaked with black paint. Even from here he looked wild, dangerous. Sarah's mouth went instantly dry and her heart began to jackhammer. She wanted to go to him, to touch him. God, she loved that man…a man she could never have.

December escorted the doctor to a Jeep waiting on the far side of the helipad, but Hunter stopped. He turned slowly, looked at her. He must have known she was there, must have seen her from the air. He stood still, just watching her, the slowing rotor blades whipping his black hair about his head.

Sarah couldn't hold back; his power over her was too great. She ran across the sand to him. "You…you're okay," she said breathlessly as she reached him, her simple words belying the tornado of emotion churning through her heart.

He took one stride toward her, yanked her into his arms and pressed his mouth down hard over hers, claiming her, holding her tightly, stroking her hair as he kissed her roughly, his tongue meeting hers, searching, needing. Sarah melted into him, hot emotion burning her eyes, searing her body. He pulled back suddenly, gazed deep into her eyes. "I missed you, Sarah."

She glanced away, afraid of what was coming next, of what must be said.

He lifted her chin, forcing her to look at him. "Sarah?"

"Irish!" December yelled from the Jeep. The engine was running, the doctor waiting, the pathogen waiting for him.

Hunter glanced at December, then back at her, not easing his hold. But a look of worry had shifted into his eyes. "Sarah," he said, his voice low, urgent. "We have to talk. I have a plan—"

"A plan?"

"For how we can be together. I want us—"

Her heart lurched sickeningly. She had to say it. She couldn't allow him to think there was a future for them. "No, Hunter."

He went stock-still. The rotor blades stopped turning, leaving only the whisper of the breeze through the dune grass at their feet, the thump of waves on the shore and the purr of the vehicle waiting across the helipad.

"No?"

"I can't be with a man like you. There…there is no us."

Confusion rippled across his features. "Sarah, I love you. I want to be with you. I—"

She pressed her hand over his mouth. "Don't do this."

"Irish! Now!"

He flicked his eyes to the Jeep, torn between duty and her. Again. She'd forced him to make the choice once, at great cost. She never wanted to put him in that position again. It wasn't fair.

He gripped her face suddenly with both hands, his gaze ferocious. "Sarah, I *know* you care for me. I *know* you want me. I've seen it in your eyes. I've felt it in your body. Tell me you don't want me, Sarah!"

Her throat went tight. She couldn't talk.

Desperation flared in his eyes. His hands tightened against her face. "*Tell me!* I want to hear you say it."

Tears welled in her own eyes. "I…I love you, Hunter. I want you with all my heart—more than you'll ever know. And I can't thank you enough for what you've done for me…in ways you'll never understand. You saved me. But…" Emotion snared her voice. "It—we—won't work."

His lowered his face to hers. "You love me. I love you. Isn't that enough?"

She shook her head. "You'll kill me, Hunter. I won't be good for you—"

"Irish!" December barked. "They need you in the war room ASAP!"

His eyes, lit with a mad kind of fury, tunneled right into her soul. "Just wait for me, okay? Promise me you'll wait, so that we can talk."

"No," she said softly. "I don't want to wait, Hunter."

The Jeep horn sounded. Despair clouded the mercenary's eyes, then turned to white-hot anger. "You're lying."

The horn sounded again.

"Go, Hunter," she said. "They need you. Go do your thing." *Go save the world.*

He spun on his heels and stalked over to the waiting vehicle.

Nausea churned her stomach, but tears, release, would not come. She was empty, a husk ready to blow in the wind. She wiped a smudge of black paint from her face as she watched him swing himself into the Jeep. He was one of the most incredible men she'd ever met. She loved him. And he loved her. He'd proved it in the most profound way. Yet she couldn't have him. She watched him go, a cloud of dust boiling behind the vehicle as it disappeared over the ridge.

15:00 Alpha. FDS Base, São Diogo.
Monday, September 29

Sarah pushed open the heavy door that led to the war room, and noticed immediately that Hunter wasn't there. A mix of relief and pain punched through her. It had been almost three days since she'd seen him disappear in the Jeep. He hadn't come looking for her, and she hadn't gone looking for him. He'd probably seen that she was right, that this was for the best. For both of them. So why did it hurt so much?

Sarah stepped into the room and the four men seated around

an oval table looked up instantly. The sense of presence and power they exuded was immediate and tangible. A prickle of awe ran over her skin.

The dark-haired man at the far end stood as she neared the table, his silver eyes appraising her with cool, calculated concentration. He was tall, well over six feet, his face all rugged angles. She noticed he had a scar that sliced from the corner of his left eye all the way down to the base of his jaw.

"Sarah, thank you for joining us." His voice was accented with French and something more guttural she couldn't quite place. "I am Jacques Sauvage. You know Rafiq Zayed here, and this is December Ngomo. I believe you've met briefly." He turned toward the white-haired man seated to his left. "And this is Dr. Jan Meyer." Sauvage held his hand out to her, palm up. "Please do take a seat."

Her eyes flicked around the table. There were two vacant seats. She chose the one closest to the door, eyeing the renowned Dr. Meyer. She'd heard about him. Every medical professional who worked in Africa had. He was an internationally renowned expert in rare tropical diseases, affiliated with the Prince Leopold Institute in Belgium, Europe's answer to the CDC.

"We've gone over Zayed's debriefing report on you," Sauvage said. "And we'd like you to join us for the first portion of this meeting just to see if there is any information you feel might be inconsistent with your experience. If anything new comes to mind, please speak up. *Ça va?*"

Sarah nodded, still trying to place his accent.

"Bien." Sauvage seated himself and Dr. Meyer stood. The man looked tired, his wrinkles etched deep behind his wire-rimmed glasses. He adjusted the collar of his lab coat and hit a key on a laptop. The bank of LCD screens on the wall behind him flickered to life with images of cells taken under an electron microscope. He peered over the rims of his glasses at them.

"Sauvage has asked me to keep this brief. We've been working on the Ishonga samples around the clock for three days now." His English was perfect but his accent was heavily Dutch. "Fortunately, the integrity of the biological material was maintained at cryogenic temperatures due to the nitrogen vapor canister used during shipping."

Shipping? Sarah felt a ridiculous laugh bubble somewhere deep in her gut. Was that what she'd been doing in the Congo this past week? Shipping biological material? He didn't know the half of it.

"If you look at these slides here—" Meyer pointed to one of the LCD screens "—you'll see that the brain tissue of the Ishonga samples is riddled with holes, like a sponge. This disease has been eating through the brains of these patients." He turned back to face them, eyes intense over the rims of his spectacles. "This is *not* a virus and it's *not* a bacteria, or any other conventional disease agent. This kind of pathology—" he gestured broadly to the images behind him "—is more consistent with what we see in brains that have been infected with transmissible spongiform encephalopathies, or TSEs—"

Sarah leaned forward. "You mean mad cow?" Everyone in the room turned to look at her.

The doctor shoved his glasses up his nose. "Correct—more commonly known as mad cow disease in cattle or Creutzfeldt-Jakob disease in humans. I believe the Ishonga patients were infected with a unique, new form of TSE."

"But this can't be," said Sarah, images of the infected villagers flooding her brain. "This disease moved like wildfire. The villagers went mad and died within days, hours. TSEs take *years* to manifest. And these patients were violent—*that* doesn't happen with TSEs."

The doctor nodded. "Yes. I agree. This is highly unusual, but nevertheless I believe it *is* a form of TSE. The violence in this case actually helps facilitate the spread of the disease through the transmission of blood and saliva." He paused, pursing his lips. "Only once have I heard of anything even remotely like this—in a very rare and elusive band of bonobo chimps that live in a remote reach of the Congo Blacklands."

Every muscle in Sarah's body tensed, and for a moment she forgot the powerful men sitting around the table. "You think the bonobo disease has spread to humans?"

"I think the causative agent has been *engineered* to spread to humans."

Rafiq cleared his throat. "But if it's not a virus and not a bacterium, what *is* the causative agent?" His *R*s rolled over his tongue, his voice resonant with hints of Arabic and French inflections.

"It is my opinion that the verdict is still out on what actually causes TSEs," said Meyer. "However, the most common current scientific thinking is that the agent is a prion—a defective protein that forces other proteins in the host's brain to degenerate, leading to progressive dementia, and finally death. My theory is that someone has figured out *exactly* what causes TSEs—prion or not—and they've discovered how to manipulate it genetically. They have thus been able to create a whole new family of TSEs as yet unknown to science." He paused, eyeing the men around the table, his expression grave. "And from the description of the symptoms you have provided me with, I believe President John Elliot has also been infected with one these hybrid TSEs—albeit one that moves much, much more slowly than the Ishonga sample."

Sauvage leaned forward. "But it's the Ishonga one they're threatening to release as a bioweapon. How do you suppose they will do it if it's transmitted via bodily fluids?"

Meyer shook his head. "I don't know yet. It *could* be made

airborne, I think. Or perhaps they'd use a food or water source. I really need more time—"

"We don't have time." The deep voice resonated through the room. Sarah's heart tripped. She spun around.

Hunter McBride stood in the doorway and he looked drop-dead gorgeous. He was clean shaven and he'd had his hair cut, accentuating his eyes. He wore a crisp white T-shirt and faded jeans that should be declared sinful. He stared straight at her, right into her, and for a moment everything in her body stood still. Then her stomach churned with a sick sensation. He looked happy. He'd been away from her and he was…*happy*. She turned, forced herself to stare at Dr. Meyer, to concentrate on what he was saying.

Hunter stepped up behind Sarah's chair, gave her shoulder a quick squeeze and then went to sit in the vacant chair in front of the window. Her chest cramped tight. Hot emotion seared her eyes, but she blinked it back. How could one touch do this to her? How could he feign casual affection like this? She had to fight not to look at him.

"I'm *fully* aware of the time constraints," Meyer said coolly, eyeing Hunter intently.

"No offense intended, Doctor," said Hunter. "Just stating a fact. We have exactly two weeks to D-day now and we're no closer to the antidote."

The doctor shoved his delinquent glasses back up his nose. "On the contrary. There is one lab rumored to be working with something like this, and one scientist in particular. Her name is Dr. Paige Sterling and she's with the Nexus Research and Development Corporation in Hamān."

Rafiq tensed visibly. He placed his hands flat on the tabletop, his black eyes flashing. "How do we know this?"

"A defector from Hamān. He was brought to see me at the Leopold Institute by the French secret service two years ago.

I do consulting for the intelligence community on certain biological warfare matters," explained Meyer. "And this defector used to work in the Nexus compound. He believed the Nexus group was involved in creating bioweapons, and the Secret Service wanted to know if I thought his information was credible. But the man had no proof, and getting into the country to obtain any kind of proof is close to impossible. As you well know, Hamān is closed to all travel and all foreigners. The European intelligence community did, however, put together a task force, including myself, that has kept a watch from a distance over the years. But so far nothing has hit the radar— until now."

"But how do you know the Nexus lab is working on TSEs specifically?" said Rafiq, pressing his hands even more firmly against the tabletop, as if trying to contain something.

"I was given a list of the scientists stationed there. One of them is Dr. Sterling, an American. Both her father and mother used to work with that rare group of bonobos in the Congo I mentioned. And it was her father, Dr. Richard Sterling, who first told me about this rare form of TSE in the bonobos." Meyer ran a weatherbeaten hand through his shock of white hair, leaving it standing on end. "Richard and his wife disappeared in the Congo Blacklands shortly after he'd spoken with me. No one ever saw them again. That was about seventeen years ago. Paige went on to graduate, and continued with her parents' research. She was eventually recruited by the Nexus group. I presume they selected her specifically because of her controversial and cutting-edge work with TSEs."

December stood. "I've done some electronic digging," he said, his deep voice reverberating around the room. "Nexus, through a convoluted system of shell and holding companies, is ultimately controlled by BioMed Pharmaceutical in the U.S.—"

Sarah sat upright. "BioMed—that was the logo…the one I saw on the hazmat suits of the soldiers that attacked the Ishonga compound!"

December nodded. "*Yebo*. And BioMed, through Dr. Andries Du Toit, also supplied the militia soldier with the corticosteroid nasal spray. Du Toit is an exiled military figure from South Africa's apartheid days. He appears to have been on BioMed's payroll for several years, allegedly marketing the company's product to the African sector." December paused, shuffling the papers on the table in front of him. He found what he was looking for. "And the company that funded Dr. Paige Sterling's postsecondary education—Science Reach International—is indirectly controlled by BioMed as well." He looked up. "Science Reach International is the same company that financed Paige's parents' Congo-based TSE research before they mysteriously disappeared."

"There's a definite thread there," said Sauvage. "We need to get into Hamān ASAP."

"Do you think you'll find an antidote in Hamān?" Sarah felt a little awkward even asking the question.

"I don't doubt it," said Hunter. "The Cabal needs to control whatever it has created to be effective in the long term. For that it needs an antidote. And all the arrows are pointing to Hamān."

Sarah made the mistake of looking into his eyes as he spoke. The room and everyone in it suddenly faded to a blur and sound turned to a buzz in her head. She couldn't break the gaze. Everything unspoken seemed to hang between them over the polished dark wood table.

"Thank you, Sarah." Sauvage's voice jerked her back. She looked up sharply. His eyes were cool. He made her feel like a kid who'd been caught out in class.

"That'll be all for now," he said. "We appreciate your help." He turned to December, lowered his voice. "Get that Hamānian defector's name and get him onto São Diogo by nightfall tomorrow. We need to know *everything* he knows about the country and the lab compound. And we need to see if we can get to Du Toit without alerting the Cabal."

This was it. She was being dismissed. It was all over…in more ways than one. With a strange sinking sensation in her heart, she stood, pushed her chair back. Hunter rose, too. Sarah moved quickly to the door. She couldn't face him now. She reached for the door handle, just as Hunter leaned across her, barring her way. She caught her breath, stared at the tile floor. She couldn't look up, couldn't let his eyes suck her in again. He was too powerful and she was feeling too weak.

"Sarah," he whispered against her cheek. "Meet me at the coffee shop down at the bay at seven this evening. Okay?"

She glared at the floor tile. No, it was *not* okay. Staying on this island was going to be sheer torture. Three days had gone by and he hadn't even come over to the clinic to see her. Did he have any idea how much she missed him? How much her body ached for his touch? She slid her eyes slowly up to meet his. And her heart stalled. She suddenly couldn't say no. She'd known he would suck her in. Perhaps the dark and defiant and illogical part of herself even wanted him to.

"Okay?" he insisted, his breath warm against her face.

She nodded in spite of herself.

"Irish!"

He ignored Sauvage. "See you at seven, then." He leaned down and brushed his lips against her ear before turning to join his colleagues.

Sarah shivered, yanked open the door and stepped quickly out of the room. The heavy door swung closed behind her with a thud, suddenly alienating her from what was going on inside. She was not welcome, not part of the group even though she'd played such a vital role. And why should she expect anything different? This was their job. Not hers. It served as a stark reminder of why she couldn't live like this—on the perimeter of Hunter McBride's existence. She needed to forge a future of her own. For her and Branna.

She fisted her hands with resolve and marched down the stone corridor, knowing in her heart she would not—*could* not—show up at that café.

18:30 Alpha. São Diogo clinic.
Monday, September 29

Hunter found her sitting in a chair by the window, watching their baby sleep in a white hospital cot. The setting sun was turning Sarah's hair copper and painting a soft gold glow over Branna's skin. He stood in the doorway and watched in silence for a moment, a voyeur savoring a vignette of Madonna and child. Purity and peace, he thought, fingering the pouch in his pocket—a picture of life and hope and future. *His* future.

He swallowed the hard knot of emotion in his throat and stepped into the room. Sarah glanced up and shock flared in her features. Hunter could immediately see in her eyes that she'd never had any intention of coming to meet him.

He'd feared as much.

That's why he'd come here first. To save himself the disappointment, to cut rejection off at the head, to not give her a chance to say no. And he'd come as soon as he could get away from the war room. He'd been planning this moment for the last three days, but now, looking into her eyes, he had a sinking feeling she had already slipped from his grasp.

He nervously fingered the soft pouch in his pocket again. He couldn't seem to think of the words he needed. Hell, even guerilla warfare didn't do this to him. He was actually afraid. And he knew why—he had something to lose now. If he hadn't lost it already.

He said nothing, mostly because he was worried he was going to say the wrong thing. He moved over to the crib, kissed baby Branna on the forehead, aware of Sarah watching his every move. Then he stood to his full height, squared his shoulders, sucked in his breath and turned slowly to face her. He held out his hand.

She stared at it.

"Come," he whispered, careful not to wake Branna.

Sarah hesitated.

He leaned forward, grasped her hand and coaxed her to her feet. She resisted, her brows lowering in confusion.

"You *have* to hear me out before you turn me down, Sarah," he whispered. "Will you come?"

Her eyes flicked nervously to Branna, then back to him. She nodded.

He led her outside, sat on a stone bench and drew her down beside him. Dry pink bougainvillea petals rustled in the evening breeze and the Atlantic in the distance looked like beaten copper under the setting sun.

Hunter felt awkward, unsure of where to start. He had a sense he was only going to have one shot at getting this right. But Sarah spoke first.

"Hunter, I've put in adoption papers for Branna."

This was already getting away from him. "You'll just have to redo them, then."

Possessive passion flashed in her eyes. "I want to give her a home, Hunter, a future. I want her to be my child."

Everything he'd dreamed of was unraveling right in front of him. "She's *ours,* Sarah. I want *my* name on those papers."

She faced him squarely, lifted her jaw. "Look, I understand you brought her into the world and that you—"

Lord, he was hopeless at talking. He'd already walked into a minefield of his own making. He groped in his pocket, pulled out the pouch, shoved it into her hands, cutting her off.

Her eyes flicked between the pouch and him. "What's this?"

"Don't talk. Enough talking. Just open it." His heart slammed hard against his ribs. *"Please."*

Sarah studied him for a moment. Then she looked down at the velvet pouch he'd pushed into her hands. Slowly she peeled back the midnight-blue fabric to reveal a small translucent, golden pebble. She rolled it slightly in her palm and it caught the bronze light of the setting sun. She knitted her brow. "What is it?"

"Diamond. I got it in Luanda. That's where I've been these past few days." He reached out, closed her hand tightly around the stone, not giving her the opportunity to hand it back. "I wanted you to decide on the cut. I…I want you to decide on the shape, Sarah." He paused. "Like I want you to decide on the shape of our future. I…" He swallowed hard, took the leap. "I want you to think about being my wife."

Sarah's stomach bottomed out. Her jaw dropped and her head began to buzz. Her mouth went completely dry, words defying her. She couldn't even begin to articulate the thoughts that raced through her brain. She could literally feel the heat of the raw stone trapped in her fist. A diamond in the rough—like him.

"I want you to marry me, Sarah," he said again, as if she hadn't heard the first time.

She opened her mouth to speak, but he placed his fingers over her lips. "Before you say anything, you need to know that I'm not going back into the field. I've already discussed it with the guys. No more fighting. I'm going to requalify as a surgeon—"

"You…you *can't.*"

"Why not?"

"You can't…just change. I mean…" She looked into his eyes. "Hunter, what I mean is that your job is who you *are*. You belong out there. I can't even begin to expect you to change who you are for me. I don't want that. You'd regret it in the long run, and if you're unhappy, I'd also end up regretting it, too. I can't let you to do this for me."

She tried to hand the diamond back to him, but he tightened his fist around hers, pressing the stone into her flesh. "It's not for you, Sarah. It's for *me*, for *us*—for me, you and Branna."

She studied his face, bewilderment swelling in her. "You…you're dead serious, aren't you?"

"Of course I am." He took her shoulders in his hands. "See, Sarah, I'm not changing, I'm just going back to who I was—who I really am. And you helped me get there. You forced me to face something in myself. You showed me there's something inside of myself that I just cannot hide from anymore. You made me pick up that scalpel again. You made me feel what it's like to save a life again."

His eyes glistened. "You showed me how to stop running, Sarah." His grip tightened on her shoulders. "Do you understand how dead serious I am about this? I'm forty-three years old next month. I want you. I want Branna. I want to be a family. I want to be a doctor again. I want *you* as my nurse, as my wife—by my side. And I want to eventually work here, at this clinic. I want to be here for the islanders, for the FDS troops." His mouth twisted with emotion. "Nothing in the world is going to change my mind, so please don't turn me down, because then I'm going to be lost as all hell—and a bloody danger in the field."

She couldn't talk. Tears streamed down her face.

He wiped them away with the rough pad of his thumb and snorted softly. "I just realized how that must sound. This is not only about me. I think I can offer you something, too. I can offer you a home. Love. Hell, I'd give you the world if I could."

Sarah stared into his eyes. Was this really possible? She'd gone into the heart of Africa, found the courage to stare death in the face, and she'd come out with the child she'd dreamed of having. A man who loved her. A sense of home.

"I love you, Hunter," she whispered.

He smiled with such relief that she could feel it in his limbs. "Well, at least that part is sorted out. Now will you have that diamond cut and set, and wear it while you think about when you'd like to get married?"

She laughed through her tears. Then cried, and laughed again. She opened her hand and looked at the pebble in her palm. Rough. Rare. Precious. She wiped her face, stilled, looked up at him. His face was all raw emotion—a rough sculpture of power and vulnerability. She closed her hand around the pebble. "You know something, McBride?" she said softly. "You're damn good at keeping your promises."

He raised a brow. "I am?"

She sniffed, wiped a tear from the end of her nose. "You made me a promise back on the Shilongwe. You promised that if anyone could get me home, you would."

He smiled. "And you told me you had no home."

She smiled back happily through her tears. "That didn't stop you from getting me there."

"No," he laughed. "I guess it didn't." Then his face turned serious. "Would that be a yes, then?"

Sarah kissed the man she loved. "That would definitely be a yes."

Epilogue

Sauvage set the bottle of brandy and two glasses on the table. "So, Irish is leaving the field."

Rafiq said nothing and the darkness hid his expression. But Sauvage didn't need to see his face. He could sense the brooding intensity in his colleague. He felt it in himself.

He sat in silence, staring at the twinkling lights of the island homes up on the hill, and he smiled wryly in the dark. So there was redemption for some. If Hunter had found it, where did it leave men like himself and Rafiq?

Out in the shadows, that's where. He knew nothing about Rafiq, but he did know redemption was not possible for a man like himself. Not with his past.

Sauvage poured himself a glass, set the bottle down carefully. "You okay with going into Hamān?"

Rafiq's eyes flashed in the dim light. "Yeah. Why?"

"You've been quiet."

Silence.

He sipped his drink, welcoming the warmth of its caress down his throat. "You're the only one for the job," he offered, unnecessarily perhaps. "You speak the local dialect. You look the part. We wouldn't be able to get anyone else into the country without raising suspicion." He paused, took another sip. "You're more than perfect."

"I know. I am from Hamān."

Sauvage stilled, held the brandy in his mouth for a moment. This was the first clue he'd ever had about Rafiq's past. He said nothing, the weight of the revelation somehow reverent. Finally he spoke. "Will this be a problem for the mission?"

Rafiq's eyes glittered in the moonlight.

"No. It will not."

* * * * *

Don't miss A SULTAN'S RANSOM,
the next chapter in the thrilling new miniseries,
SHADOW SOLDIERS
By Loreth Anne White

When Rafiq Zayed is sent to Hamān to kidnap a suspected terrorist, he never expects to find Paige Sterling innocent, a victim of an elaborate—and dangerous—setup. But to save both their lives, he'll have to trust the scientist with his secrets—and his heart.

On sale November 2006
Wherever Silhouette Books are sold.

Dear Reader,

When a man joins the French Foreign Legion, he must sever all ties with his past. He may not be married, own a bank account, vehicle, or take even a photograph with him. He can hold no allegiance to his country. He must be prepared to speak only French, bond instantly with foreigners, and die in some of the most hostile reaches of the globe.

It's an extreme choice—one often made just for the chance to come out with a new identity. But who would do this? Why? And what if it was lost love that drove a man to those infamous gates at Fort de Nogent?

From these questions my SHADOW SOLDIERS emerged— three warriors with armored hearts and no pasts. Now soldiers of fortune, they are handed one mission that could forever change the shape of the world's future. But first, they must find the courage to love again.

This is Hunter's story....

Loreth Anne White

RUN, ALLY! Don't be fooled by him. He's evil. Don't let him touch you!

But as the forbidding figure came through the mists toward her, Ally knew she couldn't run. His features burned with dark malevolence, and his physical domination of everything around him seemed to hold her like a net.

She'd heard the tales. She knew all about the Wolverton legend and the ghost that haunted The Willows, an elegant old mansion lost by Micha Wolverton nearly a hundred years ago. According to folklore, the estate was stolen from the Wolvertons, and Micha was killed trying to reclaim it. His dying vow was to be reunited with the spirit of his beloved wife, who'd taken her life for reasons no one would speak of, except in whispers. But Ally had never put much stock in the fantasy. She didn't believe in ghosts.

Until now—

She still didn't understand what was happening. The figure had materialized out of the mist that lay thick on the damp cemetery soil. A cool breeze and silvery moonlight had played against the ancient stone of the crypts surrounding her, until they joined the mist, causing his body to thicken and solidify right before her eyes. That was when she realized she'd seen this man before. Or thought she had, at least.

His face was familiar…so familiar, yet she couldn't put it together. Not with him looming so near. She stepped back as he approached.

"Don't be afraid," he said. His voice wasn't what she expected. It didn't sound as if it were coming from beyond the grave. It was deep and sensual. Commanding.

"Who are you?" she managed.

"You should know. You summoned me."

"No, I didn't." She had no idea what he was talking about. Two minutes ago, she'd been crouching behind a moss-covered crypt, spying on the mansion that had once been The Willows, but was now Club Casablanca. And then this—

If he was Micah, he might be angry that she was trespassing on his property. "I'll go," she said. "I won't come back. I promise."

"You're not going anywhere."

Words snagged in her throat. "Wh-why not? What do you want?"

"If I wanted something, Ally, I'd take it. This is about need."

His words resonated as he moved within inches of her. She tried to back away, but her feet were useless. "And you need something from me?"

"Good guess." His tone burned with irony. "I need lips, soft and surrendered, a body limp with desire."

"My lips, my bod—?"

"Only yours."

"Why? Why me?" This couldn't be Micha. He didn't want any woman but Rose. He'd died trying to get back to her.

"Because you want that, too," he said.

Wanted what? A ghost of her own? She'd always found the legend impossibly romantic, but how could he have known that? How could he know anything about her? Besides, she'd sworn off inappropriate men, and what could be more inappropriate than a ghost? She shook her head again, still not willing to admit the truth. But her heart wouldn't play along. It clattered inside her chest. The mere thought of his kiss, his touch, terrified her. This wildness, it was fear, wasn't it?

When his fingertips touched her cheek, she flinched, expecting his flesh to be cold, lifeless. It was anything but that. His skin was smooth and hot, gentle, yet demanding. And while his dark brown eyes were filled with mystery and wonder, there was a sensitivity about them that threatened to disarm her if she looked too deeply.

"These lips are mine," he said, as if stating a universal fact that she was helpless to avoid. In truth, it was just that. She couldn't stop him.

And she didn't want to.

* * * * *

Find out how the story unfolds in…
DECADENT
by
New York Times *bestselling author*
Suzanne Forster.
On sale November 2006.

Harlequin Blaze—*Your ultimate destination*
for red-hot reads.
With six titles every month, you'll never guess
what you'll discover under the covers…

MICHELE HAUF

FROM THE DARK

Michael is a man with a secret. He's a vampire
struggling to fight the darkness of his nature.
It looks like a losing battle—until he meets
Jane, the only woman who can understand his
conflicted nature. And the only woman who can
destroy him—through love.

On sale November 2006.

nocturne™

USA TODAY bestselling author

MAUREEN CHILD

ETERNALLY

He was a guardian. An immortal fighter of evil,
out to destroy a demon, and she was his next
target. He knew joining with her would make
him strong enough to defeat any demon.
But the cost might be losing the woman
who was his true salvation.

On sale November, wherever books are sold.

nocturne™

Save $1.⁰⁰ off

your purchase of any
Silhouette® Nocturne™ novel.

Receive $1.00 off

any Silhouette® Nocturne™ novel.

**Available wherever books are sold, including most
bookstores, supermarkets, drugstores and discount stores.**

Coupon expires December 1, 2006. Redeemable at participating
retail outlets in the U.S. only. Limit one coupon per customer.

RETAILER: Harlequin Enterprises Ltd. will pay the face value of this coupon plus
8¢ if submitted by the customer for this specified product only. Any other use
constitutes fraud. Coupon is nonassignable. Void if taxed, prohibited or restricted by
law. Void if copied. Consumer must pay for any government taxes. Mail to Harlequin
Enterprises Ltd., P.O. Box 880478, El Paso, TX 88588-0478, U.S.A. Cash value 1/100
cents. Limit one coupon per customer. Valid in the U.S. only.

5 65373 00076 2   (8100) 0 11265

SNCOUPUS

nocturne™

Save $1.00 off

your purchase of any
Silhouette® Nocturne™ novel.

Receive $1.00 off

any Silhouette® Nocturne™ novel.

Available wherever books are sold, including most bookstores, supermarkets, drugstores and discount stores.

Coupon expires December 1, 2006. Redeemable at participating retail outlets in Canada only. Limit one coupon per customer.

RETAILER: Harlequin Enterprises Limited will pay the face value of this coupon plus 10.25 cents if submitted by the customer for this specified product only. Any other use constitutes fraud. Coupon is nonassignable. Void if taxed, prohibited or restricted by law. Consumer must pay any government taxes. Mail to Harlequin Enterprises Ltd., P.O. Box 3000, Saint John, New Brunswick E2L 4L3, Canada. Limit one coupon per customer. Valid in Canada only.

52607136

SNCOUPCDN

REQUEST YOUR FREE BOOKS!

2 FREE NOVELS
PLUS 2
FREE GIFTS!

Passionate, Powerful, Provocative!

COMING NEXT MONTH

#1439 CLOSER ENCOUNTERS—Merline Lovelace
Code Name: Danger
Drew McDowell—Code name Riever—is curious to know why
a recently fired defense attorney has developed a sudden interest
in a mysterious WWII ship. When the mission takes a bizarre
twist, the two must work together, while fighting an attraction that
threatens to consume them both.

#1440 FULLY ENGAGED—Catherine Mann
Wingmen Warriors
Pararescueman Rick DeMassi never thought the woman he'd
shared an incredible night with years ago would be his next
mission. But when a stalker kidnaps her and his daughter, this
air force warrior must face his greatest fears and save the two
most important women in his life.

#1441 THE LOST PRINCE—Cindy Dees
Overthrown in a coup d'état, the future king of Baraq runs
to the only woman who can help him. Now Red Cross aide
Katy McMann must risk her life and her heart to help save a
crumbling nation.

#1442 A SULTAN'S RANSOM—Loreth Anne White
Shadow Soldiers
To stop a biological plague from being released, mercenary
Rafiq Zayed is forced to abduct Dr. Paige Sterling and persuade
her to team up with him in a race against a deadly enemy...and
their growing desires.

SIMCNM1006